THE CASE OF THE DISTANT
RELATIVE.

THE CASE OF THE DISTANT RELATIVE

JILL DARRAGH

Rangitawa
PUBLISHING

The Case of the Distant Relative published by Rangitawa
Publishing, Feilding, New Zealand 2012.
2nd edition 2018.

rangitawa@xtra.co.nz
www.rangitawapublishing.com

ISBN 13:978-0-473-22321-2

"Although we are still political outcasts, the promised land is in sight! Year by year we have been winning our way...our forces have been growing in numbers, not by any transient wave of enthusiasm, but by sheer logical reasoning, and the hard work performed by our members."
Kate Sheppard – Franchise Superintendant.
Address to the Annual Convention of the women's Christian temperance Union,
March 1893.

"Nothing in the world is hidden forever. Sand turns traitor, and betrays the footstep that had passed over it; water gives back to the tell-tale surface the body that has been drowned...Hate breaks its prison-secrecy in the thoughts, through the doorway of the eyes...Look where we will, the inevitable law of revelation is one of the laws of nature: the lasting preservation of a secret is a miracle which the world has never seen."
Wilkie Collins. *'No Name'* (1862)

CHAPTER ONE

Sunday March 12th, 1893.Wellington, New Zealand.

'Ladies we must work even harder for reform if we are to succeed with this new petition. Go out onto the streets, into the workplaces, the factories and shops. Spread the temperance message to all our sisters and persuade them to sign up for suffrage!'

Sophia Holmes felt excited as she rose to her feet to applaud the speaker. Around her the audience cheered, crying out their support for the stirring words delivered by their Chairwoman. This was only the second meeting of the Women's Christian Temperance Union Sophia had attended, but already she was swayed by the rhetoric and willing to do her best to enable the goal of votes for women in this, the farthest colony of the Empire.

The public hall in central Wellington was decorated with banners proclaiming the WCTU motto 'For God, home and humanity' and rosettes pinned to the jackets of the committee members stated the same refrain. Enthusiasm filled the air endowing everyone present with a sense of purpose, and the possibility of being involved in a historical landmark for the women of New Zealand.

Every one stood as the pianist took her place at the upright piano at the side of the stage, playing the opening chords to the suffrage verse that was displayed on a large board that was suspended over the stage, for all to read and join in.

The streets are filled with snares that lurk
In the wayward children's path,
Yet people say that women's work
Is still by the lonely hearth.
But the stagnant air of the world is stirred
By the voice despised so long;
The woman's voice in the land is heard-
The words of a strange new song.
We'll know the worth of a purer youth,
When women rule with men,
For love of virtue and peace and truth
Shall save the world again.

As she sang, Sophia gazed around at her
neighbouring supporters. Mostly women and a few men,
of many different occupations, she guessed, by their
dress and their accents. They were all determined in their
efforts to succeed in controlling the sale of alcohol
through gaining votes for women, who could then serve
on liquor licensing committees. If the Government could
be forced to accede to their wishes and pass the Electoral
Reform Bill this year, women could register to vote in the
coming General Election. Sophia enjoyed this moment of
unity as the song finished and many of the crowd started
to leave. She wondered if she was, at last, achieving a
sense of belonging here in New Zealand; of at last
leaving her British upbringing behind. It had been an
enormous decision to sail to the other side of the world
and begin a new life in this distant colony even though
circumstances had forced it upon her. Sophia still had
moments when she felt isolated and lonely even on such

occasions as this. Outwardly she was seen as a successful businesswoman who was independent and popular with her clients but doubts about the wisdom of her choice still crept up on her at the most inauspicious moments. The exhilaration and sense of escape to a new life she had experienced on the voyage to New Zealand largely abated once she settled into a routine, and she found herself hoping that life wasn't always going to be so humdrum. She often felt that her natural curiosity could be used to better effect than in running a secretarial agency but was happy enough to have a steady income and not have to rely on anyone else.

These pessimistic thoughts caused Sophia to shake her head slightly, as she noticed a man trying to extricate himself from the row of seats directly to her left. Dressed in rather shabby black clothes, his hat pulled low over his eyes, with a silk scarf wrapped around his face, he glanced her way briefly, endowing her with the same shrewd, rather calculating look that he then cast over the occupants of the hall. Sophia wondered if he was looking for someone in particular but her attention was disturbed as she was handed a sheaf of pamphlets to distribute. When she turned back towards the man, he'd gone, his seat having been pushed aside crookedly. Intrigued by his demeanour, she looked to the rear of the hall only to see him leaving. As she bent to pick up her bag from the floor, she caught sight of a pipe lying under his chair so she walked along the row of seats and picked it up. With the intention of returning it to the man, she manoeuvred her way through the crowds and opened the entrance door. She peered through the rain, where she saw him entering a horse cab further down the street, but although she called out and waved, he took no notice. As the carriage drove off in the rain, Sophia shrugged, returning back inside to the warmth of the hall, where she examined the pipe. Beautifully carved with two monkeys supporting an ivory bowl with the stem set into an ebony mouthpiece, it had a silver band round the stem with a finely engraved garland of tiny leaves surrounding the initials "S M". It looked valuable and its owner would no doubt want it returned. Sophia carried it over to the Branch Secretary who was closing up her Minute book and gathering up the considerable pile of correspondence that had been presented to the meeting. She turned away to open a small leather suitcase as Sophia tapped her on the arm.

'Excuse me, but this has been left behind. Do you hold on to lost property?'

'Oh dear,' said the woman peering at the pipe over the top of her spectacles. 'It looks valuable. Did you see who left it?'

'A rather seedy looking man who certainly didn't look as if he would own something so ornate,' admitted Sophia. 'Perhaps he stole it, but I don't really want to take it to the police.'

'No dear. They're more likely to accuse us of stealing it if they hear where it was found. Would you take care of it and perhaps he'll contact us?'

Dubious about this, Sophia gave her name and address to the Secretary, who introduced herself as Mrs Elenora Briggs.

'I'm Miss Holmes, 5 Willis Street. That's my business address.'

Tucking the pipe carefully inside her bag, before going to join the queue to receive a cup of well stewed tea, Sophia wondered what would happen if its owner did turn up to claim it. She'd deliberately given her business address to Mrs Briggs as she didn't wish the man to arrive at her home demanding the return of his pipe. She supposed she would recognise him but she was concerned that she might have to hand it back to a thief. Although I can hardly ask him if it's stolen, she thought.

'Sophia! Over here!'

Turning, Sophie saw her friend Tilly waving and pointing to an empty seat beside her. She collected her cup of tea and moved carefully in the jostling crowd away from the kitchen, to reach the chair.

'Wasn't the Chairwoman just so persuasive, ' said Tilly. 'I declare I felt ready to run out on the street and start marching. I'm filled with enthusiasm.'

Laughing Sophia agreed with Tilly Sergeson, a true star of Wellington society who could always be relied on to support any cause asked of her. Her wealthy older husband gave her free rein to lead the life of a philanthropist and social butterfly as long as she didn't interfere with his racing stables. Luckily Tilly's only interest in race meetings was that they offered her a convenient parade ground for showing off her latest fashionable outfit, so the marriage worked well. Tonight she looked splendid, if subdued for her, in a dark green silk skirt and matching jacket. Her hat seemed to defy gravity, perched at an impossible angle on top of curls that were constrained by a mesh net. Pheasant feathers arched down from the brim and tickled her chin, which Sophia, far more conservative and a lot less wealthy, privately judged to be intolerably itchy. However, Tilly also had her serious side and could be relied upon for sensible advice. In contrast to her more diminutive friend, Sophia was a tall slender woman, whose clothes reflected   good   taste   but   sober   intentions.

Unmarried, both by choice and circumstances, she appeared to those who met her, to move seamlessly among all levels of Wellington society, an apparently friendly, self assured female well suited to the opportunities opening up for women in this, the most distant settled country of the British realm. How she sometimes struggled to maintain this outward character was known only to her.

'I think it will come to that, don't you?' agreed Sophia. 'It seems we will have to take stringent action to get the Bill passed even if our Ministers appear to support it. I just hope it's not raining on the day we take to the streets, I am so frustrated with trying to remove the mud from my boots every night.'

'With Seddon bound to become Premier I am doubtful of success. Alfred says he's hand in glove with the liquor merchants for all his rhetoric about women's rights. He and his Liberal cronies are not to be trusted at all according to Alfred.'

'Really? Where did Alfred hear that?'

'At his Club. There's a great deal of compromising chicanery going on, if you ask me. Alfred keeps his ear to the ground, and I'm bound to say some of the gossip he brings home is unrepeatable.'

Tilly pretended to fan herself, as Sophia leaned closer hoping to hear what was so dreadful.

'No,' said Tilly over dramatically. 'I can see you want me to tell you, but I'm not going to soil my lips!'

'Oh don't be so boring Tilly. You know I rely on you to add a bit of spice to my life.'

'No!' Tilly was emphatic but then she moved closer, conspiratorially. 'Suffice to say that certain people in very high places frequent some very low places.'

'Ah, I understand what you mean. No I don't think I want to know either.'

Smiling at each other in complete understanding, they realised that another woman had seated herself close to them in an effort to attract their attention. In complete contrast to Sophia and Tilly, she was dressed in the brightest of colours. A low cut bodice under an open yellow jacket barely covered her large pale skinned breasts whilst her skirt was emerald green with a flounce of grimy white lace edged petticoat showing beneath. Perched high on her head, anchored with an enormous pearl pin, a hat, even more extravagant than Tilly's, supported feathers, bows and lace, whilst her face, although carefully made up, was bright with colour. She smiled at them both, extending her red satin gloved hand to Sophia who took it doubtfully in a quick shake, stopping herself from recoiling at the strong cheap perfume that emanated from the woman.

'I'm Susie Post. Pleased to meet you I'm sure. Don't mind if I join you? I've never been here before. Not really my line if you know what I mean.'

She gave a meaningful wink to the two women. Sophia smiled back nervously and wondered what the woman was going to say next.

'Still... got to support woman haven't you? Really important that, ain't it?'

'Well the more of us the merrier. That's what I say,' offered Tilly ever adept at trivial social chatter. 'I'm Tilly and this is my friend Sophia.'

Sophia would have preferred to stay anonymous in the circumstances but supposed Tilly was only being polite. Susie produced a small pewter screw topped flask from her bag, pouring a healthy helping of what appeared to be gin, into her tea before offering it to the two others, who quickly declined, looking round nervously to make sure none of the strictly teetotal ladies present had noticed.

'And what do you two do then?'

'I'm just a boring stay at home wife,' responded Tilly with some irony, much to her friend's amazement. 'Sophia is much more interesting. She runs her own secretarial business.'

'A business woman eh? I'm very impressed by that. I did think of starting my own place for a while, but I couldn't afford a decent house so I just rent a room now. My gents don't mind; it's nice and private, right upstairs at the back of the place. I let Mrs Protheroe do all the work, take responsibility. Much easier that way.'

'I imagine it is,' said Sophia dryly, but her slight sarcasm was lost on Susie. 'Can we expect to see you here again Miss Post?'

'Oh I don't know. I only came to give a donation from one of my clients. He wasn't wanting to do it himself. He's quite a private person. But I've got a bundle of leaflets to give out. I'll pop one into my clients' pockets before they leave. That's an easy way to distribute them!'

Susie gave a loud laugh which caused a few women around them to look at her with distaste.

'That's a good idea,' agreed Sophia quickly to distract her. 'I can put them in with the typing we do then my clients will get them too!'

The two friends looked on as Susie got to her feet a little unsteadily, the feathers and bows on her hat bobbing around with her swaying movements. Observing her progress was something akin to a sailor walking on the swaying deck of a boat. She was seemingly oblivious to the women who moved quickly out of her way as she left the hall. In London, Sophia had seen many women like Susie when she attended Court proceedings with her father, but until now she'd never really wondered what it might be like to be forced into prostitution. She admitted to a certain dubious admiration for a woman who seemed so cheerful in the light of her circumstances and the risks involved. For a moment she wondered if Miss Post had a man who really genuinely cared for her before a light tap on her arm brought her back to reality.

'She's a little unusual,' understated Tilly. 'Still we do need all the support we can get so one mustn't be too critical. Now Sophia, please let me take you home. I brought the carriage tonight. Arthur is at some boring Jockey Club meeting and another committee member took him.'

Sophia sighed and nodded, then stood up and stretched, pleased to accept Tilly's invitation. The thought of going home alone in the rain was most unappealing as she recalled the feeling of unease that she'd felt in the presence of the man who had left the pipe behind. It was on such occasions as these that she sometimes wished she did have a male to escort her through the city streets, but that was unlikely she told herself firmly. I must stick to my principles she thought as she smiled at her friend.

'That would be wonderful. It was raining quite hard when I looked out a few moments ago. I don't like those smelly cabs, so you can spoil me. I've just got to pay my subscription if you'll wait a moment.'

Joining the queue of people waiting to hand over

their money, Sophia eventually reached the front and handed her membership fee to the branch Treasurer Mrs Robertson. She glanced at the contents of the cash box as her receipt was being written out, astonished at the sight of the several one hundred pound notes within.

'That's seems a great deal of money,' she commented as she waited.

Lavinia Robertson nodded.

'I was so surprised when I opened the envelope. It was that woman Miss Post. She said she'd been asked to donate it from one of her friends. I hardly felt I could refuse it when she was so insistent although I do have my doubts about its provenance if you get my meaning.'

A look of disapproval and distaste on the woman's face left Sophia in no doubt as to her thoughts regarding Miss Post and her clientele. Curiosity overcoming her discretion, Sophia blurted out, 'Good heavens! She was talking to us a few moments ago and mentioned something about it. It seems odd that someone would trust her with such a large sum. Did she say why he wouldn't give it to us personally?'

The Treasurers natural reticence was swayed by Sophia's comments and apparent knowledge.

'Apparently, or so she said, he wishes it to be anonymous but she did request a receipt for him, but I had to make it out to her since she wouldn't reveal his name.'

'She must have some rich friends,' commented Sophia cynically and then for no apparent reason she recalled the mysterious man sitting near her. Was he the benefactor of this money? Had he been watching secretively to ensure that Susie handed the donation over to the Society? Perhaps his clothes were a disguise, which would explain why he was the owner of such a beautifully carved ivory pipe?

'Yes, well we mustn't jump to conclusions must we? We can't look a gift horse in the mouth as the saying goes!'

Lavinia closed the lid of the cash box to hide the contents from anyone else. She turned the key firmly and patted the lid.

'I shall pay it into the bank as soon as possible tomorrow. I shall be quite nervous having all that money in the house tonight!'

***

Down near the harbour where tiny dilapidated wooden cottages housed occupants used to the stench of the Wellington wharves and rats running feely in open drains, Meg Williams backed into a corner for safety, as her drunken husband staggered through the door of their one roomed hovel. He stood in front of her swaying slightly, his eyes watering from the candle smoke. He was a large burly man, but what had once been the hard bulk of muscle was now replaced with the flab of a beer drinker. She started to tremble as he stared at her. She could see rage and frustration building up in him, as his hands curled, poised to deliver punishment to her.

'Where's my supper you lazy cow?'

Bob Williams raised his fist as she went to the small coal range and carefully spooned out a helping of steaming greyish stew onto a battered tin plate. The sight of her reddened hands shaking seemed to enrage him further as she cautiously placed the meal on the rough wooden table. As she retreated, his hand clutched her arm in a painful grip, his ragged fingernails scratching

19

her bare skin below her rolled up sleeve. He reeked of beer and the stench of his rotting teeth made her avert her face.

'What do you call this? Wouldn't feed pigs on this you idle bitch.'

Picking up the plate, he tipped it over her arm forcing a scream out of her as the scalding food seared her skin.

'If you gave me more money, I could feed you better,' Meg whimpered, but he flung her down on to the dirt floor, her thin undernourished frame no match to his strength. Williams stared down at his wife with loathing before he kicked her hard in the ribs. Blood dripped onto the floor as she bit her lip against the pain, curling up to protect herself from his boots, but, to her immense relief, he moved away from her in apparent disgust.

'I'm going down to the pub for a decent pie. You'd better clean yourself up before I get back,' he threatened, then spitting on the floor near her face, he left, slamming the battered front door. Slowly sitting up, Meg rocked herself back and forwards, gasping from the pain of this latest assault, unable to sum up any excuses for her husbands' behaviour. If only she had somewhere to run to, some sort of refuge but there was no-one who would take her in. She and Bob had no relatives, and with no money she wouldn't be able to feed herself. Eventually, she found the strength to pull herself to her feet and sit down at the table first managing to dip a rag into a bucket of water near the stove which she wrapped around the burn on her arm, wincing as it touched the blistered skin.

Finally, as she attempted to clean up the spilt stew, Meg knew she should try and eat some herself but her appetite was gone. She opened the front door and took a step outside to look up and down the street. The autumn night was unusually mild but there was a hint of rain in the air. Soon there were clouds of moths fluttering inside the kitchen around the candle lantern. Her head throbbing, Meg leaned against the door frame nursing her arm, breathing in shallow gulps and wincing at the pain in her side from Bob's vicious kick. This part of the city, Grainger Street, near the fish market, had its own specific pungent aroma of raw sewage mixed with the smell of tarred ropes and salt. Meg hated it with all of her being. She racked her brains to think of ways to escape from her drunken bully of a husband but apart from taking to the streets and begging, nothing occurred to her. Once she'd suggested to Bob that she try and get a job as a house cleaner but he'd turned it down flat, letting his pride get the better of necessity.

With a loud sigh, she retreated back inside her one roomed home wiping her eyes with a dirty rag she found in her apron pocket. Quietly, she reached under the old mattress, pulling out a creased leaflet that she'd found blown into the gutter outside. She had to lift it close up to the lantern before she read it again.

WOMEN'S TEMPERANCE UNION.

UNITE AGAINST DEADLY ALCOHOL.
JOIN OUR MOVEMENT NOW AND
WORK FOR EQUALITY, JUSTICE AND
A BETTER LIFE FOR OUR CHILDREN.

Meg liked the sound of this. How she would have liked to attend one of these meetings, had her circumstances been different. All the other women in this street had similarly hard lives like her. One or two of them relied on prostitution to supplement the few shillings housekeeping they managed to cajole from their men. Meg's refusal to debase herself in this way, her constant struggle for cleanliness set her apart from what support she might have gleaned from the female community close to her. The only uniting factor for all the women in this slum community was the drunken debauchery of their men-folk, the attendant violence that was perpetrated upon them and the constant fear of losing their children to typhoid. Meg's opinion of these women was low. She despised their coarse language and their filthy clothes. Whatever went on in her home, she'd always kept herself as clean as possible, for her own self esteem. It was the one thing she could control in her life.

Well, she thought, holding the leaflet as if it were a talisman, what price self respect now? I've got nothing to be hoity toity about have I? Being clean is all well and good, but being fed is better. I bet the ladies who belong to the Temperance Union don't have drunken husbands coming home every night to beat them. Gazing over her wretched domain, she sighed. How had she come to this? The answer, of course was quite clear to her. Bob Williams had been quite a catch when she'd met him. She'd been a kitchen maid at the Grand Hotel and he'd taken a fancy to her. She'd been flattered by this tall strong wharf worker and they'd soon been married. Once she'd had little Betty, Bob had changed, bitterly disappointed not to have a son. When the small girl died, he became brutal towards her and she had hoped that when Peter was born, her husbands' attitude would become kinder. How wrong she'd been. By then the drinking had become a way of life for Bob and she became more and more frightened of him. The loss of their second child meant his behaviour became increasingly erratic and his employers less and less willing to give him the responsibility he'd once enjoyed. With smaller wages coming in, they'd been forced to move into the pitiful one room of this ramshackle house, where she now sat, battered and bruised.

Eventually she doused the lamp and curled up on the truckle bed, placing her burnt arm on top of the blanket to keep it cool.

***

Boysie Smith crouched down behind the shrubbery in the pouring rain cursing the elements. Earlier that evening it had been a fine autumn night, so the sudden downpour as he'd reached the house had taken him by surprise. If he'd been able to read the weather forecast that day, he would have known that northerly gales with rain were expected after the floods of the previous week however, not having the extra pence to purchase a newspaper, he was ignorant of this. The water was trickling off the brim of his flat cap, seeping down through his jacket collar. He'd soon discovered that even this close to the house, under the eaves, there was little protection. It hadn't been a very productive night so far, and now he was keen to return to his room at Annie Wall's boarding house. His mouth started watering as he thought about the nine penny fish and chip supper he could be sitting down to, at the Grand Oyster pub next door. Must be easier ways than this, to making a few bob, he thought. Carriages had come and gone up this driveway. Gentlemen had arrived

23

and left, but in the dim light of the porch lantern, he was unable to recognise any of them. To make matters worse they were all sheltering under umbrellas or hats pulled well down to protect and disguise themselves. The last person to arrive had been one of the women who lived there so she was no use to him.

Pulling out his pocket watch, a very nice gold hunter purloined quite recently from a punter at the races, he squinted at it to discover the time. Nearly midnight he thought, probably nothing to stay for now, but as he started to straighten up and stretch his back, he heard a woman scream. Boysie listened but the cry was stifled almost as soon as it happened. These women, he thought, they do anything to make the punters believe they're enjoying themselves. He'd had enough experience of women and their tricks to last him a lifetime. He indulged himself in a few memories from his younger, more affluent days when the girls had been pleased to see him, gratifying his senses with flattery and cries of satisfaction. Now he was reduced to skulking in a wet shrubbery listening to other men get their pleasure. Boysie shook the drips from his hat, quickly drawing back behind the laurel bushes once more, as the front door opened and someone came out. He could only see the outlines of a tall figure, swathed in a long black coat, but then the man stopped, turned to face the house as he glanced up at the windows on the upper floor. The weak lamp light showed a dark bearded face, not unusual, but this beard was different. It appeared to Boysie that two long streaks of lighter coloured bristles ran down from the corners of the mouth to the chin. Delighted at spotting this distinguishing feature, he followed the man quietly down the driveway, keeping in the shadows. His prey strode off down Grainger Street towards the quays, no doubt in search of a cab.

As he stood watching, Boysie, blackmailer, pickpocket and occasional police snout when he was really hard up, smiled. It shouldn't be too hard to spot that fellow again with that beard. He'd looked furtive enough and should have a nice guilty conscience about visiting the ladies in that house. Chuckling, despite the rain, and his very moist clothing, Boysie mentally rubbed his hands together at the thought of a possible windfall, once he'd discovered the man's identity. In his experience none of the gentlemen wanted their nocturnal visits to Mrs Protheroe's to be known by their nearest and dearest. They were always willing to stump up with a few shillings to prevent that happening by buying his silence.

Finding a few pence left in his pocket, he set off in the same direction as his possible victim, towards his favourite Grand Oyster bar which he hoped would still be open. A few ales and some fish and chips would end the night very nicely, he decided. He could sit in the bar in comfort out of the rain, pondering his next move to trace the bearded man.

CHAPTER TWO

Monday March 13th 1893.

The morning after the meeting and the encounter with
Susie Post, Sophia sat at her typewriter, making hard
work of deciphering the handwritten notes her client had
given her to transcribe. In vain she'd offered to take his
letters down in shorthand, but Mr Isaacs was old
fashioned like many of the older businessmen who came
to her office. He simply didn't believe she could read
back accurately, what appeared to him to be a jumble of
scribbles. It had been hard, at first, persuading her clients
that her secretarial skills were worth the fees she charged,
but now her agency was thriving, she'd employed
another lady to help out. She was proud of the fact that
her secretarial agency offered professional typing and
minute taking skills second to none in the capital city.

   As she sat at her plain oak desk it occurred to
Sophia that it had been nearly a year since her arrival in
New Zealand after the horrendous death of her father in
England. Her determination to run her own business
had succeeded. She'd found this shop in Willis Street,
quite close to Stuart Dawson's the jewellers, and
converted it into a very effective office. Clients were
greeted in the front reception area with an imposing
carved oak counter that separated them from a large back
office out of the public view. Sophia had chosen to paper
the walls in a neat striped design which she felt gave the
entrance a formal appearance. In the back office twin
desks upon which two Remington typewriters neatly

placed, gave an air of efficiency that impressed her customers on the rare occasions they were allowed to enter this inner sanctum. A plain table, filing cabinets and shelving completed the furnishings but unlike the reception area this room was softened by an iron fire grate adding warmth and comfort. Sophia liked the way the flames reflected in the brass coal scuttle standing on the tiled hearth, reminiscent of her old nursery in London. The wooden mantle carried a small selection of personal item; a silver framed photo of her father stood alongside two small china vases that had belonged to her mother and a small jar contained seashells she'd picked up on Brighton beach, as a child. Outside the building, painted in neat script, on the veranda awning was the sign *Wellington Secretarial Agency*.

Sophia's assistant, Mrs Una Johnson, ensured that all the shelves were neatly stacked with various sizes of paper, the book keeping records perfectly in order and the filing system impeccable. Una was married to a school teacher whose income forbade any extravagance so she'd approached Sophia a few months earlier and asked for employment. Gradually the two women had established a routine and a friendship that ensured that in Una, Sophia employed the trusted person she required to keep the business running whilst she was called out to take dictation. Gradually over the months, Una had mastered the Remington typewriter and was intent on learning Mr Pitman's shorthand as fast as she could. Although inexperienced in business, the young woman had made some astute suggestions to her employer which had improved the income and increased the customer numbers.

Finishing Mr Isaac's letters, at last, Sophia removed the carbon paper from the top three copies he required, placing the pages in a folder ready for his signatures. She inserted one of her Votes for Women leaflets inside, hoping he wouldn't take offence.

'Here's a nice cup of tea for you,' said Una, reaching over to place the hot drink beside the typewriter. 'I've ordered the new ribbons for the machines. There's some other letters to post so I'll just pop down to the letter box later.'

'Thanks Una. Golly I'm glad I've finished that job. Just look at my fingers. I'll have to go and scrub them before I touch that biscuit! Carbon paper makes my hands appear as if I was working in a dye factory.'

Una laughed at the thought of her employer doing such a job and went on with her filing. When Sophia returned from the wash room, she stretched her back before sitting down again. Because she found long periods of sitting at her desk rather a strain, she had, daringly, given up wearing her corsets to add some comfort to her working day. Admitting this to Una, a few weeks ago, she was surprised at her shocked expression.

'Heavens! No-one knows do they? I'm respectably clothed aren't I?'

But...,' Una stuttered. 'It's all right here I suppose but surely when you are in company you put your stays on.'

'Well yes I do if I have to wear a formal gown, but that doesn't happen very often. I was reading an advertisement in the paper just recently regarding something called "electric corsets"! It said that they cure headaches and backaches. I think it has more to do with magnetism than electricity. It all sounds most uncomfortable. I read that in America there's a movement towards women wearing trousers or knickerbockers as they call them, for bicycling.'

'Oh! No! I could never bring myself to do that,' said her scandalised assistant. Sophia watched as Una's cheeks went bright pink at the idea, not catching on to the teasing tone of her employer as she continued, 'You'll be taking off your petticoats soon. Whatever will they come up with next?'

'Don't worry Una, I was only teasing. I promise you that I won't embarrass you by coming to work in trousers, but the petticoat idea is worth thinking about. Even Kate Sheppard recently said that *we must be ourselves at all risks* and I did toy with the idea of buying a bicycle until I realised I'd have to push it up the hill to get home. I could have free wheeled all the way down to work though.'

Sophia was well aware that Una thought involvement with the Suffragette movement was giving her all these outlandish ideas.

'Oh Una, we'll have to agree to disagree on some things! I think I'll post the letters if you don't mind. It's a nice day after last night's rain and I'd like to buy a newspaper.'

Pinning on her hat and buttoning her jacket, Sophia left the office, turning to her left to walk down Willis Street. She crossed over carefully, weaving her way between the traffic, trying to avoid the horse manure that never seemed to be removed from these central streets. After posting her letters at the central Post Office, Sophia purchased the early edition of the *Evening Post* from a newsvendor, deciding to sit in a small park to read it as the weather was reasonably fine today. Flicking through the pages she noticed various comments about the Temperance Union, and a speech by a Member of Parliament stating,

'Those who seek for equality with men are the unfortunate victims of the feminist movement, the 'over-educated female book fiend', the short-haired he-women, the shrieking sisterhood, the few who dress without taste and talk slang!'

I must ensure he gets one of my leaflets, thought Sophia. I'll post it to him. What a prig the man sounded; how sure of himself. How are we ever going to succeed in getting the vote when there are privileged men like this one allowed to publish such biased views. Although she knew the *Evening Post* was supportive of suffrage she was still disgusted as she folded up the paper, tucking it under her arm as she started off back to the office.

***

In Willis Street, Meg gazed longingly at the shop windows. When she woke that morning she could hardly believe her luck when she realised that her husband was nowhere in sight and had obviously not returned in the night. Hunger drove her out and she was rewarded when she found some stale bread in a bin behind the local bakery. The baker had spotted her rummaging for the scraps but hadn't shouted at her. It occurred to Meg that this might be an omen for a better day for her as she wandered along. A window display of bright fabrics caught her eye but as she lingered in front of the drapers shop, a sudden jolt and startled movements by the horses tied up nearby, made her turn round. Her old shawl pulled tightly around her, she kept walking as the earthquake struck. It was over in a few seconds but, then, as she heard loud hoof beats coming up behind her, Meg looked back to see a startled horse careering straight at her, a runaway dragging an empty dog cart behind it. Forced back into the nearest doorway, she screamed as the beast reared up in front of her, its' hooves smashing into the window beside her.

As she tumbled away from the danger, Meg felt strong arms hauling her inside the doorway where she ended up in a tangled heap on the floor. The horse stood shuddering outside, it's front feet placed in the spot where Meg had been standing. Its' sudden frightened protest over, it submitted to its owner who, out of breath from his chase, grabbed the trailing reins, swore loudly and hauled his recalcitrant animal backwards onto the road where he inspected the damage to the vehicle, which had sustained a bent axle. He ignored Meg's predicament completely.

'Good heavens, that was close,' said a woman's voice close to Meg. 'Are you all right?'

Meg tried to sit up but groaned aloud as her ribs protested sending a knifelike pain searing through her chest. She was forced to take the hand the woman held out to her, easing herself up to lean against what appeared to be a shop counter.

'Thank you, oh thank you,' she gasped, her face beaded with sweat from the pain and the fright.

She looked up to see another lady peering anxiously down at her. 'The earthquake must have upset that horse. Look, they've tied him up now and he's as quiet as anything. Shall we try and lift you up. Have you hurt your side?'

'It was already hurt. If you can please help me up, I'll get on my way. I don't want to be a bother to you.'

Looking up into the woman's clear brown eyes Meg felt something pass between them. This lady knows what's happened to me, she thought, she understands and an unaccustomed sense of relief went through her.

'I'm not allowing you to go anywhere until you've had a strong cup of tea,' said the first lady. 'Oh! I'm Miss Holmes and this is Mrs Johnson. This is my secretarial agency.'

Seeing the determination overlaid by kindness in the two faces looking down at her, Meg capitulated. She could see that these ladies wanted to take charge of her and were not going to let her go on her way easily. She swallowed and felt the saliva start in her mouth at the thought of a hot drink.

'I wouldn't say no to the tea thank you. I'm Mrs Meg Williams.'

Helped by the two women, Meg got to her feet slowly, fighting to hide the pain she was suffering. She walked carefully behind the counter into a neat office, where Miss Holmes made her sit down at an empty desk. When her tea was placed before her with a dainty plate of mouth watering buttery shortbread biscuits, she managed to take ladylike nibbles at her piece so as not to appear too hungry. However, she noticed that her rescuers looked very concerned; watching over her as if they suspected not all was right. It was very obvious, she supposed, that she was extremely hungry, and Meg noticed Miss Holmes exchanging a look with Mrs Johnson who nodded back in confirmation.

'Mrs Williams, excuse me for asking this, but I have a very curious nature, as my friends are always telling me, I can see you are in pain and I wonder if perhaps you would like me to fetch a Doctor to see if you're badly hurt?'

'No, no.'

Meg was horrified at the thought of causing any more bother although the temptation to tell her troubles to these two kind women was almost overwhelming. However she realised If Bob found out she'd seen a Doctor, he'd be even more furious with her and that was enough for her pride to stay intact.

'Well... can I at least get you a cab to take you home?'

Shaking her head, Meg grasped the arm of the chair with her uninjured left hand managing to stand up stiffly, but the effort cost her dearly. Every time she moved she gasped with the pain of her bruised ribs and as she faltered, her knees wobbling, Miss Holmes reached her side, taking her gently by the shoulders, pressing her back into the chair.

'Please let me help you, take you to my house and give you a good meal. That was a terrifying experience. You must give yourself time to recover.'

'You don't have to do anything for me Miss,' whispered Meg, overcome with this unexpected kindness. 'I'm the one who owes you a debt after you pulled me away from that horse.'

'Nonsense, anyone would have done that. I could hardly ignore somebody in danger hurtling through my door?'

Meg saw her smile sympathetically but her expression changed as she suddenly noticed the rag binding Meg's left arm.

'What happened to your arm?'

The dirty makeshift bandage that Meg had bound

her arm with was now hanging loose, and all the events of the last night flooded back. Her eyes filling with tears she slowly unwound the rag, revealing the blistered skin which was already becoming infected. Miss Holmes wrinkled her nose but didn't flinch from looking closely at the burns and appeared to make her mind up without hesitation.

'Una, would you call a cab please? I won't take no for an answer Mrs Williams. I'm going to take you to my home where I can treat this for you. If it doesn't improve in a few days I shall insist on taking you to my Doctor.'

Meg was past protesting as she watched Sophia don her hat and coat. She meekly followed Sophia out into the street and into the waiting Brougham Mrs Johnson had managed to flag down and sat, quietly in awe of the lady who seemed to be determined to look after her, as the horse moved away, pulling hard at the load as he plodded up to the Terrace. Arriving at an entranceway with large white wooden gates, the cabbie directed the horse to turn in and walk up the semicircular driveway. Halting in front of the porch of a sizeable house, with a freshly painted dark green door, the cabbie waited while his two passengers climbed out and Miss Holmes paid him.

'Somewhere in here, I have the key,' laughed her hostess, delving into her large bag. 'Ah here it is.'

Meg watched nervously as Miss Holmes opened the front door with a large ornate iron key, beckoning her guest inside. Afterwards, she recalled walking across an expanse of black and white tiled floor, past a sweeping stairway and along a corridor into a large and well equipped kitchen. Told to sit at the table, she waited whilst Miss Holmes fetched water, towels and bandages.

'This is going to hurt I'm afraid, but the Boracic powder will cool the burns down.'

Gritting her teeth, Meg allowed this kind woman to treat her arm, bandaging it with clean linen.

'What a lovely kitchen,' said Meg. 'How many people live here?'

'Only me,' said Miss Holmes, and then appearing to feel some sort of explanation might be due to her patient added, 'I know it seems extravagant. I mean, one person having this huge house to themselves, but I just fell in love with it. It's about thirty years old and it belonged to an old lady who died. She didn't have any family so I bought it fully furnished, sheets, blankets, the lot just as she left it! It was a bargain and I know you'll appreciate that Mrs Williams. We women are always looking for value for money aren't we?'

'I suppose so,' said Meg doubtfully. 'I've never had enough to go round let alone save any.'

'Gosh no, that wasn't very tactful of me was it? Still my good fortune can be yours too. There are plenty of spare bedrooms in the servant's quarters at the back here. Why don't you stay here until your arm is healed? It will give your husband time to cool down perhaps? Oh there I go again! I'm only guessing that he hurt you like this, and you don't have to tell me, but I have seen women like you before. That's the reason I joined the Women's Temperance Union to fight drunkenness and abuse.'

'But I've got nothing with me, no spare clothes. Not that I've got many to speak of,' Meg answered softly. 'I found one of your lot's leaflets. I wanted to join too but...'

Miss Holmes seemed to understand her predicament and nodded. Meg was glad when she steered the conversation onto practical matters.

'Well, there are plenty of spare aprons and caps in the cupboards here and I'm certain there are some skirts and blouses that belonged to the old lady. Perhaps we can make and mend some things?'

Meg realised that Miss Holmes had a look of expectancy; the expression of someone used to issuing orders. While her pride made her slow to accept charity, she thought about the one roomed hovel she'd left, in comparison to this clean and comfortable home and the evident kindness being shown her. Was this an omen of better things to come? She might never get another chance to break away from Bob. She really had little choice when her terror of her husband far outweighed her distrust of her luck in meeting Miss Holmes and she made her decision.

'Thank you Miss, I'd like that very much but you must let me do something in return. Cooking, cleaning. I'd feel much better if you let me help out here.'

'Well I'll gratefully accept your help but nothing heavy mind you, until you are fully well. To tell the truth it will be very pleasant to come home to a house with the lamps lit. I've only lived here for about three months and it has been a little lonely. I'm sure we'll deal very well together.'

Meg was surprised and touched when Miss Holmes reached out and patted her on the arm in an affectionate gesture of sisterhood that went straight to Meg's heart.

CHAPTER THREE

Tuesday March 14th 1893

'That was the best soup I've tasted in a long time.'

Sophia pushed her bowl to one side, gazing with satisfaction, at the transformed woman standing on the opposite side of the long scrubbed kitchen table. Meg's cheeks had already lost the pinched grey look from yesterday morning and her benefactor was pleased to note how rapidly a good night's sleep could take effect.

'It's easy to make good soup when you've got all the right ingredients,' said Meg, busying herself at the coal range.

'I think I've discovered a treasure in you Meg,' said Sophia sincerely. 'Can I persuade you to stay here as my housekeeper and cook? I'm sure we could reach an agreeable arrangement that would suit you.'

'But what if my husband finds me? He's a terrible bully. He'd make me go back to him. I couldn't expect you to sort him out.'

'I don't see how he would find you. After all, no-one knows you are here except Una and he's hardly likely to run across her. If you wish I can make enquiries to see if he is looking for you?'

'No don't you go near him. He's dangerous. I don't know what he'd do if he found out I'd run away.'

Meg's agitation increased rapidly as she talked, so Sophia made the decision to drop the subject although still determined to persuade Meg to stay. After a helping of Spotted Dick pudding and custard her resolve was even stronger!

Picking up the previous night's *Evening Post*, Sophia, as was her custom, scanned through the front page quickly to see if there were any mentions of the suffrage movement. There was a long article regarding prohibition that argued that the colony would be in financial straits without the taxes and duties gathered by the Government on liquor sales. The writer stressed that cutting down on services and increasing other more personal taxes would never make up the shortfall if alcohol was banned completely.

Sophia was in two minds over this assertion and she turned the page where the murder of a woman the night before, was briefly reported, then suddenly, her eyes caught a small headline. Reading it to herself, she looked over to where Meg was about to make a pot of tea, scooping out the leaves from a tin tea caddy Sophia's father had owned since her childhood, and which never failed to remind her of breakfast with him before he departed for his chambers every day. Rising from the table, Sophia quickly grabbed the pot holder, lifting the heavy iron kettle off the range before Meg attempted it and caused herself more pain. She'd pointed out the hot water tap at the side of the Shacklock range to Meg, but it seemed too new fangled for her to cope with yet, and she persisted in using the old kettle. As she poured the boiling water into the tea pot, Sophia tried to work out how she could soften the news she has just read.

'Meg,' she hesitated. 'This will be a shock for you but there's a report in the paper that a body was pulled out of the harbour yesterday. I'm afraid the police have identified it as your husband.'

Meg lifted her head, silently walking over to the table where she picked up the paper. She read the column slowly, her lips moving then shaking her head, a grim expression on her face, turned to look at Sophia.

'They don't say how he died, but he must have been unconscious before he went into the water or someone shoved him. He could swim quite well. Even dead drunk he could swim. It says here the police are looking for me but I'm not going to the police. They'll be thinking I pushed him. They're bound to think I'm the guilty one.'

Sophia gazed at her quite sadly and shook her head.

'No of course they don't. They'll just want to see if you know what might have happened. It doesn't say he was pushed or anything remotely suggesting that. It's more than likely it was a terrible accident, so you must go Meg. They'll want to know about funeral arrangements at the very least. Think about that.'

'Never,' declared Meg. 'I'm glad he's dead. Now I don't have to be frightened any more. He was a brute and if someone did push him in the water, then I'm glad. They can plant him in a paupers' grave for all I care. I don't have any money to spend on his burial and if I did I wouldn't be wasting it on him I can tell you!'

Taken aback by this vehemence, Sophia could only shake her head and try to think of a solution that would be acceptable to Meg who she sensed, was becoming increasingly confident in her new found independence.

'Well... would you like me to go to the police and see if I can find out anything?'

'Only if you don't tell them I'm here or they'll come to find me.'

'No. I promise I won't reveal your whereabouts, but it really would be better for you if I see what the police want and then when I've proved you aren't a suspect it can all be sorted out. If we don't discover what happened then suspicion could hang over you for the rest of your life and I'm quite sure you don't wish for that.'

Nodding her head doubtfully, Meg returned to pour the tea, but she was very quiet for the rest of the evening.

CHAPTER FOUR.

Wednesday March 15th 1893.

The front reception office of the Wellington Central Police Station in Manners Street was crowded and smelly. Outside the wind had returned, rising strongly to whip the harbour into white capped waves. Holding her skirts in tightly, Sophia edged past an anxious young couple, a rather fraught old lady and nearly tripped over the bundle of an extremely dirty tramp before she was able to reach the counter. As she waited for the attention of a busy Constable, she hoped to achieve her errand and leave as soon as possible. Finally, she was attended to by a very harassed officer, who peered at her suspiciously over the top of his wire rimmed glasses as if she was a criminal.

'Yes madam what can I do for you?'

Sophia looked at the burly uniformed man on the other side of the counter, summed him up and smiled sweetly, trusting in charming manners to expedite the situation.

'I've come about the body in the harbour. Bob Williams? There was a report in the *Evening Post.*'

'Have you got some information for us,' enquired the Constable in the same dour tones. He appeared completely oblivious to any feminine wiles but that only hardened her resolve. His eyes darted over Sophia's shoulder towards the throng of waiting humanity, as if he was searching for somebody more interesting or more in need of his attention.

'Yes. It concerns his wife,' answered Sophia, not wasting her smile this time. She deliberately moved directly in front of him, blocking his view of the room as he was slightly shorter than her. 'The report said the Police are looking for her.'

'Ah. Then you'll be requiring Detective Butler. One moment please,' he proclaimed, bringing his attention back to her, then looked down at her left hand in a completely obvious manner, even though she wore gloves.

'May tell him your name please?

'Miss Holmes,' said Sophia patiently, clasping her hands together on the worn, pitted wooden counter top as he disappeared through a door in the rear wall. She was spared a long wait because almost immediately he returned, with a tall man in a neat, but well worn black suit, who Sophia judged to be a few years older than her, perhaps thirty five?

'Miss Holmes, please come this way,' the man said politely, as he lifted a hinged part of the counter up to usher her through. 'Please follow me.'

Sophia walked after him down a dark corridor into the depths of the building their footsteps echoing on the wooden floorboards. A strong smell of carbolic disinfectant mingled with cigarette smoke and other odours she preferred not to identify. Finally he stopped at an open door, stepping aside to let her pass. She found herself in a grim little room, its only furniture, a table and two chairs. One high window provided the only light, restricting the view to the fast racing clouds and a few seagulls hovering in the wind currents. She noticed where initials and dates had been scratched in the grey painted brick walls as the detective pulled out a chair on one side of the table for her then sat opposite. Pulling out a notebook and pencil from an inner pocket, he licked the tip and wrote the date.

'Your full name please?'

Noticing the distinct lack of social niceties, Sophia sat up straight and became assertive.

'Miss Sophia Holmes and you are?'

'Detective Jack Butler, I'm in charge of investigating the Williams case.'

'I hadn't realised it was that serious...I mean, to be called a case,' asked Sophia raising an eyebrow at him in query, but he didn't respond to her curiosity.

'Address?'

Sophia wondered why this was necessary but she complied, then before he could start again decided to seek some sort of control of the interview.

'I'm here to represent Mrs Williams so my personal details aren't really relevant.'

'I decide that, Miss Holmes. Let's continue, do you know the whereabouts of Mrs Williams?'

'Not exactly,' said Sophia cautiously. 'But I can assure you she didn't push him into the harbour.'

'Perhaps she didn't but she might have stuck the knife in his back before he fell.'

Sophia guessed that Butler was gauging her reaction and fought to keep her face impassive at the mention of a knife attack which brought sudden sickening memories back. She swallowed hard hoping he put her reaction down to natural shock. She imagined that it wasn't often a woman like her came within his ambit but didn't think there was anything out of the ordinary about herself. Plainly dressed, her neat dark grey jacket and skirt complemented her brunette hair coiled neatly under a smart straw hat that was tied firmly under her chin with a silk scarf to avoid it being blown off in today's typically strong Wellington wind. Sophia understood that she was not beautiful, but she possessed large brown eyes under well shaped brows which she frequently raised in response to his questions. She had often been told that she was an attractive woman when she smiled and she made it abundantly clear that she wasn't worried about being questioned by Detective Butler; in fact she quite enjoyed it in a perverse way. Knowing he was inwardly amused, as she digested this information, she knew that he was quite unprepared for her matter of fact response. Resting her wrist on the table edge, she stretched out the fingers of her gloved left hand frowning down at them slightly, as if picturing what had happened.

'So he was murdered? I did wonder. Well that's all right then. Meg has nothing to be worried about.'

She smiled at this point noticing that her calm dismissal of his statement threw him off balance for a moment as he cleared his throat.

'I... can assure you Miss Holmes that many women are quite capable of killing their husbands, especially abused ones like Mrs Williams. We've established her husband treated her very cruelly. Even in a rough neighbourhood like Grainger Street it was noticed.'

'Where was the stab wound?'

'In the right hand side of his back. Probably punctured his lung,' responded Butler.

Sophia judged that he had revealed this fact before he could stop himself as he hastily continued, 'But that's in confidence. I shouldn't have revealed the manner of his death to you.'

'Oh I'll keep it strictly entre nous,' responded Sophia lightly, putting put a finger to her lips in a gesture that she suddenly realised was overly coquettish in the circumstances of a police interview. Now it was her turn to quickly make a pretended cough, allowing her to spread her hand over her mouth before she continued. 'But of course, you must accept that definitely means Meg is innocent. First of all she has several cracked ribs and she's left handed; added to that, her left arm and hand are badly scalded where he poured boiling stew over her earlier that night. She's not in a good way physically. It's quite impossible to imagine she would have followed him to the docks in those circumstances.'

'Well thank you for that. It looks like you've just removed a key suspect from my list with your amateur sleuthing'

His sarcasm was not lost on Sophia who gazed steadily back at him in silence with a prim expression, until he dropped his eyes to his notebook. She thought he had quite a pleasant face, clean shaven but possessing a grim expression that seemed to be its normal fixture. His dark wavy hair was rather longer that the normal short back and sides cut that most men favoured, but although she deemed him quite presentable, she was not impressed by his attitude, understanding now, why the plain clothes police in New Zealand did not have a spotless reputation. Many of them were recruited from the beat constables, straight off the street with little experience in dealing with people who weren't involved with crime. Finishing his notes, he finally raised his head, tapping his pencil on the table.

'May I enquire why Mrs Williams hasn't come to see me?'

'Well obviously, first, she's not well enough and secondly, she's too frightened of the police. I gather she's had some bad experiences with her husband running foul of the law.'

Butler sighed and stared at Sophia, continuing to tap his pencil on the table, expressing his impatience succinctly.

'Most people are only frightened of the police if they're guilty,' was his trenchant comment.

'Well I don't think that's correct at all. I myself haven't found this to be at all pleasant and I certainly don't feel guilty about anything. Now, if that's everything, can I go?'

Jack Butler became aware that he was losing control of this situation and that unless he could come up with a very good excuse for detaining Miss Sophia Holmes, he was going to lose face with this entirely exasperating young woman. Acknowledging to himself that he was unable to find any valid reason to stop her leaving, he grudgingly escorted her to the front door of the Police Station where he decided to be a little more diplomatic.

'I would appreciate it if you could persuade Williams to talk to me. Her husband's body will stay in the morgue until she lets us know where she wishes him buried.'

'I'll venture to inform you that she's quite happy to let him have a pauper's grave. She's not exactly a grieving widow. She has no money at all for any other arrangement. But I will ask her. Good day Detective Butler.'

Sophia turned and walked briskly back down the street but she sensed that Butler watched her with a wry smile which she might have interpreted to mean that he thought Miss Sophia Holmes was a worthy opponent.

CHAPTER FIVE

Thursday 16th March 1893

Scratching her head and rubbing her eyes, Sophia bent low over her desk as she endeavoured to decipher the spidery copperplate hand writing of another of her elderly clients. She was extremely pleased when Una brought her a cup of tea.

'Una? Can you read this?'

Placing the cup and saucer carefully on Sophia's desk, Una took the letter and puzzled over it. Pursing her lips she read it and then re-read it.

'I can't make head or tail of it. Did he tell you what it was about?'

'It's a complaint of sorts to Kirkaldie and Staines department store. As I recall he told me his wife had purchased him a new waistcoat there for his birthday but he had to return it because it was the wrong size. They refused to exchange it so now he's writing to the manager to demand his money back.'

'Well perhaps you could put that in your own words and when he comes to pick it up you can check with him.'

'I suppose so but between you and me, he is a most difficult fussy man.'

'Oh, I nearly forgot,' said Una. 'This letter was hand delivered to you just now.'

She handed Sophia an envelope with an embossed seal.

'The High Court?   What on earth have I done now?'

Reaching for her paper knife, she slit the envelope open and drew out a folded note of thick good quality paper.

'It's from Sir James, my Godfather. He wants me to take afternoon tea with him today if I can.'

'That's short notice,' said Una curiously. 'It must be about something important.'

'Perhaps I really offended the detective yesterday and he's reported me!'

Una looked worried, but Sophia laughed at her,

'I'm only joking Una. I expect Sir James feels guilty because he hasn't seen me for a while. It's most likely today is the only free time he has. Judges are always so busy. I'll just dash off a reply and perhaps you can get it delivered for me?'

***

Promptly at three o'clock that afternoon Sophia was shown into Sir James Mclauchlan's office. The air smelled of fragrant smoke from a cigar left burning in the large greenstone ashtray on the massive desk. Her Godfather, the most senior High Court Judge in New Zealand, rose from his carved mahogany, leather padded chair, striding across the vast wood panelled room to greet her with a fatherly hug, his neatly trimmed silver beard tickling her cheeks.

'Sophia, my dear girl, it's been too long. How are you?'

'I'm well Sir James and yourself and Lady Muriel?'

'Oh can't complain you know. Muriel's getting a bit stiff in the joints these days but we're both still surviving. Now come and sit down and let me introduce you to Detective Butler.'

Sophia turned abruptly, completely taken by surprise as the police officer she'd met just the day before, came forward from the back of the room. To her eyes he appeared a little sheepish in his behaviour but she dismissed this idle thought as wishful thinking not wanting to seem too ungracious at his presence in this formidable room.

'We've met,' was their simultaneous answer as Sir James motioned for them to sit down at a table set in a large window alcove with deep red velvet curtains roped back at either side, framing a view over the harbour. A large silver tray with a fine china tea set and a plate of dainty sandwiches sat on the linen lace edged tablecloth.

'Can I pour you a cup of tea Miss Holmes?'

Sophia nodded at Butler's question, waiting alertly for an explanation for his presence as she took the tea from him, placing the fragile bone china carefully down on the table. She noticed how well the policeman poured the tea from the heavy silver pot, with not a drop spilled as he'd handed it to her with a steady hand. Her Godfather beamed at them both, and it was obvious to Sophia that he was keen to relate why he'd invited them here. Taking a deep drink of his tea, he wiped his moustaches on a napkin, cleared his throat loudly and launched into his explanations.

'Sophia you must be wondering why I've asked you to come here at such short notice? Butler has presented me with a dilemma in a new case he's working on that I feel you may be able to help us with.'

'I was under the distinct impression that he doesn't approve of amateur sleuthing,' was Sophia's rather tart response. 'So I'm not all sure what I can do?'

'Oh come, my dear. It's in your blood, you know. Surely some of your cousin Arthur's intuition and imagination must have been handed down. I'm certain your father would have agreed.'

Butler looked puzzled at this comment from his host and raised an eyebrow at Sir James who was only too pleased it seemed to a reluctant Sophia, to reveal all her secrets.

'Sophia is related to the great author, Conan Doyle.' explained Sir James. 'I feel certain that his amazing talent for concocting those tales has been passed down to her. She has a knack of getting to the heart of problems and prying out all the finest details. We've seen it happen time and time again over the years as she grew up.'

He smiled at Sophia who gathered her thoughts to offer some sort of defence before Detective Butler could jump to any conclusions about her talents or lack of them.

'My Godfather's enthusiasm for my family ties runs away with him at times I'm afraid,' she said gently, not wishing to offend Sir James, of whom she was very fond. 'Conan Doyle is, or was, I think I should say, my late father's third cousin. I doubt if we even have a teaspoon of the same blood in our veins. As for my inheriting his extraordinary imaginative deductive skills, I hardly think so. All I can say is that I do possess a healthy curiosity and perhaps we share that in common. It is a weakness of mine to want to tie up loose ends neatly and unfortunate that my name is Holmes. I was much teased about it as a youngster. It appears that Conan Doyle may have used our name for Sherlock on purpose, to pay respect to my father's legal skills. Or so the story goes although I have no proof of it.'

'Have you ever met him?'

Jack Butler was eager to know. He was an avid reader of all detective stories and was keenly interested in the history of crime solving. Finding himself in proximity to a woman who had an actual connection to one of his favourite authors was mildly intoxicating to say the least. Sophia, who was well practised in answering questions on the subject, but who thought she might have left it all behind in England, patiently explained the circumstances to this new acquaintance.

'Only once, very briefly as a child, when he came to visit my father about a legal matter concerning one of his books. My father was a criminal defence barrister. I hardly saw Conan Doyle that day so I really can't describe him. As I recall I let him into the house, shook hands and showed him into my father's library. Nothing more than that. I'm afraid it was hardly a significant moment in my life. He appeared quite ordinary to me.'

'I wish we knew what happened to Sherlock Holmes. Do you think Conan Doyle intended us to believe he died at the Reichenbach Falls Miss Holmes? Perhaps it was Moriarty who died?'

'I have no idea except to say that a friend wrote to me from England recently to say that the latest writings from Conan Doyle indicate the character may have been seen in Tibet tracking the Abominable Snowman. It all sounds rather farfetched to me but I do hope he's kept the character alive. We may never find out. After all it's been nearly two years according to the book, since

Sherlock is supposed to have disappeared. Perhaps Conan Doyle simple got bored with writing about him.'

'It's a shame you are not better acquainted with him then you could perhaps write and ask?'

Butler had to be satisfied with the shake of her head that Sophia offered him as a reply to his pensive question. Both men nodded in agreement with her rueful expression, then surveying his empty teacup, as if reading his fortune in the tea leaves before placing it gently back in the saucer, Sir James cleared his throat again, placing his large hands on his crossed legs, leaned slightly forward, as if balancing his body against a strong wind and continued.

'We've asked you here on a rather delicate matter my dear. It requires someone who can be discreet; a person who also understands the fine nuances of politics. I think you fit the bill perfectly but it's probably better if I ask Detective Butler to explain to you.'

Jack Butler pushed his chair back from the table and crossed one long leg over the other. Sophia was quite impressed by his highly shined boots, wondering why they weren't dusty and muddy like her own, from the unpaved streets outside. He appeared to be weighing up his approach to Sophia who lifted her eyes from his feet and gazed calmly at him with her hands demurely folded in her lap.

'On the same night that Bob Williams was killed, there was another murder. A most vicious and unpleasant attack on a prostitute, who lived in a fairly well run brothel. She was strangled, her clothes torn off and the words 'No Votes' carved across her chest.'

'My God!'

Sophia was genuinely horrified. She swallowed

hard and placed a hand to her lips as she turned away to look out of the window, quite sickened by this lurid description. A vivid picture of the event came before her eyes and she turned to her Godfather who, she knew would appreciate her feelings. He looked anxiously at her, fully aware that she might not be able to cope with this news but she nodded silently at him as Butler gave her no time to recover from her squeamishness and continued as if he'd not noticed.

'She was left lying on her bed with several of the latest Suffrage leaflets scattered around her and one stuffed in her mouth.'

'Susie Post,' said Sophia in a whisper turning back to him. 'Was it a woman called Susie Post? At Mrs Protheroe's?'

'Yes,' said a surprised Butler. 'How did you know that?'

'I met her at our meeting earlier that night. She came up and introduced herself to me and my friend Tilly. She had a bundle of WCTU leaflets like the rest of us. I remember she made a joke about giving them to her clients. That seems in rather poor taste now doesn't it?'

'Is there anything else you can recall about her?'

Thinking back to that evening, Sophia talked about Susie Post sitting with them and the conversation the three of them had shared. She frowned in concentration as the two men listened to her.

'She told us that one of her gentlemen, as she called him, had given her a donation to give to our cause. He wanted to remain anonymous so she'd brought the money.'

'Do you think that was true?'

'Oh yes. I saw it myself when I went to pay my

subscription. There was a large bundle of notes in the open cash box and I was naturally curious so asked the Treasurer Laura Robertson about it. She said there was several hundred pounds from Miss Post's secret friend. Apparently she'd been insistent on having a receipt for the money.'

'Sounds like the man wanted proof she'd actually given it to the right person.'

'Did you find the receipt? It was probably in her bag.'

'No...' said Butler thoughtfully. 'We went through the contents of her handbag but that certainly didn't turn up. Could be the person who killed her took it. Indeed he may have been one and the same, the killer and the donor of the money. But why would he want a receipt made out to Susie Post?'

The policeman shook his head, evidently puzzled at his own question.

'Possibly they could be the same man,' said Sophia considering this. 'But you should also consider that she may have met this mysterious donor straight after our meeting to give the receipt to him before she went back to her room. He could be quite innocent of all this. When she left all she said to us was that she had to get back to business. Strangely enough there was a man sitting in the same row as me who left very abruptly when the meeting ended. Later I did wonder if he was the donor and he came to ensure she gave the money and didn't cheat him.'

'Can you give me a description of him?'

'Yes...' said Sophia doubtfully. 'But it could fit any of the men in the hall that night, dark clothes, a cap well down over his face and scarf quite high round his chin. I felt he was scrutinising me when I caught his eye but I couldn't honestly say why. I found a pipe under his seat after he'd left and tried to catch up with him but he took a cab and didn't see me waving.'

'A pipe?' asked Butler. 'Where is it?

'It's here somewhere in the bottom of my bag,' said Sophia. 'I'd forgotten all about it until now.'

She felt around at the bottom of her handbag and found the object. Holding it out to Butler she said, 'It looks valuable. I wondered if it was stolen.'

As he turned the ivory pipe over in his hands, the policeman pursed his lips.

'It's wonderfully carved. I think you're correct Miss Holmes in thinking it valuable. Are you absolutely sure this man dropped it?'

'Well no... I mean it could have been someone else sitting next to him, only it makes more sense that it was his. It wouldn't have rolled along the floor and if it was moved by a foot, surely that person would have felt it?'

Butler nodded and handed it back to her.

'Promise me that if this man does try and meet with you to get this, you will try and find out who he is.'

'I'm not sure I would feel at all safe now that you have mentioned he might be a murder suspect. Can't you keep it Detective Butler? Then I could simply send him to you.'

'Well...' Butler paused. 'If he is guilty he certainly won't wish to show his face to a policeman Miss Holmes.'

'I suppose you are correct in that but it makes me very uneasy.'

As Sophia pushed the pipe deep down into her bag again, Sir James eyed her keenly as if coming to a conclusion, then nodded at the detective.

'The reason I requested that you both come to talk to me about this particular murder, which came to my notice through Butler, is that as you may know, Kate Sheppard the Franchise superintendant of the WCTU, and Muriel are close friends and correspond regularly. Kate is becoming increasingly alarmed at the series of misfortunes and setbacks that are plaguing the WTCU and the Women's Franchise League particularly here in Wellington. She is of the opinion that they are not coincidental but are being put in place by some very powerful people.

As the most senior High Court Judge, I have to take this seriously but I have to be very careful not to be too biased. Premier Ballance and his Cabinet might not be best pleased if he thought I was too much in favour of the suffrage movement. There are enough rumours flying around this town regarding Dick Seddon's positive attitude in public for the Electoral Reform Bill and his private opinions against it. It's obvious to all of us that with Ballance ailing, Minister Seddon is a powerful political force.'

'Well... we all know the liquor barons are against us, but would they stoop to murder? Surely Seddon wouldn't condone that?' Sophia asked Butler.

'We think they would, indeed already have. Why Susie Post was chosen I have no idea, but her death has all the hallmarks of a devastating plan to further blacken your cause. We're almost certain of it and obviously money is no object so there is at least one very wealthy man involved.'

Sophia nodded at Butler's statement giving her full attention to his words but becoming anxious about his reasons for telling her. In a matter of a few days she had indirectly been involved in two murders and her usual calm demeanour was becoming slightly ruffled. She wondered if her companions realised that she didn't feel as intrepid as they hoped she was but decided to make her own mind up if she could be of any help rather than be coerced or flattered by Detective Butler.

'Without putting you in any danger, we would like you to keep your ears and eyes open at your meetings. If, for example, you are made aware of any other prostitute donating money, try and prevent her from leaving and call the police.'

Despite concurring with this, Sophia felt there was a more important fact that should be pursued and she also thought the chances of a policeman being available when required at a moment's notice was unlikely.

'While I can agree with that, I hardly think it's likely the killer would repeat the scenario. It would be too risky now that the police are alert to the possibility. If I were you I would focus on that receipt. I have a feeling that's the key to all of this. Did Mrs Protheroe not see who the visitors were that night? I always pictured those Madams ensconced firmly in the entrance to their houses so they could keep an eye on the visitors.'

If Sophia's knowledge of brothel management shocked the two men, they hid it well. Sir James, because he was aware that his Goddaughter had been quite deeply involved with her father's cases, and Butler because he felt he didn't know Miss Holmes well enough to comment, although his curiosity was piqued about her back ground.

'I grant you that's usually the case but unfortunately on this occasion, Mrs P., who is a bit too fond of a gin or two, retired to her room early that night and was dead to the world. Didn't hear a thing according to her and to be fair, her room is on the ground floor at the front of the house well away from the murder scene. However, it's not to her advantage to point the finger at any of the men who frequent that place is it? I imagine they could make life very difficult for her if she wasn't discreet enough to protect her livelihood.'

'Perhaps if you put a report in the newspaper asking for witnesses, someone might come forward? There may be somebody who does have a conscience,' suggested Sophia.

'I did allow a very brief report of the death in the *Evening* Post but somehow I doubt that any of the men who visited the place that night, would wish it known, Miss Holmes, but it may be worth a try. We've kept a more detailed story out of the paper so far. I have an informant who might come to me if he hears anything about the house that night and it's worth his while. I may try and contact him if he doesn't come forward.'

'Ah yes,' said Sophia. 'I do recall that report but when I read about Bob Williams I completely forgot about the woman's death.'

Sir James rubbed his hands together, pleased at the progress of the conversation.

'Well it sounds an excellent suggestion, Sophia my dear. There Butler, didn't I tell you she would come up with some good ideas. She'll have the case solved for you in no time at all. I can tell Mrs Sheppard that it's all under control.'

His two visitors looked astonished at this

sweeping statement but made no comment. After a few more pleasantries with her Godfather during which he urged her to come on a shooting party at the weekend and issued an invitation to have dinner with he and his wife, Sophia and Butler left, making their way out, through long corridors, onto the street where Sophia intended to wait for a passing cab. It was evident that Butler, feeling he should make polite conversation and not leave her too abruptly, should use the chance to find out a bit more about her past.

'May I ask why you decided to come and live in New Zealand Miss Holmes?

'Oh...,' Sophia hesitated before replying with a much practised explanation that had served her well on most occasions. 'When my father died I was left on my own. Sir James and Lady Muriel wrote and urged me to come for a holiday. I never intended to stay permanently but when I'd been here a few weeks I realised there were business opportunities here so I decided to stay. There's no mysterious past to intrigue you Detective Butler.'

'I'm surprised you can shoot Miss Holmes'

'Only clay pigeons I assure you. I have absolutely no wish to kill anything. My father insisted I learn. He used to drag me off to Scotland for pheasant shooting holidays but I was quite content with target practice. I really prefer something lighter than a shotgun. The American ambassador in London was from Wyoming and he taught me to shoot a small Derringer when I was younger. He used to call me his little English Annie Oakley! A bit of an exaggeration I may say. It's been a long time since I fired a gun.'

She felt her lies hang between them like a red misty banner but only Sophia was aware of it as Butler smiled.

'What an accomplished woman you are Miss Holmes. A crack shot from the sound of it and an accomplished typist. If you'll forgive me remarking, it is an odd combination of talents. Shall I flag down this cab for you?'

'Thank you,' said Sophia formally. 'Oh and please don't take notice of all that Conan Doyle and Sherlock stuff and nonsense Sir James was telling you. It really is of no consequence. Honestly I don't possess any special skills and I'm quite sure you are perfectly capable of solving Miss Post's death without my help. May I ask how it is that you seem to know Sir James so well?'

'I've had to present several cases to him as Judge. He's always been most helpful when I've had to discuss matters with him in chambers, unlike some I could mention. Anyway, he let drop that he knew Mrs Sheppard was concerned about the campaign so I thought it best to let him know about Susie Post. I had no idea he would take it so seriously though, in advising you.'

'Yes but as I said before I'm sure you will quickly solve the murder without any intervention from me.'

'I can't help but be impressed though,' said Butler, apparently touched by her genuine modesty, as he handed her into the cab. 'I apologise for that remark about amateur sleuthing but I really had no idea who you were.'

Well that was precisely how I intended it, before Sir James let the cat out of the bag, thought Sophia. I do hope he can be discreet from now on.

***

That evening after supper, Sophia sat at the kitchen table and read to Meg from the *Evening Post,* an article entitled 'Fooling the Women'.

'Listen to this Meg. It says that the Minister of Labour addressed the Tailoresses' Union last night in a speech with a *"strong Pocksniffian flavour"*. I shall have to look that word up. Anyway, it was apparently,

"a nauseous mixture of cant and hypocrisy". The writer says that, *"Mr Reaves posed as a friend of down-trodden women and he urged them to unite for their own protection, but he carefully refrained from promising to use his Ministerial position to aid them in obtaining the only endowment by which their union can be rendered really effective – the possession of the franchise. He told then they would get this some day. He did not tell them- as he ought to have done, if he desired to tell the truth- that they had been deprived of this power last session through the dishonest intrigues of the Ministry of which he is a member, and that the same Ministry is now using every means in its power to prevent them exercising electoral rights at the next election. He pretended to advocate the equality of the sexes, while he and his colleagues are doing all they possibly can to keep one sex in political subjection to the other."*

'That's bold reporting isn't it?'

Sophia nodded at her housekeeper and continued to read aloud.

'It goes on to say how Mr Reeves deliberately avoided the subject of equal pay and patronised his audience, treating them as ignorant and weak. Oh! It makes my blood boil to read of a politician speaking like this. It's insulting to all the women in New Zealand.'

She threw the newspaper down on the table in disgust.

'I'm sure there'll be a debate about it at your next meeting,' offered Meg.

'You can be assured of that,' snorted her employer. 'You can use that paper to light the fire with Meg. That's all it's worth.'

'At least you know the *Evening Post* supports the cause,' said Meg endeavouring to placate.

'Yes there is that. It would be nearly impossible to progress if we didn't have some of the editors on our side. I believe the Christchurch Press is in complete opposition to women voting and electoral reform. That makes it extremely difficult for Mrs Sheppard. Apparently she purchases a page in the *Prohibionist* magazine and uses it to print articles about suffrage.'

Picking up the paper again she read on through the article.

' "*Soft words butter no parsnips,*" *and the women of the colony in working out their political, social and industrial salvation, need expect nothing more than soft words, cloaking treacherous actions, from Mr Reeves and his colleagues.*'

It occurred to Sophia that, not only did she and Tilly have to keep their ears and eyes open regarding the Post murder, but also to ascertain the underlying and devious innuendo of any political gossip that might occur within their orbit. On a more whimsical note she read that,

"Miss Sara Spilsbury, an eccentric lady' and Mr G.H.Powley had been nominated for a vacancy on the Auckland City

Council... The lady is chiefly notable as a breeder of St Bernard dogs."

It was evident in the following article that the writer considered this lady unsuitable for the position. Sophia quickly came to the conclusion that possibly it was the fact that Miss Spilsbury was unmarried and standing for political office, rather than her proclivity for dogs that the other candidate found objectionable. Before she folded the paper, it occurred to her that whilst she chose to remain unmarried, it might prevent unforeseen problems.

CHAPTER SIX

Monday 20th March 1893

The tattered newspaper blew across the damp grass in a skittish dance, wrapping itself around Boysie Smith's legs as he sat on a park bench in the early morning light, eating his breakfast, consisting of a stale bun he'd cajoled off a baker. He hadn't been able to afford a breakfast at the Grand Oyster this morning. He hoped something would occur today to improve his financial position or he'd have to go back to petty thievery which was becoming increasingly risky in the city.

'Drat', he said out loud, startling the ever present pigeons, gathered around his feet, alert for any crumbs he might drop. Pulling the paper away, he was about to screw it up when a headline caught his eye. His literacy skills being a bit on the slow side, he spread the paper out and smoothed the creases, his lips moving as he slowly spelled out the words.

"Murdered woman – Police seek help."

Taking the last bite of his bun, Boysie chewed carefully with his few remaining teeth and thoughtfully went on reading, oblivious to his surroundings.

"Police are baffled by the vicious killing of a woman on the 13th March. Miss Susan Post was attacked in her room at the Protheroe residence, Grainger Street. Appealing for any witnesses to come forward, Detective Butler told our reporter

that all information received would be treated with the greatest of discretion."

Boysie digested this then roared with laughter, causing a great ruffling of pigeon feathers amongst his faithful flock. The Protheroe residence, he smirked, these reporters are too namby-pamby to call a spade a spade. Bordello's more like it, in my book, he thought. Then he read the date again, lifting his fingers as if counting. Hang on a minute, he thought, that must be the night I was there. He looked around as if worried somebody could overhear his thoughts, read the article once more, then wiped his hands down the sides of his trousers as he gazed into the distance deep in thought. He realised it could have been that man he'd seen, the one with the streaked beard, but if he told the police he'd likely lose the chance of recognising and blackmailing him. On the other hand, Inspector Butler was known to be generous with his informants if they gave him something useful. Money in the hand for a bit of trivial information was easy work. Weighing up his options, Boysie made a decision, stood up and brushed himself down, much to the delight of the pigeons, who surged forward to clean up the miniscule remains of the bun. Folding the paper under his arm, Boysie walked towards the park gate whistling cheerfully. Halfway down the hill going towards the centre of the town he stopped to watch a fire blazing a few streets away. Satisfied that it was nowhere near his lodgings in Willis Street, he continued on.

***

Putting her knife and fork together on her plate, Sophia sighed.

'Nothing beats a good plate of bacon and eggs Meg. That was a perfect breakfast, thank you.'

Smiling at this, Meg removed the dirty plates from the kitchen table looking round, disturbed, as a loud knocking on the back door startled them both. Placing the dishes in the sink, she straightened her apron and went to see who it could be this early in the morning. Sophia heard an exclamation of surprise and then Meg came back into the room with an elderly man who appeared to have been near a bonfire, with a smoke begrimed face and shirt. Clutching his cap in his hands, his hair tousled and his clothes smelling strongly of charred wood, he stood awkwardly inside the door.

'It's Bayliss, Miss,' Meg announced rather unnecessarily to her employer.

'I can see that,' Sophia said as she rose from her seat. 'Whatever has happened to you? Come and sit down. Meg will get you a cup of tea.'

Bayliss, a sturdy middle aged man, sat down heavily at the kitchen table and wiped his face on his sooty shirt sleeve which didn't help his appearance one iota. Sophia was used to seeing him dirty as he came to garden for her once a week, but this appeared entirely different.

'I'm sorry to come to work like this Miss Holmes,' he apologised. 'But my boarding house burnt down early this morning. I lost everything. Just got these clothes, that's all.'

'Better fry up another lot of bacon and eggs Meg,' responded an ever practical Sophia. 'Now tell me all about it... No...on second thoughts, first go and wash your face and hands then you'll feel a bit better. Your face looks like a Maori tattoo with all that black soot in your wrinkles!'

Bayliss managed a weak smile as he went out to the laundry and they could hear him scrubbing at his hands. When he returned his appearance had improved but his hands trembled as he sat down. Stirring several spoonfuls of sugar into his mug of tea, he took a long drink while the two women waited patiently for him to tell his story.

'I was fast asleep and I'm woken up by all this yelling. I managed to pull on these clothes and opened my door. The hall was filled with smoke but I got down and crawled out into the street. I was lucky my room was on the ground floor but two of them upstairs didn't make it. Poor bastards. Oh...sorry Miss.'

Sophia waved aside his apology for his language and told him to continue.

'Well by that time the building was well ablaze downstairs and I guessed that the smoke got up to the next floor and did for them. The fire engine arrived but there was nothing they could do by that time. There didn't seem to be enough water. It all seemed to happen so quickly. One minute I was dead to the world, the next I'm out on the street destitute. I've got to find somewhere else to live now, so I can't work today Miss Holmes. I'll make it up to you after I find a place.'

'Why don't you stay here for a while,' suggested Sophia after a moment's thought. 'There's a big room empty at the end of the servant's quarters. It must have been a Butler's room I think. Anyway there's a bed and plenty of space for an easy chair and a desk if you want.'

'Oh I don't know...,' hesitated Bayliss staring down at his work roughened hands. 'I can't afford very much. I've only got what I earn from my gardening jobs. It's not that I don't appreciate the offer Miss...'

Sophia realised his pride wouldn't let him take charity so she made a suggestion on the spur of the moment.

'How about I give you free board and lodging? To earn your keep you can make us a large vegetable garden and I'd also like a green house built. There's plenty of work here, painting the house and decorating. I know you're capable of all those things. It would be quite nice to have a man in the house too, make us feel safer. Meg can do with a hand bringing in the coal and lifting heavy washing, until her ribs heal. You'd be doing us a favour too. Please re-consider it?'

Bayliss looked down at his hands again as if they contained the right answer to this proposal, exhaled loudly, then replied, 'Very well Miss. It's a bargain. You won't regret it I promise.'

Going to the dresser, Sophia reached inside her handbag and produced a banknote from her purse.

'I'm sure I won't. Now you need to go and buy yourself some new clothes and boots. I'll give you ten pounds to cover everything. You don't need to pay me back until you can afford to. Meg and I will make the bed up for you and we'll expect you back for lunch. Don't forget to buy several lots of underwear and socks. Meg only washes once a week.'

With this practical advice ringing in his ears, Bayliss put on his cap, and with obvious reluctance, took the money from Sophia and went off to shop.

'More work for you Meg I'm afraid,' apologised Sophia.

'Well we could hardly turn him out could we?'

said Meg. 'One more's not going to make much difference is it? And you're quite right, it will be handy having someone to help in this big old place.'

Sophia inwardly smiled to herself at Meg's use of 'we', but was glad her new housekeeper accepted the sudden addition to the household so readily.

'Perhaps we could have some chickens out in the back yard too? I mean now that we've got Bayliss to look after them.' Meg ventured. 'He could build a hen house.'

'Why not? I'm sure fresh eggs are much better for us and useful for your baking,' said a resigned Sophia, who was finding that Meg, although efficient in her duties, was increasingly ambitious to improve things. To think that just a few short weeks ago she'd been a happy spinster, subsisting on her own in the house, and now she had acquired a housekeeper/cook, and a gardener/handyman. She was beginning to worry that she'd come home one day to find a milking cow at the back door and a dog and a cat in the kitchen.

***

That evening, Sophia read a letter in the *Evening Post* out to Meg, who she'd discovered had an avid interest in politics in general and women's suffrage in particular.

"Sir- Will you be good enough to allow me to suggest to the Government through your columns, at this period of such strong and persistent advocacy of women's rights- Female Suffrage and the many other positions and privileges they lay claim to-that on the occasion of preparing the next batch of J.P's. a few names be drawn from the fairer sex should be

placed on the roll, if for no other reason, that when cases are being heard between persons of different sexes- more especially between husband and wife- a lady should have an opportunity of taking a seat on the Bench, when perhaps some of the supposed lords of creation would have a better chance of having strict impartiality shown to them than I am afraid is at present the case, through perhaps the uncalled for gallantry of its present sole occupants.

I am &c. A. Nemo."

'I wonder if A. Nemo is a woman or a man? It's hard to tell,' mused Meg.

'Well whatever gender they are, it sounds as if they have Labour leanings,' replied Sophia.' It says here that the Labour Party is circulating ideas for their election campaign. One of them is to give every adult a vote, after one month's residency in the country, for Parliamentary, municipal and local board elections. I shall seriously consider voting for them if that's the case, especially if the Electoral Reform Bill doesn't succeed under Seddon.'

'I'll support that,' said Meg eager to please her new employer.

'They also talk about bringing in an eight hour working day, free education and best of all the licensing of liquor to be controlled by the people.'

'Things change so fast these days. It's all very well them wanting free this and free that, but who's going to pay for it all? That's what I wonder,' was Meg's practical approach to all these mooted reforms.

'The working man and woman, that's obvious,' sighed Sophia. 'In other words Meg, you, me and Bayliss, to name just three!'

The two women nodded at each other in mutual

agreement as Sophia continued to read.

'Ah...you remember me telling you about Miss Spilsbury, the dog breeder who is standing for the Auckland Council? Apparently all the Councillors have threatened to resign if she's elected to fill the vacant chair. Isn't that so typical of men? They are acting like a lot of spoilt children!'

'I'm beginning to feel quite sorry for her. I hope she sticks to her guns,' said Meg.

'Yes I do too...Oh I know what I meant to do,' said Sophia going to the dresser and rummaging in her hand bag. 'I haven't had time to read these new leaflets from the WCTU. There's supposed to be a mention of taxes in them.'

Pulling out a pamphlet, she returned to her seat where she scanned through it rapidly before nodding and reading it to her cook.

'It's titled IS IT RIGHT.

"IS IT RIGHT that your mother, your sister, your wife, or your daughter should be classed with criminals and lunatics, or be treated as aliens from a foreign country? Many women have to pay Land or Income Tax.

IS IT RIGHT that their money should be taken and no representation given them?

IS IT RIGHT that while the loafer, the gambler, the drunkard, and even the wife-beater has a vote, earnest, educated and refined women are denied it?

IS IT RIGHT that a capable women, who farms her own land, should be thought unfit to use a vote that is given to the most ignorant of her men servants?

IS IT RIGHT that an educated woman can be trusted to teach a school, and yet not be trusted with a vote that is given to the boys she had educated before they have her years or knowledge?"

'That's telling them,' said Meg. 'I especially liked the bit about the wife-beaters. That appeals to me.'

CHAPTER SEVEN

Wednesday 22nd March 1893

Halfway through the week, thought Sophia, as she hurried down MacDonald Street on her way to work, holding her coat tightly against her body. Autumn was beginning to make an impression on the weather. There was a chill in the air, which added to a cool brisk breeze made this morning quite unpleasant. Sophia coughed as she walked along, unavoidable inhaling the smoky air. She recalled telling a friend in London that she couldn't wait to get away from the fogs in the city to go to New Zealand for some fresh air. Unfortunately she hadn't realised that Wellington was just as reliant on burning coal for its heating, cooking and industries as London and she'd soon had to get accustomed to the ever present grime and soot here, the same as the congested atmosphere she'd grown up with in England. Reaching Anderson's, the china and glass merchant, she couldn't resist stopping to admire the beautiful porcelain dinnerware displayed in the windows. Perhaps one day I'll give a grand dinner party she thought, but then again...

Entering the front door of the Agency, glad to be inside sheltered from the wind, she picked up the post Una had left in a neat pile on the counter, from the Saturday delivery then made her way out into the back office. At the same time, her assistant came out of the passage that led to the back door, looking puzzled.

'Good morning Sophia. Did you leave the back door open?'

'No, we always keep it locked.'

'Well it was wide open when I arrived just now. I went out there to wash my hands and discovered it,' Una said frowning.

They both walked to the rear of the building past the kitchen and storeroom. Una had shut the door again, but when Sophia looked closer she could see the inner bolt had been forced open and was hanging loosely by two screws.

'I think you'd better go and find a policeman Una. This appears deliberate to me. While you're gone I'll check to see if anything has been stolen.'

Una nodded and went on her errand to wait outside until the constable came past on his regular beat, as he was obliged to, every twenty minutes or so, while Sophia returned to the main office and slowly inspected it. Nothing appeared to be disturbed at all. Walking around the desks, she tried to recall how she'd left everything placed on Friday night when the two of them finished work before locking up the premises before the weekend. All she noticed was a carbon paper on the floor next to her desk that had hardly been used. Picking it up she put it back in the manufacturers flat box, making a note to remind Una to be a bit more frugal with office stationary, but nothing else caught her attention as being out of place or missing. Running her hands over her desk drawers and checking the safe produced no clues. After a few minutes Una arrived back with a police constable who inspected the door, listened to Sophia's comments and wrote everything down carefully in a small black notebook.

'Well Miss Holmes. Seems nothing has gone missing so I suggest you get a locksmith in pronto to mend that door. I'll report this to the desk Sergeant and I'll tell the boys on the night shift to walk round the back of this building at night to check everything is safe. That rear alley is as black as pitch at night so I don't suppose anyone saw anything. Probably just street urchins,' was the constables opinion as he left.

'Pretty strong children to force a door like that,' remarked Una. 'If you ask me, boys would have made a mess in here if they'd come in. Perhaps someone is deliberately trying to frighten you.'

'Why would anyone do that?' said a surprised Sophia. 'I don't think I've got any enemies. Thank goodness no harm is done and the typewriters are still here. They could be worth stealing I suppose except they are heavy items to carry away. Perhaps whoever it was simply changed their minds when they realised there was nothing worth stealing and they couldn't get into the safe.'

***

Later that day, Sophia was surprised to receive a visit from Detective Butler. She noticed how tired he looked but supposed his was the sort of occupation that couldn't be carried out in regular normal working hours. Smiling at him, she beckoned him through into the back office.

'Good afternoon. Would you care to join us for a cup of tea? Have you come about our break in?'

'I was hoping you'd offer,' he had the grace to smile, removing his hat and seating himself at the office table. 'And no I'm afraid I hadn't heard about any break in here. I actually came to tell you there's a bit more news on the Susie Post case.'

Sophia quickly told him about Una's discovery of the open back door this morning then recalled why he'd come to see them.

'Oh, did someone come forward after reading the newspaper?'

'Yes one of my regular informants, actually. He tells me he was lurking outside the Protheroe house that very night, hoping to recognise any of the men going in and out, so that he could blackmail them.'

'He sounds most unpleasant,' sniffed Una, betraying her rigid morality.

'He's a nasty man but he's proved worth listening to in the past so I have to give some credence to his observations,' acknowledged Butler.

'And who did he see?' Sophia asked anxiously. 'Did he recognise anyone?'

'Not one of them, according to him. He explained that they were all very circumspect in hiding their faces with hats pulled well down or mufflers pulled well up, and of course it was raining quite hard by then. He just caught a glimpse of one chap who came out and looked up at the first floor windows. The porch light shone on his face but it was flickering badly. Boysie noticed he had a strange sort of colouring to his beard. Light streaks going from the corners of his mouth down under his chin. Well that's how he described it but there are so many bearded men around none of us really notices if the whiskers are distinctive or not.'

'I don't think I've ever seen anyone answering that description,' mused Sophia.

'If he's our man he's most probably shaved it off by now if he's canny,' said Butler. 'We'll just have to keep our eyes skinned to see if we can spot him even though there's no proof that he was the murderer. He could have been a client of one of the other women, although none of them seems to remember him. They're all playing innocent of anything going on in that house even if they are very frightened of being the next victim.'

'All cats are grey in the night,' said Una reprovingly. 'Those men that use those girls know they can rely on their discretion. Women like that are never going to help the police if it interferes with their livelihood.'

'It will interfere worse for them if he kills another one,' stated Butler flatly. 'Anyway that's not all I'm afraid. I expect you've heard about the boarding house in Dixon Street that burnt down on Saturday? It was arson...'

'Yes, my gardener Bayliss lived there for years,' Sophia interrupted him. 'He arrived at my house very distressed about those men dying and now you're saying it was deliberately lit?'

'It was started in the coal shed at the back of the house. That's why it generated so much heat. Someone set a fire using Suffragette leaflets, then scattered a few of them outside so we'd get the impression the Temperance Union was to blame, or that's what we think he did. Apparently the old man who ran the boarding house is a real misogynist and hates women full stop, especially the Suffrage movement. He had this sign up in his window.'

Butler reached inside his coat and pulled out a tattered smoke grimed, folded poster which he spread out on the table top. Sophia leaned over and read out loud.

NOTICE TO EPICENE WOMEN

ELECTIONEERING WOMEN
ARE REQUESTED NOT TO CALL HERE.

They are recommended to go home, to look after their children, cook their husband's dinners, empty the slops, and generally attend to the domestic affairs for which Nature designed them.

By taking this advice they will gain the respect of all right-minded people-an end not to be attained by unsexing themselves and meddling in masculine concerns of which they are profoundly ignorant.

Joshua Briggs, Dixon Street, Wellington.

'Well he couldn't put it plainer than that,' Sophia commented. 'Still I suppose he hardly deserves to have his house destroyed because of a poster. I can't believe there are such bigoted men still left in this world.'

'Many of them I'm afraid,' nodded Butler who smiled rather smugly as he continued. 'You'll no doubt be pleased to know that I'm not one of those. However we're treating the fact of the leaflets left there, very seriously. There does appear to be a link to the Post murder unless... can you think of anyone at all in your movement who would act in this extreme way? Have you heard any threats against men like this, even half joking ones?'

Shaking her head, Sophia looked at Una who was reading the poster again. Neither of them could imagine anyone they knew performing this dreadful action against Mr Briggs, however badly he felt about the Franchise movement. Biting her lips together unconsciously, Sophia thought about all the implications this new anti-suffrage outrage raised. It was apparent to her that there was an extremely dangerous man on the loose in the city and the terrible crimes he had initiated were starting to affect her life in too close a manner. Turning to the others she voiced her conclusions.

'First Susie Post's murder was made to look as if it was someone against women getting the vote and now this, which could equally be called murder in my opinion, is set up to appear like revenge on behalf of the women's movement. It's brutal but complex as if it's all been planned in advance. It certainly doesn't seem spontaneous,' she pondered. 'I can't help believing there will be more of these actions. It's becoming apparent that Mrs Sheppard may well have grounds for her anxiety.'

'That's what I'm increasingly coming to believe myself,' agreed Butler. 'I have two possible suspects. Mrs Protheroe tells me that Susie Post had quite a serious boyfriend although I suspect he was her pimp, if you'll excuse me using that word. But she hasn't seen him around for a while. Mind you she seems to be conveniently blind when it suits her. I've been asking around to see if I can find him.'

'Well I suppose it could be a crime of jealousy, especially if she had a rich new man in her life?'

'You could be right but it seems odd that he'd kill her if she gives him money. These men usually resort to a good beating to keep their girls in line. They just administer enough pain to remind them who is boss.'

'Ouch!' Sophia winced at the thought. 'If that's the case I really would prefer you take the pipe.'

'No it is much safer with you. I was quite surprised to find out that Mrs P. doesn't own that house. She disclosed that she manages it for the owner.'

'Who is?' Sophia leaned forward in anticipation.

'A gentleman by the name of James Huxley.'

'That sounds familiar,' said Sophia.

'It should do. He's the owner of several properties in Wellington. The most important one is a large warehouse on the quays where he stores all his imports, mainly liquor.'

'That would appear more than a co-incidence,' offered Una. 'Have you spoken to him?'

'No I imagine he's not going to be easy to interview. He may not even know what the house is being used for. So many of these wealthy men let their lawyers deal with all their property. If these events are being orchestrated by the liquor barons it's going to be very hard to infiltrate their ranks. They could well have hired a professional thug to carry out their wishes. Men with their wealth and political influence don't take kindly to being questioned by the police. Soon as we start our enquiries they'll be hiring fancy lawyers to protect their interests. I've come up against this sort of thing before and it was akin to hitting a brick wall, not to mention the political implications if I start treading on too many toes.'

Both Sophia and Una were well aware of the sudden frustration in his voice.

'Perhaps Mr Huxley does know about the bordello? Perhaps he was even a client of Susie's? He could be the originator of the money,' suggested Sophia. 'What we really need is someone who can move amongst these people at social gatherings, gathering information, who won't arouse their suspicion. That person could keep their ears and eyes open for clues.'

'We seem to have plenty of clues,' said Butler dolefully. 'They're leaving them all over the place but nothing to get us heading in the right direction.'

'Red herrings,' added Una earnestly. 'Like Sherlock Holmes was always on about.'

'Oh please don't bring him into this,' groaned her employer. 'Although, I must admit you may be correct, Una. Perhaps we are being misled and there's another reason lying behind all this mayhem that we're missing, but for the life of me I can't guess what it could be.'

'Returning to your suggestion of an insider, can you think of anyone who we could trust? It goes without saying I can't use any of my low-life informants. They don't move in those circles at all.'

'Well the only person I know is Tilly Sergeson. She spends a great deal of her life at soirees, dinner parties and the like. She picks up the most indiscreet gossip I've ever heard. In fact some of it I haven't heard because she says it's too indiscreet even for her to reveal!'

Sophia laughed at the others and tapped her nose. Jack Butler showed an unexpected interest in this opportunity to gather information, gossip or not.

'Can she be trusted not to tell anyone but us what she hears? It's useless asking her if she's loose tongued. Any information she gleans needs to be exclusively for us. Can we rely on her discretion?'

'I can assure you that Tilly never reveals much about herself to anyone but her closest friend and that's me,' replied Sophia, quite interested in his use of the word 'us', which led her to think that he had accepted her part in the investigation. 'If I explain the circumstances she'll leap at the chance to be useful rather that her usual ornamental self. Best of all she's a strong supporter of the Temperance Union even if she does have a penchant for champagne! And yes, her husband does know quite a few politicians and liquor barons who are invited to the house frequently.'

'Can I ask you to arrange a meeting with her then? As soon as possible I think, then we can find out who she's likely to meet as her social diary fills up.'

Agreeing to talk to Tilly the next evening at the next WTCU meeting, Sophia showed Detective Butler out. Reluctantly returning to work, her mind raced at the latest developments and how she would have to break the news to Bayliss that his boarding house and all his possessions had been lost by a deliberate criminal act. These senseless acts were beginning to remind her of the reasons she had left London, a dangerous city for women on their own.

CHAPTER EIGHT

Thursday 23rd March 1893.

Even though she was once again sitting in a packed meeting, Sophia's thoughts kept straying to the possibility that a murderer could be in this very hall, infiltrating the movement. She wondered if Jack Butler had managed to trace Susie's boyfriend and puzzled over how she could engineer Tilly into helping with information. A strong nudge from her friend, brought her wandering attention back to the proceeds as the Chairwoman rose to her feet.

'Ladies and gentlemen, I would like to read you some quotations from staunch leaders of our movement. Let their clarity of thinking and fine reasoning become an inspiration to us all. First of all, Marian Hatton, who last year addressed a public meeting at Waimate with these acute personal observations.

"It used to be argued that, women's brains being smaller than men's, women must be an inferior being. Then it was discovered that a calf had a larger brain than most men, so by the same process of reasoning, the calf should be the superior animal of the two!"

The Chairwoman of the WCTU held up her hand as her audience erupted into laughter. She waited, allowing herself a wry smile, until this had died down, before continuing to consult her notes for the next quote.

'Also last year Jane Smalley said." *It takes infinitely more brains to train our children than to rear sheep, and yet are not many of our members of Parliament farmers?"*

Sophia and Tilly, sitting together, both roared their appreciation at this astute comment, clapping loudly with every other member of the audience. Their Chairwoman looked out over the enthusiastic crowd and nodded.

'I can see we all agree with these ladies. However, to return to gravity again, I must emphasise the essential need to keep ever to the forefront of our minds, that it is these same men, these elected representatives that we have to bring our utmost persuasion to. Ours has been a peaceful movement and long may that continue in light of the hardships endured by our sisters in England. The new petition is gradually gathering momentum and at the last count we had achieved nearly twenty thousand signatures, but we need so many more. Our aim is to present the final document to Parliament by the end of July so we only have four months to go. I would ask all of you who are able to place the petition sheets where people can sign them, to take one tonight. Even a few signatures will help to swell the numbers when they are all combined. The sheets will all be glued together in one long piece. It will be a grandly dramatic gesture when Sir John Hall rolls it out in front of Parliament. We must let nothing stop us now ladies and gentlemen. This petition must succeed where our last one failed through lack of numbers, then surely the Government will take heed and put the Electoral Reform Bill to the vote in a positive manner.'

Once again applause filled the hall, several people cheering and stamping their feet in acclaim.

'So, ladies and gentlemen, once again I urge you to please take a petition sheet from the table at the back of the hall before you leave. Thank you all for your supportive attendance on such a cold night.'

Tilly turned to Sophia and said, 'You can put one on your front counter.'

'Yes I will,' Sophia smiled. 'I'm going to put a poster up in my window too. It's an easy way of nailing my colours to the mast as they say!'

'I must admit to being quite aroused by all this rhetoric,' owned Tilly, who was resplendent in a dark green and purple dress tonight. 'Although I honestly feel that there isn't too much I can do to help besides handing out leaflets.'

Sophia saw her chance to raise the suggestion of Tilly keeping her ears open for any gossip relating to the cause.

'Ah... we mustn't be pessimistic. All these small actions can add up to larger pressures on the Government, and...well... actually I was going to ask you to do something. Can you come to my office tomorrow morning? There's someone I'd like you to meet who needs the help of someone like you rather badly, with a very serious matter that affects our movement. They think there's a special task that you could do personally that may have a big impact on events.'

'Oh? Can't you tell me now?'

Tilly looked expectant, waiting for her friend to elucidate further but Sophia just put a finger to her lips shaking her head in a conspiratorial manner.

'This is far too public a place to talk about it, and anyway it's not really my place to tell you. I'm sorry to be so mysterious but I promised to keep mum.'

'It must be serious then if you're being so melodramatic,' said Tilly. 'Now I shall lie awake all night speculating on what it could possibly be. Wild horses won't keep me away.'

'Don't mention wild horses to me,' shuddered Sophia. 'I had enough experience of those last week with poor Meg nearly flattened in my doorway by that runaway.'

'That's right,' recalled Tilly concerned. 'How is the poor woman?'

'She seems to be settling in very well. Her injuries are all healing and I certainly can't complain about her cooking. I shall have to ask for smaller portions. It appears she thinks I need feeding up! Bayliss isn't complaining, I might add. I don't think he's ever had meals like them.'

'I hope your food accounts aren't going to be too horrendous then?'

'No I must say she seems to keep within the budget I set her but so far so good. It will all be revealed at the end of the month when the grocery and butchers bills arrive.'

'I do love good food but I really have to watch my weight now or I will have to get my dresses let out. I think I'd die of embarrassment if I had to do that. I have a particularly extravagant outfit to wear to the races next weekend. Why don't you come with me? We can park the carriage next to the course, put the roof down and have a picnic if the weather's fine enough.'

'Yes... thank you. I'd love to come with you,' agreed Sophia much to her friend's surprise. 'I could do with a nice day out to blow the cobwebs away and that will be just the thing. I'm sure I can find a suitable dress to wear without outshining you!'

Tilly missed the irony and was pleased at this acceptance, but if she had been able to read Sophia's thoughts she might have been uneasy. The opportunity, to perhaps spot the bearded man or to overhear pertinent gossip for Butler, was of far greater appeal than the horses, to the amateur sleuth, as she now thought of herself!

***

He lay on his bed in the early morning light, too exhilarated to sleep. It was all going exactly to the plan just as he'd been asked. Of course he'd thrown in a few refinements of his own but those wouldn't come to the knowledge of the one who mattered. As he'd done on previous nights he brought to mind the thrill of feeling his hands tighten around Susie Post's neck. She'd been so excited to find him waiting for her, appearing so at ease in the seedy surroundings of her room. Reaching into her bag, she'd handed over the precious receipt to him and then arranged herself in a seductive pose against the cheap satin cushions on her bed.

'I think I've earned a little reward,' she'd said beckoning to him. 'Are you going to pleasure me?'

She'd mistaken his hands caressing her shoulders, for affection. When they started to tighten around her neck, she'd wriggled and kicked out, as she tried to escape him but her struggle didn't last long. Falling back limp on the bed, her face purple, mouth open, a trickle of saliva on her chin, she'd resembled the silly bedraggled doll lying on the pillow beside her. Almost lovingly he sliced open her blouse with his beautiful knife, pulling the cheap material aside to reveal her corsets. It was with infinite care that he sliced into her pale flesh to write his message. There wasn't much blood now that her heart was still, just a few drops that he leaned forward and touched his tongue to. Savouring the salty taste, he sat up and reached for the leaflets that had spilled out of her bag when she'd dropped it carelessly on the floor beside the bed. Standing he surveyed the body, placing the tracts around like offerings to an idol. Susie's staring eyes still seemed to be watching him and he cursed, screwing up a pamphlet and forcing it into her mouth. Placing the reminder of them in his pocket with the receipt, he'd quietly left after ensuring there was no-one in the downstairs hallway to witness his exit.

There was no doubt in his mind, when he recalled that night that he'd acted with genius. Feeling his body react at the pleasurable thought he'd just invoked, he gasped and gave himself over to the forbidden excitement for a few glorious moments as a reward. This thrilling moment was his private secret, something he didn't have to share or report.

Satiated, he continued to revel in the memories of his crimes, although he preferred to call them his 'retributions'. Could there be a more perfect way of pleasing oneself, he wondered? He could still smell the smoke of the Dixon Street fire on his old coat. He only had to bury his nose in the rough tweed to inhale the scent of elation. The deaths of the two lodgers had been an unexpected bonus although he regretted he hadn't been able to watch their demise. It took some of the pleasure away from the escapade nevertheless it was successful in attracting public attention, playing on the emotions of those who were against the suffragettes, exactly as they'd planned on all those long nights when sleep was impossible.

Walking the city streets after midnight had become essential to his well being. It suited his moods to sit on the quay, watching as the sea mists rolled in across the water. The lonely echo of the fog horn was music to him. Absorbing the mingled odours of tar, stale fish and heavy coal smoke from the foundry chimneys, he felt revived and ready to forge on with his set tasks. Alleys lit by flickering gas lamps, away from the bright electric lights of the main streets, suited his mood. His favourite haunt was the Bolton Street cemetery where he could sit in the doorways of family crypts and smoke a calming cigarette. The dead fascinated him. He often wondered if he should have studied medicine. Given the chance he would have enjoyed standing in a dissection class, pouring over a cadaver to discover its inner secrets.

Through his bedroom curtains, he could see daylight. With a deep sigh, he turned on his side and let sleep come to him.

CHAPTER NINE

Friday 24ᵗʰ March 1893.

The bell jangling discordantly on the front door, announced Tilly's arrival at the Agency. Sophia came forward as her friend pushed it open allowing a gust of wind to howl into the reception area, blowing papers around and almost causing the door to slam.

'I've got it,' a male voice said as Tilly stepped inside, holding on to her hat in one hand as she attempted to stop the door flying back with the other. Sophia watched as Butler, entering behind Tilly, took a firm hold on the door and closed it with a bang.

'Thank you. What a terrible gale today. My eyes are full of grit from the street,' Tilly smiled up at him although Sophia guessed this wasn't strictly true as she'd seen Tilly step straight out of her carriage outside the office. Sophia ushered them both through into the back office, where Tilly immediately sat herself down at the table, unpinned her hat and started fussing with her hair which, as usual looked immaculate.

'Tilly, how are you?'

Sophia greeted her and then turning to the detective who had followed them into the room.

'I'd like you to meet Detective Butler. This is my friend Mrs Sergeson.'

Tilly stood, holding out a kid gloved hand which Butler shook briefly and as she sat down, Sophia could see her assessing him with a connoisseur's eye. He was tall, dark but not strictly handsome, probably in his mid thirties. His hair a trifle too long but quite attractive; good teeth and neatly dressed, his eyes a dark blue with laughter lines etched deep. Sophia could almost read her friend's thoughts and knew that Tilly had completely forgotten what she'd been told the night before, and was no doubt indulging herself in a fantasy that this might be a preamble to Sophia announcing her engagement to this strange man. She could sense that Tilly was caught up in this reverie, and was probably momentarily quite hurt that she hadn't been told about his position in Sophia's life. However, as soon as he started to speak, Sophia saw her friend's confusion rapidly dispelled as he related the details of the Post murder, the tragic boarding house fire and Kate Sheppard's worries about the plotting she believed could be behind events such as these, which were occurring so suddenly.

'And so we, that is, Miss Holmes, Sir James and myself, are in agreement that you may just be the person who can ferret out any small details that may come your way in your social life,' concluded Butler, showing his good teeth in a very confiding smile to Tilly.

'I'm very flattered you should ask me. I certainly will help if the occasion arises.'

Sophia frowned at Tilly who was inclined to flirt, to ensure she realised that this was not a social occasion and these were life and death occurrences that she was being asked to help with.

'Of course, as Sophia has no doubt told you, I do hear some very intriguing snippets. Perhaps I'd better keep a notebook in my purse from now on so that I can jot down any pertinent details correctly. I don't wish to make any mistakes in case I have to testify in court.'

'I sincerely hope you don't have to be involved in anything like that Mrs Sergeson, but even vague references to the WTCU or the brewery owners and their political friends would be of interest to me. It's always astonishing how little 'snippets' as you call them, can be pieced together like a jigsaw to give a complete picture.'

Tilly eagerly agreed to help even if outwardly showing a slight disappointment at his comment about her non-appearance before a Judge and jury. Sophia kept a straight face but she imagined Tilly was already envisioning the sober jacket and skirt she would wear, with the merest soupcon of colour in her hat, and of course her jet black drop earrings barely brushing her slightly rouged cheeks.

'Sophia has agreed to accompany me to the races on Saturday. That's a most excellent place for gossip, especially in the Members Stand. Everyone tends to drink heavily there; they become very voluble as the day wears on. We may well glean some titbits for you, Detective Butler.'

'Yes indeed,' agreed the policeman politely.

Taking her leave, Tilly sailed out of the office and Sophia and Jack watched her braving the wind before climbing into her brougham, giving them both a cheery wave.

'She seems a strange choice of friend for you?'

Butler's comment surprised Sophia as she turned back into the building.

'Why would you think that?'

Leaning back on the counter, facing the street, the detective put his hat on, pulling it hard down to prevent it being blown off.

'Oh don't take that the wrong way. You appear to

be so different but I suppose you do have a common interest in the Franchise movement.'

Sophia smiled knowingly.

'You mustn't judge a book by its cover Detective Butler. Tilly may seem like a social butterfly but she existed in extreme hardship before she married Arthur Sergeson. She had to survive on a pitifully small annuity. She found a position at a milliners shop and her husband Arthur was the owner's brother. But never mistake Tilly for being empty headed. That's far from the case.'

'I bow to your greater wisdom then. Let's hope she uses her talents to reveal some answers for us.'

***

Sitting in the bar at the Grand Oyster, Bayliss was enjoying a glass of strong stout after a hard days digging in what was to become, Sophia's new vegetable garden. He'd eaten the large plate of mutton stew that Meg had produced for the evening meal and then excused himself to walk into town. Since the boarding house fire, he often went to this bar to meet up with some of the other single men who'd also been made homeless by the arson and were now living next door at Mrs Wall's, but so far tonight, none of them had arrived ensuring the bar was reasonably quiet for a Friday night. Stretching his legs out in front of him, he took another pull at his glass, re-lighting his pipe again, tamping it down to enjoy a long satisfying pull at it. Meg and Sophia had banned this odorous object from the house almost immediately he'd moved in, but he was so grateful for his new comfortable circumstances that he'd agreed to abstain from smoking on the property. In a way, the enforced rationing of his smoking enhanced the pleasure and he had to admit it saved him money!

'Allo mate. Can I join you?'

Bayliss looked up at the man in front of him and wasn't impressed. Small and untidy, with a reptilian greasy appearance was how he would have described him, but if the man was looking to steal something then Bayliss was rather larger and stronger. He nodded at the stranger who put his jug of beer and his half empty glass on the table and sat opposite on the wobbly legged bentwood chair that the gardener had avoided.

'Boysie Smith, pleased to meet you,' the man grinned, showing a mouth better kept closed, with yellowed and blackened teeth. 'You stayin' at Annie's?'

'Bayliss... No, I was up at Dixon Street until the fire. Got another place now.'

'Bad job that,' offered Boysie, looking suitably grim. 'I heard it was deliberate. What sort of bastard kills good blokes like that eh?'

'A mad one I'd say,' agreed Bayliss. 'I lost everything. All gone in the blink of an eye. Pity that sod if I ever get my hands on him.'

'Not worth swinging for a mad bloke though. Best let the police sort him out, that's what I say.'

Boysie took a long drink, wiped his mouth on a filthy rag that may once have been a handkerchief, that he pulled from a torn pocket then, replenished his glass from the draft ale in his jug.

'Here,' he offered the jug, noticing Bayliss had finished his stout. 'Like a top up?'

'Kind of you but I only have one.'

Bayliss decided to sound reticent, not trusting this offer from a complete stranger. He conjured up a slightly sarcastic tone. 'Have to take it easy. My landlady belongs to the temperance crowd. She wouldn't be happy to see me rolling in drunk or even a bit tipsy! It wouldn't be worth upsetting her, believe you me.'

'Oh! The ladies! Where would we be without them? Here's to them all.'

Boysie raised his glass in a mock toast before taking another huge swallow, his scrawny Adam's apple prominent as he tipped his head back, revealing a smudged tattoo on the side of his neck, possibly done in prison thought the gardener.

'I know where I'd be,' acknowledged Bayliss. 'In the doss house probably. Thanks to Miss Holmes I've got a good bed and the best meals I've had in years. I'm not going to break her rules. No sir!'

'Boarding house is it then? The name's not familiar to me and I thought I knew all the places round here.'

Something in the query alerted Bayliss. He gave his answer careful thought.

'No. She's my employer. I'm a gardener, an odd job man if you like.'

'Ah...A private house then? Very nice if you can get a live in job like that I expect?'

If Smith expected a response from his drinking companion, he was disappointed. The two of them sat in silence for a few minutes watching as the bar filled up with working men. Muddy boots stamped on the bare wooden floor, voices were raised loudly in greetings, arguments and the occasional swearing. Gusts of laughter overruled the chatter as the customers relaxed after a long working week. The smell of frying fish permeated the bar from the kitchen at the rear. Boysie appeared to be wrestling with some inner thoughts as he turned to his companion.

'You said your landlady, Miss Holmes, was involved with the temperance lot? Is she a teetotaller then?'

'Yes. Mind you, I have seen her take the odd shot of scotch with her meal but all in moderation. She's very keen on getting women the vote. Goes to the meetings every week.'

Bayliss saw no harm in divulging this sort of information.

'Interesting,' Boysie pondered these remarks for a few seconds then appeared to come to a decision if the look in his eyes was anything to judge by. 'Hope she's careful that's all.'

Bayliss was instantly alert. Was this the reason this stranger had introduced himself, to cast aspersions on Miss Holmes? Bayliss knew where his loyalty lay and he didn't like the way Smith's insinuation might lead.

'What do you mean?'

'There's some powerful men against it,' offered Boysie. 'Ruthless bastards especially where their incomes might be threatened. Wouldn't put it past any of those booze barons to fight dirty to protect their wealth. That whore that was murdered at Mrs Protheroe's, she was giving out the leaflets. The killer carved, 'No Votes' on her bosom. Nasty work.'

'How do you know that? Do you know who did it then?'

Bayliss was deeply shocked as he digested this information.

'Don't be daft. Do I look like I'd consort with that sort of man? No... between you and me, I sometimes hear things from the police 'cos I help them a bit you know, for a few shillings. People tell me things and I put two and two together, keep my eyes open.'

'You're a nark,' guessed Bayliss with distaste.

'Yeah, but don't look at me like that. I'll have you know I've helped bring several criminals to justice. Dangerous bastards who'd still be walking the streets, if it wasn't for men like me. Sometimes I feel quite proud of what I've done for the cops. Anyway, as I said before, keep an eye open for any trouble round your landlady because it's odds on she knew the tart. Could easily have met her at one of those meetings.'

Emptying his glass, Boysie sniffed loudly, stood up, stretched and left the table as abruptly as he'd arrived disappearing into the dense crowd around the bar. Bayliss sat deep in thought, recalling the conversation, wondering if he should tell Miss Holmes what this unpleasant little man had told him so openly. He found it hard to believe she would have an acquaintance with a prostitute but then he'd also come to realise how she didn't discriminate between people. He only had to think of her treatment of Mrs Williams and himself to see that as a perfect example. She'd always been even handed with both of them; even took her meals with them as if they were all equals; part of a family.

The gardener stood stiffly, edging his way through the jovial clients of the Grand Oyster, out into the street and the damp coolness of a Wellington night, starting his walk up the hill to the Terrace, thinking lovingly of the cosy new room that awaited him. On reflection he decided to wait a while before relaying his conversation with Smith. There were other ways he could ensure Miss Holmes was kept safe.

CHAPTER TEN

Saturday 25th March 1893

Standing on the balcony of the Members Stand, Sophia looked down over the finish line at the Trentham Racecourse. The forecast rain had held off and hundreds of eager punters milled around the betting stands while many more were packed along the white picket fence surrounding the winner's enclosure. Several horses were being led around waiting for their jockeys to be hoisted up into the saddle by the stable lads. Tilly stood next to her husband as his favourite horse was led out. Sophia could see that her friend had a rather forced smile on her face as people came up to her and Arthur, to appraise the animal.

Earlier Tilly had given her two betting slips. She'd chosen Awerua Rose and Heather Bell as their horses in the main trophy race, but Sophia had no idea of their winning ability, trusting that her friend was more knowledgeable. Raising a small pair of binoculars to her eyes, she squinted as she gazed over the crowd from her vantage point, trying to pick out any familiar faces, bearded or not, but to no avail. The constant movements of the race goers, the waving of arms to place bets and to greet acquaintances, made recognition almost impossible. Placing the binoculars back in her bag, she sipped at the glass of lemonade that a waiter had brought her as she waited for her friend to join her before the first race started. Aware of a group of three men standing next to her, Sophia turned slightly to look at them. Their conversation was quite heated, which caused her to turn away but her curiosity kept her within earshot.

'Of course you can rely on me, Luxmore. If I tell you it won't pass, then it bloody well won't pass!'

This came from a portly grey bearded man who, to her astonishment, she recognised as the Liberal politician Richard Seddon, who was more than likely to become the next Premier, if Mr Ballance's health did not improve. He was addressing another older man, also bearded who was accompanied by a much younger man, possibly barely twenty.

'Glad to hear it Seddon. There'll be untold bankruptcy if you don't deliver the right result. The brewing trade will be destroyed if those harridans get on the licensing committees so it's imperative you get this sorted out as soon as possible. We can't afford to allow women the vote before the next election. It will be a disaster if they put the Labour party into power. Apart from anything else, an eight hour working week would shut me down. '

'Calm down. It's all agreed. When the Bill comes to the upper house, then it will fail.'

'This time yes, it will, but you can't delay the Bill for ever. There's every chance the Labourites will win women over to their side. They're promising all sorts of idiotic things, eight hour working days, votes for women. What the devil's going to happen then? You need to have a plan, put some sort of legislation together to protect the industry.'

'I can't be seen to be favouring you Luxmore. Lobbying me like this in public is too risky. Anyone might guess what you're up to. You will have to curb your impatience and wait for the outcome of the debate like everyone else. Now if you'll excuse me I have official duties to attend to before I have to mix with race goers a bit more,' was the terse reply from Seddon as he walked away.

The man called Luxmore turned, watching the Member of Parliament with a sour look on his face, before moving towards another group of men. Sophia turned around abruptly, on purpose, bumping into the young man, spilling her drink over his coat.

'Oh! I am so sorry,' she said, adopting a breathless voice that she hoped sounded sincere. Stepping back, the recipient of her splashed lemonade, smiled down at her, starting to brush the drops of liquid off his jacket.

'Quite all right Madam? Miss...?'

Sophia whisked his handkerchief out of his top pocket and patted at the marks on his jacket in a motherly fashion, all the while smiling up at the tall blonde haired young man in, what she hoped was a coquettish manner, from under the brim of her hat, a splendid concoction of white straw and pink feathers.

'There that's better... Miss Holmes,' she said extending her gloved hand towards him.

'It's a pleasure to meet you, Miss Holmes. Richard Luxmore at your service,' he said removing his hat which allowed his straight fair hair to fall down over his eyes, which were sandy lashed and pale blue. Sophia carefully folded his handkerchief and returned it to his pocket. He'd held her hand just a fraction too long until Sophia had gently withdrawn from his clasp.

'Do you have a horse here today Mr Luxmore?'

'No not me. My father has several. That was him standing here just now nagging away at Seddon. I'm just tagging along being a dutiful son.'

Richard Luxmore smiled at her in an over friendly way and, although she knew herself to be several years older than him, she felt almost flattered by his interest. "almost" being the important word she told herself.

'I always think It must be hard for politicians to have a private life,' she wondered out loud, in an effort to encourage him to share the details of the conversation she'd partially overheard, even though she'd come to a rapid realisation of its content.

'Possibly,' Luxmore replied in bored tones, then he drew closer to her and she could smell the whisky on his breath. 'Tell me about your private life Miss Holmes. What brings you to the races? Are you a devotee of the sport of kings?'

Although disappointed that he hadn't revealed anything, Sophia decided to lead him on a bit further, making her tones confiding as he leaned intimately towards her in the crowded room.

'I'm a business woman Mr Luxmore. I own a secretarial agency. You could say I'm a career woman. One of the owners invited me here today, thus why I'm up here in this stand and not down with the masses which is where I probably belong. I'm afraid I know very little about horses in a racing or any other capacity.'

'Fascinating,' said Richard although he didn't sound at all interested. 'Would that be the Holmes Secretarial agency in Willis Street?'

'Indeed it is. You know it then?'

Sophia couldn't help her eyes widening in surprise as Luxmore laughed easily at her astonishment and explained.

'Rather a coincidence us meeting here isn't it? I

noticed your place a few days ago when I was looking for another business in Willis Street. I recall you have an Electoral Reform poster in your front window.'

'Indeed I do,' replied Sophia. 'Can I ask if you support us?'

'Oh I don't get involved with politics Miss Holmes. Leave all that to the old man. I just like to enjoy myself when I can and not get too serious about life.'

Richard Luxmore raised his glass, winking at her in rather a familiar fashion and then turned to greet another young man who had been standing near him.

'Huxley old boy! Come and meet my new chum. Miss Holmes this is Quentin Huxley.'

Sophia smiled, offered her hand then took a step back and assessed the young men in a more critical manner. They were both dressed in very expensive suits with brocade waistcoats, exuding wealth and the air of spoilt sons. Richard Luxmore's raffish attitude set her teeth on edge for no strongly apparent reason. It's probably just his youth she told herself, deciding he wasn't deliberately offensive. She turned her attention to Huxley who held out his hand.

'Such a pleasure to meet you Miss Holmes. Any luck with the gee gee's?'

'I'm afraid not so far. Does your father own a horse Mr Huxley?'

'No but I'd like to. Wonderful here today isn't it? I'd come every day if the races were on. Not much else to do in this city. Richard and I will be forced to follow into the family businesses but we manage to have a bit of fun until that happens. Can't get too anxious about the future.'

'It must be pleasant to have no worries,' was the

only polite comment Sophia could think to say on the spur of the moment to this apparently spineless young man.

'Oh I wouldn't say that was quite the case Miss Holmes. One tends to worry about all sorts of things, you know? What colour cravat goes with this waistcoat? Are my shoes sufficiently shined? The list goes on and on I can assure you. Appearances are so important don't you think?'

Quentin Huxley put an arm around Luxmore's shoulders as his friend nodded in agreement.

'Mm... I suppose everything is relative. It all depends on ones circumstances,' she said deciding to follow her instincts about this young man. 'What business is your father in Mr Huxley?'

'Oh. This and that you know, mainly importing, furniture and household goods, liquor and luxury food stuffs.'

Sophia took a sip of her lemonade in an effort to give herself a moment to gather her thoughts. So this young man was the son of the owner of the house where Susie Post had lived. She would have loved to ask him more but prudence kept her quiet and anyway she found that her composure, was rapidly disintegrating as she listened to the arrogance of these two youths. She wondered if they were deliberately trying to unnerve her but she realised that they were just shallow young men not long out of school, probably lacking the intelligence to deceive her. Luckily she spotted Tilly coming towards them and turned to greet her friend.

'So sorry to desert you like this,' breathed Tilly, rather out of breath from the climb up the stairs. 'I couldn't get away from all those people pressing in on us to look at the horses. I had quite a battle to make my way through the crowd to reach this stand. I was certain I was going to lose my hat.'

'That's quite all right. Let me introduce Mr Luxmore and Mr Huxley. This is my friend Mrs Sergeson. Her husband has a horse running today. They are quite the young man about town, Tilly. I think they are as interested in fashion as you are.'

'Pleased to meet you both,' responded Tilly politely, but looking a little puzzled by these sudden new acquaintances of Sophia's.

'Pleasures all mine,' said Luxmore smoothly and then his interest in them obviously waned. 'Ladies if you'll excuse me I think I may go and try and track my father down before he throws away the family fortune on the next race. I can't allow the old man to leave me destitute! Come Huxley.'

The two women watched as he threaded his way through the groups of race goers, his friend close at his side.

'I think they are a bit young for you dear,' suggested Tilly.

'You're right... but Richard may also be a useful contact to encourage. He's the son of Luxmore the brewery owner. You will never guess who they were talking to and what I overheard...'

CHAPTER ELEVEN

Tuesday 28th March 1893

As she finished off the ham sandwich Meg had packed for her lunch, Sophia sighed, reaching for her cup of tea and her unread copy of last nights' *Evening Post* to delay the moments before she had to continue to work.

'I see that Queen Victoria has arrived in Florence and the Princess of Wales and the Duke of York have paid a visit to the Pope amid great ceremony.'

'It's another world isn't it,' remarked Una from her desk. 'Hard to believe it's spring time in Italy. Lucky royal family not having to endure Wellington weather. I expect they only go overseas where the weather is going to be nice.'

The morning had proved so busy Sophia was seriously thinking of hiring another assistant to help in the agency. There appeared to be a sudden interest in typewritten business letters but she couldn't help wondering how long it would be before employers had their own secretaries to do this work. She returned to her typing after her brief lunch break, and finally came to the end of a long and complicated report for the annual meeting for investors in a Wellington iron foundry, removing the sheets from her machine and taking out the carbons. Carefully aligning the copies on her desk she screwed up her nose at the blue ink on her fingers again, but as she stood to go and wash her hands, she saw a policeman entering the front door.

'Good afternoon. Can I help you?'

Sophia moved to the counter, offering her best customer greeting smile to the officer. He looked at her squarely with no hint of pleasantness in his manner.

'Miss Holmes?'

'Yes that's me,' Sophia said.

'You are required to accompany me to the Central Police Station Miss. Immediately if you please.'

'Whatever for? Can you tell me?'

Puzzled, Sophia put her head on one side and regarded him uneasily. There was a distinctly unfriendly air about the man, an officiousness she associated with someone only used to dealing with wrongdoers.

'I'm just obeying orders Miss. Detective Butler said I was to bring you in and not to take no for an answer.'

He shuffled his large feet in their sturdy black boots, his face remaining stern and unrelenting. His use of the expression, 'bring you in,' sounded more like a demand to a possible criminal than a polite invitation to an innocent person.

'Oh... well if he wishes to speak to me, it must be about something we were discussing recently,' offered a slightly relieved Sophia. 'I'll get my hat and coat.'

Her journey, accompanying the Constable down Willis Street to the Police Station was silent for the entire way. It was obvious that he didn't wish to make small talk with his companion whilst Sophia was glad she wasn't required to make the effort. As was becoming quite normal these days, rain in the night had turned the busy main roads into large areas of sticky mud in places, so she concentrated on keeping her skirt clear of the detritus that was usual on the city thoroughfares in these wintry conditions. On arrival, she wiped her boots carefully on the large bristled mat provided before she was ushered through the usual waiting crowd, behind the counter and into the same small room that had witnessed her first visit here.

'Please sit down Miss. I'll inform the Detective you're here,' said the officer gravely as he turned to leave her, closing the door after him. Unable to resist, before she sat down, Sophia reached for the handle to see if he'd locked her in, but it turned freely, so she perched on the edge of the hard chair at the table obediently, arranging her skirts in a demure fashion in an effort to hide her muddy boots. She looked up as the door opened after a few minutes.

'Ah! Miss Holmes,' Jack Butler greeted her brusquely without a smile.

'Detective?'

Butler seated himself opposite her, close enough for her to notice that his shirt collar was highly starched but his jacket cuffs a little frayed. Spreading his hands out on top of a brown cardboard folder he held her gaze steadily. Sophia sat back silently, waiting for his explanation, wondering why he had adopted this manner, acting, almost as if she was under suspicion.

'Unfortunately this is not a social meeting. I've had to bring you here on a very serious matter.'

He continued to stare at Sophia in a way that she could only think of as accusing.

'Has there been a development in the Susie Post case? What have you found out?'

Her questions brought no lightening to his features causing her to tense in anticipation of bad news. She brought her hands together under the table, interlacing her fingers tightly on top of her handbag, in a hidden gesture of worry.

'No... nothing further. This is about an entirely new matter that may or may not have some bearing on that event. We shall see.'

Sophia decided that further silence on her part might be the best choice. There was a look in Butler's eyes that made her feel extremely uncomfortable so, unusually, she remained quiet, waiting for him to reveal what this summons to his presence might mean.

'Yesterday I had a visit from the Member of Parliament for Wellington. As I am sure you must be aware he sits on the Opposition benches but still he's adamant of his intention to vote against the Electoral Reform Bill in any form that might gain the vote for women.'

'Yes I am aware of his opinions. He's voiced them loud and clear in the newspaper and publicly at anti-franchise meetings,' said his listener, who couldn't for the life of her think where this conversation was going to end up. Jack Butler cleared his throat before continuing giving Sophia the impression of nervousness.

'Last Friday he received a letter that outraged him. He says it is treasonous, slanderous and immoral. Those are just a few of some of the milder words he used to me, along with several epithets not suitable for female ears.'

'Good heavens! What on earth did the letter say?'

Sophia leaned forward as Butler opened the folder and took out a letter which he placed in front of her. As she looked down at it, he saw her turn pale as she recognised its provenance.

'This can't be real,' she whispered in astonishment as she lifted it closer to read.

The letter was typewritten on the headed notepaper of the Wellington Secretarial Agency. It stated quite clearly that if the Member for Wellington were to change his mind and vote in favour of the female franchise, then he could expect a sum of five hundred pounds to be discreetly paid to him in cash. It was signed legibly in black ink, on behalf of the WCTU, by the Treasurer Lavinia Robertson.

Sophia read it through a second time, feeling numb at the audacity of this deliberate attempt to blacken the WCTU, by implicating both her and Lavinia.

'Rather foolish of you isn't it? I thought you would be above this sort of thing.'

Sophia flinched inwardly when Butler couldn't disguise the sarcasm in his voice.

'When Susie Post gave that money to your Treasurer, did the two of you concoct this prank when you saw how much she'd given the Branch?'

'You can't believe this is from me,' Sophia retorted, aghast at his insinuation. 'It's far too obvious. Please allow me some credit for not being so stupid.'

Butler nodded at her, but she wasn't sure if this was in agreement.

'Well perhaps you can humour me with an explanation?'

Mustering her thoughts, Sophia took a deep breath then pulled off her gloves, carefully inspecting the letter minutely, noting Butler's interest. Turning the notepaper over she could see some faint blue smudges where a carbon paper had slipped or maybe, Sophia wondered, these marks were finger prints. Seemingly satisfied with her investigation, she put the letter down on the table, giving him a very straight look which she was pleased to see, he found hard to hold, averting his eyes away quickly.

'Last week, someone broke into my office. I did give you the details when you called in the other day, but you seem to have forgotten. We summoned a policeman from the beat, who wrote a report. You should have that filed somewhere in this building I presume,' she asked patiently as if to insinuate that office procedure in this building might not be up to her standards.

Silently Butler held up his hand, placed the letter in the folder which he took with him as he went out of the room, leaving Sophia extra time in which to puzzle over events. A few minutes later he returned with a sheet of paper. Sitting down opposite her once more, he read it carefully, frowning over it. Placing it in the folder, he returned the WCTU letter to Sophia.

'I do recall you advising me of the event but I hadn't seen the report before. Please carry on. I'm quite sure, in my absence, you will have had further thoughts about this you may wish to share with me,' he said in grudging tones.

'Yes indeed I have,' said an increasingly indignant Sophia. 'It seems patently obvious that the burglar must have broken into my office specifically to use my agency's headed notepaper for his purpose. He used my typewriter to write this horrible letter then he's forged Lavinia's signature to ensure there could be no doubt about its origins.'

'Can you tell it's your machine?'

She sensed his credulity was being stretched but now she was on safe ground.

'Oh yes, that's the easy part to prove. You see they all have their own little idiosyncrasies. Some are hardly noticeable, like mine,' she said.' But of course when one uses a typewriter frequently these slight variations in the type become evident.'

Jack Butler was obviously fascinated by this observation, as he leaned closer, turning the letter towards him, as she pointed with a long, neatly manicured finger.

'See the letter "e"? It's slightly fainter than the other letters because it's the key that is used the most. It wears out quicker.'

'Wouldn't that be the case with any other typewriter used regularly?'

'Yes, but mine is occasionally a tiny bit crooked and if you look at that one there in the word 'female', you can see what I mean.'

By this time they were both leaning forward over the letter, until Sophia realised how close their faces were and pulled back. As she did so she noticed her fingers, still stained blue from the carbon and this jogged her memory.

'Oh... and now I recall finding a carbon paper on the floor when I was checking to see if anything was missing. I picked it up and put it back in the box. I was going to blame Una for being untidy but possibly it could be the piece used for this. You can see the blue smudges on the reverse of the paper.'

'He bothered to take a copy? That sounds a bit strange,' queried Butler. 'But, I must admit, I have heard of villains who do like to keep souvenirs of their crimes to gloat over afterwards. It's a dangerous practice if they're found though. Nothing we like better than a scrap book of incriminating evidence although it doesn't happen often.'

'I agree but we aren't dealing with a normal person are we? Another thing I can tell from this typing is that whoever did it, hasn't typed before. This has been typed using two fingers only. None of the letters have printed with an even pressure.'

'So...' mused Butler sounding as if he was starting to be impressed, against his will, with Sophia's acute observations. 'Your premise is that the intruder broke into your office with the sole intention of using your paper and typewriter to implicate the women's movement in bribery and corruption on a grand scale? You must admit it sounds a bit ambitious not to mention risky.'

'I agree, especially as he would have had to light one of the lamps to see what he was typing,' nodded Sophia. 'Perhaps that carbon is still in the box. I'll look immediately I get back to the office.'

'Which implies that this is all part of a plan that has been put into action with a devilish precision wouldn't you agree? But it still leaves us with the indubitable fact that Lavinia Robertson signed this letter. How do you explain that Miss Holmes?'

'I can't,' said Sophia shaking her head slowly, then her eyes widened, she smiled and clapped her hands together. 'Of course, it all points to the same man who gave Susie Post the donation of five hundred pounds. The exact same amount of money mentioned in the letter. That's why he wanted the receipt so he could forge Lavinia's signature from it. That's why it was missing from Susie's room.'

Butler picked up the letter and scrutinised the signature.

'If you ask Lavinia to give you a sample of her real

signature, I'm quite sure some tiny differences would be obvious,' suggested Sophia. 'Anyway I would guess that she'll rightly deny signing anything like this.'

'Yes I'll have to do that. Thank you and if you can find the carbon paper it will add to our evidence file,' Jack Butler said a little begrudgingly.

'All you have to do is find a man with blue stained fingers!'

The Inspector remained straight faced, not impressed by her joke as he looked at the fingers she stretched out in front of him with carbon stains on them.

'Can I go now?'

"Yes but I think I'll come back with you to collect the carbon. I am very interested in the new science of finger printing and there may be something I can use on that paper.'

'The smudges on the back of the letter could be prints, but they aren't clear,' said Sophia. 'But you would have to have the suspects' prints to compare them to, wouldn't you?'

Butler nodded at her reasoning, and stood as Sophia put her gloves back on and walked ahead of him, acutely aware that he had his nose out of joint, but immeasurably glad that she was allowed to walk free and hadn't been incarcerated under suspicion of bribing a politician.

Walking back to her office with Butler by her side, Sophia was full of conjecture about this latest effort to derail the suffrage movement, chattering away in her usual animated fashion as her enthusiasm to get to the bottom of the matter was not at all quenched by the gravity of the man who strode alongside her.

'Do you think we are dealing with one person or

several? she asked.

'It's not obvious yet,' admitted the policeman. 'It is plain that everything has been well planned to one end, but what that is, I have no idea. Surely one person cannot hope to influence the politicians by using such extreme methods. It may be that a group opposed to suffrage have hired a professional criminal who is working to their instructions.'

'But that's abhorrent. I can't believe things like that happen in New Zealand. We are such a quiet society, so conservative. That's one of the reasons I chose to come and live here rather than Australia.'

'In my profession I've come to understand there are always men who are willing to do the most heinous acts for money, certain in their minds that they won't be brought to justice. But I can assure you that while the public and Press express a lack of confidence in the Police, the legal fraternity and politicians alike, we're not all as stupid or corrupt as they would try and make out.'

'Of course not,' said Sophia supportively. 'I can only speak first hand of the legal profession but must assure you that Sir James is a highly intelligent man of great integrity. He and my father were at Oxford together and they both got Firsts. They were bound to be lawyers but my father became a defence barrister and Sir James a Crown prosecutor. Luckily, they never had to oppose each other in Court. That would have been very difficult for them and probably would have ruined their friendship. My father was very sad when Sir James and Lady Muriel left to come and live in New Zealand but, between you and me, he's quite keen on politics and I wouldn't be at all surprised if he was aiming to be picked for the Upper House fairly soon.'

Reaching the secretarial agency, Sophia and Butler went into the back office where she took the box of carbons out of her desk drawer. Removing the lid, she lifted out the paper she'd picked up, holding it by its edges as she handed it to the detective. He held it up to the light, studying it for a minute, paying particular attention to any marks around the edges.

'There may be something useful here.'

'If you hold it up to a mirror, it's possible you can read it,' suggested Sophia. 'Place it in one of my folders so that it doesn't get creased.'

Butler laid the paper carefully in a new cardboard folder and Sophia realised she hadn't told him about her trip to the races.

'I overheard the strangest conversation and met the son of Mr Huxley.'

'You mean the owner of the house?'

'Yes. He seemed a very spoilt young man with an equally spoilt friend called Luxmore. They both have in common father's who import liquor.'

'Do I add them to my suspects list?'

'Only you can decide that but I suppose you must investigate every avenue although I must say that neither of them appeared likely to want to indulge in violence. Far too pretty in my opinion.'

Butler gave her a sideways look at this comment.

'Well I suppose we must try everything. I'll get one of my men to find out more about them.'

Tipping his hat he took his leave.

'What was all that about?'

Una had been standing quietly watching as Sophia and Butler examined the carbon paper.

'It appears that whoever broke in here the other

night used my typewriter to write a threatening letter to the Member of Parliament for Wellington, on our letterhead paper. Butler accused me of doing it at first! Can you believe that? But then I recalled picking up that carbon when I was looking around to see if anything had been stolen. He's decided it may give him a clue if it's been used to make a copy of the letter.'

'I could be just as guilty as you, I suppose. All though, of course neither of us would do a thing like that,' Una hastened to say, in explanation of her comment.

'Certainly not, all the same I wish I knew who it was who broke in. To think they had the nerve to sit down and type something like that on purpose, knowing it would implicate me.'

'It's a horrible feeling to have the police suspect us,' stated Una dramatically. 'Do you suppose we do know who the person is? It must be someone who has been in here surely? It makes me shudder to think I may have met them, and been completely innocent of their intentions.'

'Perhaps... but I can't possibly think that any of our clients would be guilty. I would think most of them are too elderly to contemplate crimes like these.'

'I shall watch them all very carefully from now on,' decided Una with a grim expression on her face. 'I don't know. It seems you can't trust anyone these days.'

***

Sheltering from the rain under the eaves of one of the largest mausoleums in the cemetery, he laughed to himself as he thought about using the secretarial agency typewriter. It had been easier than it appeared even if he could only use two fingers. It was a master stroke to implicate the suffragette in their plans. Apparently, Miss Holmes was quite well known in the central city; her support of the vote for women easy for anyone to see from the poster in her office window. Now she would have to face questions from the police over the letter sent to the Member of Parliament and surely a police reporter would get wind of it and print the whole sorry story. How he wished he could be a fly on the wall at that interview.

They'd tried to imagine the headlines in the *Evening Post,* which might read *"Temperance woman bribes MP,"* laughing over the thought of the scandal it would cause. It had taken him some days to perfect Lavinia Robertson's signature but at last he was satisfied with his efforts and added it to the bottom of the letter. Eagerly waiting for the news to break, they'd been disappointed when nothing was mentioned in the newspaper but it only served to make them re-double their efforts to continue with everything and there was still plenty of time to contact a reporter and pass on the information if they decided it was necessary to bolster their scheme.

Then he pondered on the next step he must take. The thought of this action filled him with a sense of power even if It was risky, involving others, but he was sure he could manage it and still retain anonymity. He would, however bide his time, keep this attack up his sleeve until he was certain it would do the maximum of damage.

Stubbing out the cigarette under his boot, on the stone step of the tomb, he exhaled the smoke from his lungs, deciding to report back to the one who mattered.

The thought filled him with anticipation at the pleasure he could expect to receive when he'd spoken of his latest efforts. Turning up his coat collar he strode briskly towards the gateway of the crushed shell path.

CHAPTER TWELVE

Monday 3rd April 1893

The hall was full again despite the wet evening. Closely packed together the audience listened to the Chairwoman's rousing comments with only the occasional cough and sniffle interrupting the proceedings as they ignored their damp clothes and the discomfort.

'For those of you who haven't been able to read the *Evening Post* today, I bring your attention to the article on page two regarding the adoption of women as Factory Inspectors for the Tailoressess. I will read out the last part as it is encouraging to hear the progress being made and endorsed by Mr Mundella, the President of the Board of Trade when he spoke in England recently. He states that,

" If women had votes, the practice of paying women less than men for doing precisely the same work would quickly disappear. The work would be paid for according to its value, not according to the sex of the worker. We strongly advise the women of the colony while thankfully accepting such sops as the appointment of a female Inspector under the Factories Act, not to rest satisfied with any such minor concessions, but to press steadily and unceasingly their demand for the abolition of all distinctions of sex in respect to the exercise of political rights, of which the greatest and most essential is the Franchise."'

Mrs Dallaston paused to wait for the applause to quieten, before continuing to address the meeting.

'Mr Mundella is a wise man and a brave one. I think you will all agree with my assessment. For those of you women here tonight, who are factory workers, this must be an ambition to work towards. We must all think of ourselves as equals with men here in New Zealand, never forgetting that we are not the weaker sex. Remember, our strength lies in our numbers so once again, I urge you to add as many signatures to your petition sheets as you are able. The Women's Christian Temperance Union will not bow down to the misguided and misogynist views of our male politicians who apparently support us in public but plot against us in private.'

Another roar of appreciation caused her to pause, taking a sip of water from the glass on her table.

'The Ballance government appears hell bent on denying us the vote before the coming election but I can assure you that when those men standing for Parliament get on the hustings, they will be met by a barrage of banners, shouts and catcalls from the ladies of this organisation if they dare to oppose our rights as women. Nearer the time, I will be calling for ladies to lead teams out on to the streets of Wellington to ensure that not one single candidate is left in peace if they are against us!'

Her rousing diatribe was cheered and hoorayed from all parts of the hall. Sophia and Tilly clapped until their hands were sore and they were breathless from shouting their support.

'Marvellous isn't she?' Tilly said when the noise had calmed down. 'One can't resist being stirred up ready for the fight when she speaks like that.'

'I sincerely hope it will be just a war of words though. I have no wish to come to blows with anyone on the street,' stated Sophia knowing that of all the people in this hall, she was the one who needed to avoid any violent confrontation more than anyone of them could imagine.

'I shall take my stoutest umbrella with me. I can defend myself with that!'

'Be careful you don't break a finger nail Tilly,' teased her friend deciding to take a light hearted approach before she let her real concerns show.

'Oh! You of all people know I'm made of sterner stuff than that.'

Sophia held up her hands in acknowledgement of Tilly's strong character, and went to fetch their cups of tea. As they sat dunking their wine biscuits in a very ladylike way, they both scanned the gathering in case they had missed any suspicious person or any young woman who might be a replacement for Susie Post.

'Can't see anyone who might be a suspect,' said Sophia. 'I can't think he would try the same thing again or at least I genuinely hope not. I'm fed up with Detective Butler's cynicism about me. I really can't read that man. I wonder why he joined the Police Force? I think he would have made a good prosecutor because he certainly doesn't take anything at face value. He wants proof of everything.'

'Well of course he does, silly,' responded Tilly with unusual good sense. 'He can hardly bring a villain in front of a Judge on idle speculation and purely circumstantial evidence. Police work seems to be so much more scientific these days. They'll all have to have a degree in chemistry soon at this rate.'

'Yes, to be fair, as a member of the public, I shall expect good evidence of guilt if I'm ever allowed to sit on a jury.'

'Well that's precisely what we're working for isn't it? Women in authority, permitted to act in all aspects of daily life, which should include being a jury member.'

'And perhaps even a policewoman? I think I would make quite a good one actually.'

'Ugh! No!' shuddered her friend. 'You aren't being honest with yourself. You wouldn't like it all. Just think of all the truly awful people you'd have to deal with. You'd have to look at dead bodies and deal with prostitutes and drunks. Oh and having to wear some sort of terrible uniform! Please don't even consider it.'

Sophia paused but not for the reasons Tilly might think. Her friend's comments were all too close to the reality of her past life, a life she had been determined was not going to encroach on her circumstances in New Zealand. It was all too tempting to share her experiences with Tilly but she couldn't persuade herself there was anything to be gained by it. Her father's death and the events surrounding it would always haunt her but she saw no reason to upset other people with this knowledge. She'd asked her Godfather never to mention it to anyone and she trusted him completely.

'I was thinking more of typing the reports and serving within the Station,' she observed quite touched by Tilly's protectiveness towards her. 'Oh... I know it goes without saying you'd hate any sort of uniform I might have to wear! Still it could provide me with the opportunity to wear trousers that I've been looking for!'

They laughed together and then decided it was time to leave. Outside on the street, Sophia was greeted by a large man, who she looked at in surprise.

'Bayliss? Have you been to the meeting? I didn't

see you in there.'

'No Miss. I was just passing and I remembered you said you were going to be here tonight, so I thought I'd wait and walk back with you.'

'I was going to ride with Tilly, but thank you, I will walk with you. It's cold but it will do me good to stretch my legs. I spend far too much time sitting down. It's very kind of you,' responded Sophia as she waved to Tilly. She wondered at the sudden appearance of her gardener but was genuinely pleased to be escorted home. As they walked briskly along she racked her brains for a conversational topic until she remembered he had served in the Merchant Navy for a while.

'Do you think we will have snow? I read in the paper tonight a report of an immense ice field in the Southern Ocean. There were icebergs two hundred feet high and one was almost fifteen miles long. It's hard to imagine. Have you ever seen such a sight Bayliss?'

Bayliss certainly had seen such massive icebergs and the topic lasted all the way home.

***

The filthy, scarred table in a less than salubrious waterside bar suited Jack Butler well for his purpose. He always smiled inwardly as he approached this tavern, aptly known locally as the 'Rat Hole', but displaying a battered sign outside depicting crossed anchors with lettering too faded to read. The detective was here to dispense bribes and payments for information. His salary took these disbursements into account but the extra pay had to be carefully rationed out to those men who inhabited an amorphous gray area between crime and the law; those men who listened in dark corners passing on the whispers of crimes to be planned, theft, and murder amongst them. Men like Boysie Smith who existed on charity and the trust of criminals and police alike. There was a good gathering of the less fortunate citizens of Wellington this night. Butler sat patiently for some hours, waiting to be noticed, waiting for vital scraps of information that, pieced together, could bring someone to justice especially the prostitute's murderer. Men came and went past him, some stopping to whisper with an outstretched hand, and some ignoring him or swearing at him for what he was. It didn't bother Butler that his presence wasn't welcome by all. He'd long ago learned that a belly had to be really empty before a man's pride would force him to talk to a policeman.

Tonight he'd gathered news of a new gambling den in Haining Street, near the opium house where elderly Chinese men spent their days in smoke filled rooms, so addicted that the police turned a blind eye as long as they didn't solicit new customers. Only occasionally did they check on the occupants of this house to ensure they were all oriental men. One mariner had supplied him with names involved in theft from the wharves, another with the address of a house where stolen goods were fenced and could be bought cheaply by those in the know. It was all useful information for the police, but none of it helped in the Post case or the Dixon Street fire.

Not one of his informants besides Boysie had anything to say about these events. It would appear whoever the perpetrator was, he either didn't mix with the regular criminal fraternity of Wellington or he was so familiar they didn't notice him. Butler was beginning to wonder if the man had been specially recruited from another city. Perhaps he was better known in Auckland, Christchurch, or even Sydney, and unheard of in Wellington, which could be the reason he'd been hired by whoever was behind the anti-suffragette occurrences. Butler mentally disputed this theory. He was sure he would have heard of anyone in New Zealand who was capable of such ghastly crimes. Unless, he wondered, he had been brought over from Australia where there were plentiful numbers of hard men quite capable of such vile acts. It's all a gallimaufrey he thought to himself, as my Scots Grandmother would have said, a complete hotchpotch of suppositions. Should he suspect Huxley or Luxmore of being mixed up in this or was it simply a crime of passion, but then he surmised there does seem to be a link to the Dixon Street fire that tied it to the suffragette movement.

Some of the men who'd talked to him tonight were like children, eager to please as they counted the shillings or even the few pence he gave them. Some were angry, forced by their unemployment to eke out a living that was reliant on their ability to glean scraps of information to sell to men like Butler. At least Miss Homes had been forthright about her discoveries at the race meeting but he had the feeling that she hadn't really forgiven him for his assumption that she was the writer of the letter to the MP. Sometimes he felt her answers were a little too practised and that she was withholding knowledge of some sort that would give him a better insight into the case and perhaps her character. He shook his head unconsciously, realising that her private life was none of his business and that he should really be grateful for her help so far. It was always difficult coming

126

to rely too much on a member of the public, but so far he hadn't had much choice in the matter and he gave a wry smile as he supposed he could have done a lot worse than having a woman such as her to help him.

Near midnight, the detective stretched, drained his glass and left the place. Outside he was instantly forced to brace himself against the chilly wind howling in from Cook Strait, funnelling through the Heads into the harbour and around the streets. As usual on these occasions, the fresh air was a welcome relief from the stench of his mates in the bar. At least the southerly wind blew the ever present shroud of coal smoke away over the hills and further up the west coast. He looked forward to arriving home and scrubbing his hands red, to rid them of the smell of greasy handshakes that permeated the pores of his skin. Sometimes, he welcomed bad weather as it kept the villains at home. Tonight he cursed it as the grit whipped up by the wind, stung fiercely in his eyes, making them water, forcing him to pull his long woollen scarf up round his face as he set off for his small house with long strides.

CHAPTER THIRTEEEN

Thursday 6th April 1893

Once again, Sophia and Jack Butler were taking tea with Sir James, invited to discuss progress in their investigations. Sophia, who was still feeling a little frosty towards the Detective after his accusations, sipped her tea quietly, gazing out of the window at the low grey clouds gathering over the hills which draped down over the ridge lines surrounding the harbour, reminded her of soot stained lace curtains. The water was calm but its' very inertia belied the weather forecast for squally rain and high winds, and the bush covered slopes appeared almost black in the sombre afternoon light. She was heartily glad she was not a passenger on the ferry leaving for the South Island that was starting to edge its way out into the bay leaving the shelter of the wharf. As it made for the wide gap in the sea cliffs a mile or so further, that formed the gateway to the turbulent waters of Cook Strait Sophia could only imagine how the hull would begin to roll. These headlands always reminded her of two clawed arthritic fingers stretching out towards the South island. It was a bleak view today.

'Sophia my dear, can I pour you more tea?'

'Oh... no, thank you. That was very pleasant but quite sufficient,' she answered politely, bringing her concentration back into the formal but stylish room where all was cosy and calm despite its size. She put down her cup and saucer, moving to face the two men, listening as Butler brought Sir James up to date on their information so far. Sophia remarked to herself that he gave no hint that she had stood accused of bribery in his eyes, but calmly laid out the facts and explanations she had devised as if they were his own. Realising that he probably only wished to spare them both some embarrassment, she nodded at his assumptions wishing to appear in harmony with him in front of Sir James. What enmity lay between them must be kept from her Godfather she decided.

'It seems as if our murderer has vanished into thin air by what you say,' Sir James responded looking at Sophia. 'Perhaps he's left town.'

'Well I couldn't spot anyone with a beard like Boysie's description when I was at the races. I nearly went cross eyed peering through my binoculars trying to look at everyone,' said Sophia deprecatingly, with a smile at him. 'I did, however, recognise and overhear Richard Seddon, of all people, coming under pressure from a brewer called Luxmore. That was worth waiting for. I managed to get into conversation with Luxmore's son Richard, but he wasn't giving me any juicy gossip about his Papa, I'm afraid. I thought him rather a dilettante, a real wet week! And I felt much the same about his friend Huxley who turned out to be the son of the owner of the Protheroe house.'

'There's a definite rising of feeling regarding women being allowed to vote in the coming election,' said her Godfather. 'Last night's paper reported that the Auckland Women's Franchise League have been fiercely urging Ballance to push the Bill through, but I can't see it happening. I've met Luxmore senior. He's a self made man and a tough person to deal with from what I hear.

Can't say I warmed to him. Seddon might have some trouble there if he promises too much. Anyway I digress, please continue Butler.'

'I'm sorry I don't have anything firmer to report. It's a possibility that there might be finger prints on the letter from the carbon paper but until we get a definite suspect we have nothing to match them to,' apologised Butler leaning forward, regarding his own finger tips. Sophia noticed how elegant and expressive his hands were with slender fingers, very clean nails and no yellow staining from cigarette smoking. 'Also I have it on good authority that Huxley has a mistress set up in some comfort in the city so it's doubtful he'd want to visit Mrs Protheroe's. Anyway he's one of the less vociferous liquor baron's because, according to my informant, in order to keep his wife happy about his affair, he has kept out of the suffrage argument.'

'Well we can rule him out then I suppose. This business of finger printing is such a new science as far as the police are concerned, isn't it? You would have to be almost one hundred percent certain to persuade a jury of a man's guilt like that,' opined Sir James from his vast experience of the legal system.

'I suspect you're right but hopefully it wouldn't be the only evidence we could produce.'

'There seemed to be no new faces at our WTCU meeting on last Monday night so I drew a blank there,' Sophia said resignedly. 'I know it sounds dreadful, but one almost wishes he would strike again and make a mistake so that we could catch him. It's becoming like reading one of Charles Dickens' serials and never reaching the end.'

'Yes it does sound awful but I do understand what

you mean,' said her Godfather. 'It may be a case of softly, softly catchee monkey; much patience and attention to the tiniest of details. Something I feel you are eminently suited to Sophia. Women have a knack for noticing those little nuances that can add up to a large clue.'

'That's very flattering of you, but I'm starting to feel that I should be going through my daily life with a large magnifying glass permanently attached to my hand! If you see me adopting a caped coat and a deerstalker hat, please feel free to lock me up until I have regained my composure!'

Both men laughed appreciatively at this picture.

'Perhaps you should write to Conan Doyle and ask his advice on this case. It seems eminently worthy of a Sherlock Holmes mystery at the moment,' suggested Sir James, still smiling.

'I prefer to think of it as something Detective Jack Whicher would have loved to investigate,' mused Butler.

'That brings back memories, I must say,' agreed Sir James nodding. 'That was the Road Hill House murder case wasn't it?'

'Yes. A locked house in Wiltshire, a secretive family and a small child taken and murdered in the middle of the night, to put it in a nutshell,' replied Butler.

'I've never heard of it. Is it a real case or a story,' asked Sophia, her legendary curiosity aroused. 'When did it happen?'

'Real all right I'm afraid,' said Butler. 'June 1860 it was. The Kent family were asleep and when they woke in the morning, their little son Saville , three years old was missing. The nurse who slept in his room noticed he was gone from his bed in the early hours of the morning but she presumed he'd got into bed with his mother who slept in a room across the hallway. The nurse went back to sleep and then when she got up at about seven o'clock, asked his mother where he was. Panic ensued when it was realised he was missing.'

'Poor people, what a dreadful thing to happen.'

'They eventually found him, later that day, in the outside privy, with his throat cut. Quite horrific wounds according to the records. The local police couldn't make head or tail of it. No knife was found, no bloodstained clothing belonging to the killer either, so after two weeks, they called in Jack Whicher from the Metropolitan Police.'

'As I recall, Whicher was one of the original detectives based at Scotland Yard. He was highly respected in the Force,' added Sir James. 'I was twenty at the time of the murder, a law student with your father. We followed the case avidly and for a while because Whicher seemed to be a national hero. He had a huge reputation for arresting villains when no-one else could solve the crimes.'

'Apparently he had a knack of recognising guilt in people, even complete strangers. Amazing intuition,' said Butler shaking his head in puzzlement.

'So did he discover the murderer?'

Sophia was fascinated by the story and leaned closer in anticipation of a neat and tidy ending.

'It was extremely difficult for him. Remember that the house was locked, although a window was found ajar on the ground floor. The family closed ranks and refused to be helpful. With no solid evidence, as I said before, he finally arrested Constance Kent, the fifteen year old half sister of Saville. There were rumours that her mother had been insane, but Constance never gave way under questioning and because there was no tangible proof, she was set free. The newspapers vilified Whicher for invading the privacy of a home.'

'So it was never solved?'

'Ah yes... it was many years later confirming Whicher's original suspicions. Constance was sent away to different schools and eventually ended up in a religious seminary run by nuns in Brighton. When she was twenty one, she confessed to the murder. It seems she had succumbed to religion and had at last, listened to her conscience.'

'So Mr Whicher was right all along? He was vindicated?'

'It seems so, but he'd retired the year before because of ill health.'

'And what happened to Constance Kent?'

'She served a long prison sentence, only escaping hanging because she'd owned up to the crime then she quietly went to Australia with her elder brother William and his wife. He was a sort of marine biologist I think. She trained to be a nurse and I can tell you that she is at present alive and well, with the new name of Emily Kaye. Turns out she had a real gift for nursing and I believe she's now the matron in a private hospital in Perth. I have family in Australia and they recently mentioned her, knowing my interest in the case.'

'I don't think I would like to be nursed by her,' shuddered Sophia. 'Did she ever say why she did such a terrible thing?'

'She said she hated her stepmother and wanted to pay her back for luring her father away from her mother.' She was adamant she had no hard feelings for Saville; she just saw him as a means to an end to deprive the second Mrs Kent of the thing she loved the most. What really fascinates me about Whicher is that he started a trend in authors to write about detectives. Charles Dickens was friendly with him and even put a character in *Bleak House* modelled on him.'

'Oh I know,' said Sophia with glee. 'It must be Inspector Bucket?'

'Yes, but many other writers used him and his methods in their books, perhaps even your relative Conan Doyle's character owes much to Jack Whicher's methods of investigating. There are certainly similarities in the Sherlock Holmes books.'

'If only we could know how Whicher looked at people. Who knows, I might have been able to spot all sorts of wrongdoers at the races? What a wonderful gift to possess.'

'It has always fascinated me, how he did it. I can only assume that there are some minute facial expressions, or tics or body movements that can be interpreted in a certain way. If only I could spot a villain that easily.'

Butler laughed softly and Sophia hoped fervently that he did not develop Mr Whicher's talents. She was discomposed to think he might read evidence of her past in her looks or movements. It made her very uneasy in his company but she was distracted from these thoughts as Sir James stood up and moved to his desk and sitting down heavily in his chair, he pulled a leather covered diary towards him and opened it up.

'I think we should meet again soon, say in about ten days?'

Sophia and Butler both nodded and wrote down the appointment in their respective note books. Sophia hoped that they would have made progress by then but at the moment she was doubtful. She decided to ask at the Library if they had any records of the cases Jack Whicher had worked on so that she could study his methods to perhaps obtain an insight into the events of the last few weeks.

As they stood outside, the rain finally arrived and Sophia asked Butler what else he was working on and he laughed as they waited for a cab.

'I got called out last Sunday to deal with a group of young men at Thorndon Esplanade. They'd all stripped off and dived into the sea much to the disgust of passersby. Personally I thought they were rather brave. It was freezing but I suppose the alcohol they'd been drinking gave them courage and an immunity to the cold. They soon came to their senses when we loaded them into the police wagon.'

'I read about it. Someone signing himself or herself 'Disgusted' wrote a real diatribe to the Editor on the subject. The writer suggested that only if one is properly clothed in a decent swimming costume should one be allowed to swim there and then again only when no-one else was likely to see them. I suppose he meant in the middle of the night?'

'It wasn't a pretty sight,' owned Butler with a grin. 'They got off with a warning.'

CHAPTER FOURTEEN

Saturday 8th April 1893.

Yawning loudly, Sophia sat at the kitchen table drinking her second cup of breakfast tea. The night before, she and Una had attended the second meeting of the Wellington Shorthandwriter's Association, and while they were pleased to see several new members being enrolled, Sophia had been not a little perturbed to find they were all young male clerks. However this didn't daunt Una, who signed up for the practice sessions to be held on Monday and Thursday night, which relieved Sophia of the necessity to teach her during business hours. Sophia had arrived home feeling wide awake and hadn't fallen asleep until nearly dawn. Images of Susie Post at the meeting flashed into her mind as she tossed and turned. She couldn't stop herself wondering about the murder scene. Were there clues that Butler might have missed? What sort of knife had been used? A picture of a long sharp bloodstained blade came into her mind. Trembling, she sat up in bed and shook her head. It was several hours before she calmed down and fell asleep. Now, she was feeling drowsy and in dire need of Meg's strong tea. As her cook worked at one end of the table, kneading dough, Sophia spread last night's paper out and read out items of interest.

'Mr Seddon is coming in for criticism again. Listen to this editorial Meg.

"Mr Seddon knows perfectly well that he was not sincere in his professed desire to see the franchise conferred on women, and that it was due to his intrigue and hostility that the Bill fell through last session. As he now says the attitude of the Government is unaltered, we may reasonably expect that the introduction of the Bill next session will be a further act in the comedy, and that Ministers and especially Mr Seddon, will continue to intrigue to prevent their own Bill passing."

'The Editor is a brave man in my opinion. It's lucky we have freedom of the Press here in New Zealand. In some countries I believe he would not be allowed to write about politicians such strongly negative terms.'

'It's true though, isn't it? Everyone says Dick Seddon's a slippery customer,' commented Meg as she worked her dough with hard strokes, as if pummelling the politician's head. 'I listen to what people are saying at the shops and he's not popular with the working classes.'

'You and I think that, but he always gets voted back into Parliament so a great many people don't agree with us. The rumour is strengthening that he'll be the next Prime Minister by September, after the election, if Mr Ballance's health doesn't improve.'

'Even more power to his arm then,' said Meg with a long suffering expression on her flushed face. She put the dough into a heavy china bowl, covered it with a clean cloth and reached up to put it to rise on the mantle above the coal range. Sophia glanced at her and remembered something as she noticed the slight wince that Meg still gave as her ribs stretched upwards to take the weight of the bowl. Searching through the pages of the paper she found what she was looking for.

'I'm going to buy one of these new light weight aluminium bowls for you Meg. That's what you need. It will make things much easier for you.'

Outside, the two of them could hear Bayliss chopping wood. After the meeting last night, Sophia had found him, once again, waiting outside to walk her home and she was beginning to wonder if he thought she was in some sort of danger. Sighing she put the thought out of her head and continued reading.

'Oh good, the new Public Library is opening next week'

'You've got plenty of books here in your own library,' suggested Meg pouring herself a cup of tea and a third one for Sophia. 'You surely don't have the time to read any extra ones?'

'Yes, but many of them are my father's law books. Not what I'd call bedtime reading matter. They look decorative but there's no plot!'

'No, I see what you mean,' laughed Meg.' But I did notice a few by Charles Dickens when I was dusting them the other day. I've heard he wrote good stories.'

Sophia noticed a wistful note in this statement and realised that Meg was unlikely to have been able to obtain and read the novels in her circumstances. She gave way to a sudden impulse.

'Would you like me to read them to you Meg. He originally wrote them as serials. One episode was published at a time in a magazine. We could read one a week perhaps?'

Meg went quite pink with pleasure and nodded.

'That would be wonderful Miss. I expect Bayliss would like that too, even though he reads all the time.'

'You're right he does, but perhaps if I'm unable to read he can take over and keep you up to date with the story. We'll start with *Bleak House*. There's a particular character in that book I would like to re-acquaint myself with.'

***

The roars of the crowd at the rugby match, reached a crescendo as the Wellington half back crashed over the line to score the winning try, just as the fulltime whistle went. Jack Butler cheered with everyone, glad to be anonymous on this cold Saturday afternoon even if he found himself scanning the crowds for men with streaky beards. Desperate for a lead in his case he had decided that anything was better than spending an afternoon in his small house when there was always a slight possibility that he might spot something in the large crowd and enjoy the occasion at the same time. Of course he was soon aware that at least half of the men present wore beards of all descriptions and that he was wasting his efforts in that direction. He waited as the crowd went silent, watching the number ten player sit the ball up on a pile of sand, step back and take aim for the goal posts which were swaying in the strong wind. With a graceful, almost balletic swing of his leg, and a loud thump of boot on leather, the ball took flight, curving inwards through the uprights. The score keepers hurriedly put the new numbers up on the score board as the referee blew the final whistle before the crowds departed, happy that their home team had beaten the boys from Masterton.

The detective appreciated the effort and the fitness of the players. It had been a tough fought second half against the wind and the determination of the men from Wairarapa. The strain of battling both the elements and the opposition had taken a toll on the local team, two of them being injured in the tough scrummaging and tackles. They limped from the field at the conclusion of the match to the acclaim of their supporters. As he left the ground, Jack met up with one of his workmates who invited him for a beer. They made their way slowly back into the centre of town amid the crowds still abuzz with the winning result. The wind was so bitter, most men like he and his companion, had their scarves well up round their faces.

'Ah the dust in this town is deplorable,' said his friend Neil, spitting the grit from his mouth, that blew up from the road, as the wind gusted and forced its' way through the streets and whipped around the buildings. 'Everyone's complaining about it. There was a letter in the paper yesterday, suggesting they put down wood blocks to pave the roads. Something's going to have to be done about it soon.'

A beer soon soothed Neil's throat and his complaints and the two men spent a companionable few hours, enjoying drinks and a meal, reminiscing about cases they'd been involved in, rugby matches they'd enjoyed and their future prospects.

'Have you reached any conclusions about the prostitute's murder?

'It's one of those infuriating cases where there seem to be several suspects but no proof. I'm not short of clues but they simply don't add up to any one person. Even the motive seems cloudy at this stage. It could be aimed at the electoral reform lot or that could be a smokescreen. It's frustrating to say the least.'

'I believe it could be very difficult to prove anything if the brewery men are involved. They appear to have staunch support in Parliament and the money to cover their tracks'

'I'm praying this isn't linked to any politicians but the facts are pointing that way.'

Parting company about eight o'clock, Butler was undecided on where to go. He wondered if he could call on Sophia on some pretext, and he recalled that he still hadn't managed to meet Meg Williams. Well, now was his chance to use this as an excuse to visit the Holmes household or so he persuaded himself.

Walking down the driveway to Sophia's house, it appeared to be engulfed in complete darkness with not even a small porch light left on to signal its owner's presence. After a moment's hesitation, Butler found a side path leading around the building, followed it and was relieved to find brightly lit windows at the back of the home which illuminated the rear door. Rapping hard on it he waited until, after a few moments, it was opened by a burly older man who looked him up and down with suspicion.

'Good evening. I'm Detective Butler. Is Miss Holmes in please?'

The man nodded.

'I'll ask her,' he said in a quiet voice and disappeared down a hallway leaving Butler standing out in the cold. He turned to look at the garden but the darkness hid everything so he was unable to judge the extent of the property. Arriving back quickly, the man ushered him in silently, closed the door, locked it then motioned him to go up the passageway to an open door. Butler walked into a warm, well lit kitchen that reminded him of his mother's. A large Shacklock coal range dominated one side, with a clothes airing frame hanging from the ceiling above, whilst a wooden dresser loaded with china, stood against the opposite wall. In the middle of this large room was a scrubbed table, big enough to seat six people and very quickly he took in the sight of Sophia Holmes and another woman sitting playing cards. He also noticed three glasses of what appeared to be whisky.

'Detective Butler, this is a surprise,' said Sophia, rising from her chair. 'Please do come in. This is Mrs Williams my cook and Mr Bayliss my gardener.'

She indicated to them and Butler nodded in greeting.

'Please excuse me interrupting your evening but I was in the neighbourhood on other business and decided that I should just call to meet Mrs Williams and talk to her regarding her husband's death.'

'Ah... I see,' said Sophia looking as if she found his excuse a little lame. 'Well here she is.'

Jack smiled down at the small woman sitting opposite him. He kept his tone light and sympathetic as he began to talk to her seeing the distrust plainly obvious on her thin face.

'I'm afraid we still haven't found out who killed him Mrs Williams, but something may crop up to help. We're keeping our ears open for anything that might lead to an arrest.'

Meg said nothing only nodded at him so he pulled out a chair and decided to make polite conversation. The warmth of the room, so much in contrast with the weather outside, made him reluctant to leave.

'This seems a wonderfully cosy kitchen. Perhaps

you won't mind if I warm up before venturing out again?'

'Of course not,' said Sophia. 'Please make yourself at home.'

'Perhaps I could join in your game?'

'Do you play Poker? To my detriment I've taught these two to play and they consistently beat me,' laughed Sophia appearing more at ease with him.

'I have played, yes,' said the Detective. 'But I haven't any money for gambling I'm afraid.'

'Oh we haven't either,' said his hostess. 'If you reach into that tin there, you can count yourself out twenty buttons as a starting stake.'

'Excellent, I was wondering what those were for,' he indicated the large piles of multicoloured buttons in front of Bayliss and Meg.

'And in case you have a headache tonight, you may pour yourself a small whisky. We've found that playing cards give us terrible headaches and we need to have a tot for purely medicinal purposes,' offered Sophia with a perfectly straight face.

'Of course I have heard that the Temperance Society does condone alcohol for medicinal purpose,' said Butler with a wicked grin at Sophia as he fetched a glass from the dresser and poured a measure. 'Can I surmise that Mrs Sergeson's well known love of champagne serves the same purpose?'

'Oh you know how we ladies suffer so badly from headaches! Now I think it's your turn to deal Bayliss.'

An hour passed and Butler watched as Sophia let her staff win again and again. He noticed the pleasure on their faces as they pulled her bets into their own piles of buttons. He decided to call her bluff when Meg left the game to make supper. Bayliss went off to check the house was securely locked up and Sophia dealt out a two handed game. However, she then beat him soundly and he realised that her altruism didn't extend to a player like him who knew the ropes.

'Whoever taught you to play Poker did an excellent job,' he said as she took all his winnings away from him in a final hand.

'The American Ambassador in London. I think I told you he taught me to shoot too. Such a charming man.'

'I hope I never find myself in front of you holding a gun then if that's the case. You're too good at bluffing by far.'

'How kind of you,' she laughed but he noticed she suddenly clasped her hands tightly together nervously. 'But I can't think of anything more unlikely. Let's stick to cards. Now please join us for supper?'

Jack was only too pleased to partake of home cured ham sandwiches and a slab of rich fruit cake, noticing how pleased Meg looked when he complimented her on her cooking.

As they sat waiting for their cups of tea to cool, Sophia gave Jack an enquiring look.

'You mentioned you have relatives In Australia? Are you Australian?'

'Yes I am,' said Jack. 'And before you ask, because I can see it's on the tip of your tongue, yes, I am descended from a convict!'

'Oh nothing was further from my mind,' denied Sophia with a laugh. 'But I would like to know all about them!'

'My Grandfather was sixteen when he was arrested for picking up an apple from the gutter at a street market in London. He'd presumed it had been thrown away and took a bite before an angry stall holder accused him of stealing it. Some bystanders stood up for Grandfather but he was brought before a Judge and sentenced to deportation.'

'The law was so cruel then,' commented Sophia.

'Anyway luck came to him. When he finally arrived in Sydney, he was indentured to a builder who took him into his own home and treated him like a son. The builder and his wife had no children of their own. He worked out his seven years and then stayed on to manage the business for them. He expanded into forestry and timber and finally brought them out when they wanted to retire. It was only then that they told him the Judge who'd sentenced him had written to them in his favour, asking them to apprentice him. My father inherited everything and started a hardware store affiliated with the building company, which my two older brothers manage. I had no interest in the trade so I joined the police.'

'How extraordinary that in two generations your family has gone from convict to law enforcement,' mused Sophia. 'It's such a good example of how men can achieve success from adversity, from one side of the law to the other.'

'I'm gratified you think that. I remember my Grandfather being a very kind old man. He never pointed a finger in recrimination at anyone. I don't think he ever complained of his treatment, just always remained so grateful to the couple whom took him in.'

'Kindness can go a long way in improving people's lives,' said Sophia. 'Even the smallest gesture can mean so much to someone who has nothing. My father never treated any of his clients as if they were guilty, not even the most recidivist of them. I don't believe he even asked them if they were guilty. He preferred to think the best of them. He told me once that if he knew someone was definitely guilty of the crime, he wouldn't take them on unless there was a reasonable excuse or a legal loophole. I have to say that there nearly always was, in his opinion!'

CHAPTER FIFTEEN

Tuesday 11th April 1893.

As the office door bell jangled, Sophia went to attend the customer. Much to her surprise she was met by Richard Luxmore, who stood leaning on the counter with one elbow as if waiting for a drink to be served at a bar. He straightened up as she appeared and raised his hat with one finger. She noticed he sported a large yellow bow tie which peeped out from under the collar of his long black overcoat.

'Miss Holmes, thought I'd come and have a look at your business after our little tete a tete at the races.'

'I'm honoured you remembered me,' smiled Sophia. 'What can I do for you?'

She noticed his eyes narrow for an instant and then he smiled.

'Do you know I'd love to have a go on one of your typewriter machines?'

'I'm so sorry but we're using them both at the moment and I can't remove my work easily.'

Luxmore gazed at her as if she was making a rather irrational excuse but then he shrugged.

'Course I understand, silly of me to ask. Anyway I thought I'd deliver this in person to you. Good day.'

He put an envelope on the counter, tipped his hat again and was gone abruptly, before she could reply. Picking it up, Sophia noted the expensive stationery. She walked back to her desk and reached for her letter opener to slit the envelope. Inside was a gilt edged card.

'What is it?'

'I don't know Una. It appears to be an invitation. Give me a minute to read it please.'

The black printing on the card was clear and precise. She read it out to Una.

> *Mr and Mrs George Luxmore*
> *are pleased to invite*
> *Miss Sophia Holmes*
> *to an evening of music and dancing at their residence*
> *Saturday 22nd April 1893, at 7.30pm.*
> *R.S.V.P 'The Oaks', Tinakori Road, Wellington.*

'Good heavens, why would they invite me? I've never met them.'

'Must be their son that wants you to go,' suggested her assistant. 'Maybe he's taken a bit of a shine to you!'

'No, surely not,' responded a horrified Sophia. 'He's years younger than me and he knows I'm a suffrage proponent. On the other hand you could be right. George Luxmore is a liquor baron, hard and fast. I'm sure he wouldn't invite me if he knew how much I detest everything he stands for. Anyway it's out of the question. I can't go on my own. It would be impossible, not to say potentially embarrassing.'

'Perhaps young Mr Luxmore intends to be your escort?'

Una's slyness wasn't lost on her employer who brushed it off tersely.

'Nonsense, surely he would have said so just now

but if he thinks I 'm going to spend an evening as a wallflower waiting for his attention, then he's wrong. I'd rather stay at home with a good book.'

'Well you could always ask someone to go with you, purely as a companion,' suggested Una in kinder tones. 'The Luxmore's couldn't object to that could they? I expect so many people will be there that no-one would notice one extra.'

Una's idea stayed with Sophia for the rest of the day. It occurred to her that she might gain an insight into George Luxmore's plotting with Richard Seddon, if she had an entree into the household. Then she panicked at the decision about what to wear and decided that she needed Tilly's advice on the whole matter. Picking up the hand piece of her newly installed telephone, she asked the operator for the Sergeson's number and waited. When Tilly answered, Sophia explained the whole dilemma to her and they arranged to meet the next day to plan a campaign for the Luxmore soiree.

CHAPTER SIXTEEN

Wednesday 12th April 1893.

'Definitely not grey sweetie. Ghastly with your complexion, and this lace one is far too dated and too matronly.'

Sophia had taken an afternoon break from work and now she and Tilly stood before a large wardrobe in one of the spare bedrooms, which held all the gowns she'd worn in her previous life in London. Tilly pulled each one out critically, wrinkling her nose at the smell of mothballs. Then her face lit up as she lifted down a deep lilac dress and hung it over the door.

'This is the one. It's extraordinary, quite beautiful.'

Sophia nodded and smoothed the beautiful fabric with her hand.

'It's a genuine Charles Worth. My father bought it in Paris for me just before he died. It was made for an Austrian duchess but she rejected it as being too plain. Most of his gowns do usually have a great deal more beadwork on the bodice than this one. I've never had the chance to wear it.'

Tilly sensed the note of sadness in her friend's voice but she too, smoothed her hand against the thick satin of the swirling skirt, admiring the delicate pleating at the waist and the intricate shaping around the bodice neckline.

'I've never seen one of his up so close. It's a marvel of dressmaking. Look how cleverly it's shaped here and here,' she whispered, almost in reverence, as her fingers followed the lines of the styling. 'You'll be the envy of every woman in the room.'

'In that case I'm not wearing it. I want to be as unnoticed as possible.'

'Rubbish Sophia. You've got to wear it once before you get too old.'

'Mm,' conceded Sophia. 'Perhaps you're right. Look have you noticed that it has an inner boned bodice to give it the right shape. I don't have to wear a corset with it. That is greatly in its favour.'

'Come on. Put it on so I can see what you look like,' Tilly said excitedly. 'You'll need an admirer at your side to carry this dress off! Have you anyone in mind to escort you?'

'Well...' Sophia said slowly, not sure of Tilly's reaction. 'I thought I could ask Detective Butler because it would give him a chance to meet the Luxmore's. I've sensed that he isn't too keen on the tactics over prohibition.'

'Just as long as he wears a decent set of evening clothes,' was Tilly's practical reply, as she started to do up the tiny buttons on the back of the Worth gown. 'After all, at least you know you can trust him to behave!'

'Oh I hadn't given any thought to that or what he would wear. Do you think I should offer to hire a suit for him?'

'Good heavens no,' stated Tilly, finishing the buttons and turning her friend around to face the mirror. 'You look wonderful Sophia. You should wear clothes like this more often. Butler may not want to behave when he sees you wearing this gown!'

Turning her head and admiring the elegant sweep

of the lilac satin skirt, Sophia was satisfied that her appearance would be more than suitable for the Luxmore evening party. Her slender build was perfect for the lines of the dress and the boned low cut bodice complemented her well shaped bosom.

'I'll have to buy some long evening gloves, and some new shoes.'

'What about jewellery? You should wear long earrings I think, but no necklace.'

'I've got my mother's diamond drop earrings.'

'Just the thing and I'll loan you a diamond bracelet,' said Tilly clapping her hands in an excited mood that her friend could not match. However she did try and show some enthusiasm to please Tilly.

'I'll feel like Cinderella now you've transformed me. You must be my fairy Godmother!'

Tilly, struggling to undo all the tiny buttons she'd just fastened, wished that was true and she had a magic wand to do the job!

CHAPTER SEVENTEEN

Friday 14th April 1893.

The wet and windy weather prevailed in Wellington. The rain barely subdued the dust and grit on the streets, before the wind dried it out again. Sophia struggled to work with a scarf tied tightly over her hat and around her face. It was common to see hats being blown off, bowling down the road ahead of their owners. Many of the flags flying on public buildings were beginning to gain a shredded appearance as they flapped and strained in continuing westerly gales, the chinking noise of their lanyards providing a permanent background noise. Several sailings of the South Island ferry boats were delayed. The harbour became filled with moored ships, all awaiting a lull in the weather conditions before attempting to make their way across the turbulent waters of Cook's Strait with its treacherous currents.

'These could hardly be described as April showers could they,' remarked Sophia to Una, as, gazing out of the front window of the Agency, they watched the sheets of rain advancing down over the city deluging it from heavy black clouds that once again, cloaked the hillsides like funeral clothes. Pedestrians sought shelter under shop verandas as they found their umbrellas useless in the wind.

'I don't think we'll get any clients in today. If this keeps up, you and I will have to take a cab home. Let's have a cup of tea.'

Almost as soon as the two women had seated themselves back at their desks with their hot drinks, the door bell rang. Sophia rose and went to answer it.

'Ah Miss Holmes... a port in the storm.'

Sophia smiled politely at the young man who was divesting himself of a rain cape that dripped all over her floor.

'Mr Luxmore, whatever brings you into town on such a terrible day?'

Luxmore hung his cape and hat on a coat stand near the door then turned to smile at her.

'Ghastly isn't it? I got so bored listening to my mother-in law to be moaning about the weather to poor Mama that thought I must get out for some fresh air.'

'Well the air is certainly fresh today. No doubt about that. I didn't realise you were engaged,' said a surprised Sophia all in one breath. 'Why don't you come through and have a cup of tea with us. You can tell us all about your wedding plans.'

'Oh just the ticket. Milk and two sugars please.'

After introducing Richard Luxmore to Una, Sophia indicated a chair to him and fetched his tea.

'Wondered if you were coming to the parents' do,' he said casually. 'Hoping to have a dance with you actually.'

'That's very sweet of you, but I wouldn't want to upset your fiancée,' ventured Sophia.

'Oh you needn't worry about her,' he said in dismissive tones. 'It's a business arrangement more than anything. Her father owns a brewery that mine wants to get his hands on. Daphne's an only child like me, so he sees it as a way of cementing the two companies together for his own advantage. That's the brutal reality of it.'

'That sounds more than a trifle ruthless if you'll forgive me for saying so,' said Sophia who was uncomfortable with his use of the word "brutal". 'I wouldn't have thought that was a reasonable excuse for marrying you off to her. It's not a good basis for a happy marriage is it? I'm of the opinion there has to be an element of mutual attraction to make a partnership successful but perhaps you don't agree? How does Daphne feel about it?'

'Never really asked her,' shrugged Richard with a grin. 'Don't suppose she cares one way or the other. We've known each other since we were both tiny. Women are happy if they make a good marriage aren't they? Better than being sent off to a nunnery or becoming a teacher!'

It was obvious to both his listeners that this young man was either extremely arrogant or extremely stupid, as they listened to him laughing rather too jovially, at his own joke. Sophia reckoned that both options were possibly applicable to Richard Luxmore, and she frowned at Una before her assistant said something she'd regret.

'I suppose we all hope for at least a little romance and mutual affection in a long lasting marriage,' was Sophia's diplomatic response. 'It seems to be the best recipe for happiness as far as I can tell. Although of course, I can't speak from experience, but I'm sure Mrs Johnson would agree with that.'

'Oh yes...' responded Una quickly. 'I was lucky to marry for love and I've never regretted it.'

'Oh I like her well enough, you needn't worry on that account. We get along amicably. I think we'll be quite happy.'

His obvious dismissal of their doubts made both women uncomfortable. Una managed to offer a few comments about the weather and Sophia followed her example.

'We really are having the most dreadful winter. I do hope it stops raining by the night of your parents' party.'

'You didn't say if you are coming,' recalled Luxmore staring at Sophia with a sharp look.

'I will accept your kind invitation,' said Sophia. 'But I hope you don't mind if I bring a friend? It can be a bit difficult for a woman attending that type of gathering on her own. It will make me feel more at ease, you see, as I doubt I'll know many people.'

'Oh you want to come with a companion. Of course you'll want someone to gossip with when I'm not dancing with you. Quite understand.'

There was something wolfish about his smile that sent a tingle down Sophia's spine but she tried to ignore it as, finishing his tea, their guest pulled on his cape and hat and went back out into the rain with a cheerful,' Au revoir.'

'Well he's a piece of work, I must say,' remarked Una. 'You'd better be very wary of him. He strikes me as being as slippery as an eel.'

'I think you are right but that's a bit dramatic Una. He's certainly very sure of himself but I expect all young people are these days. I'm a bit out of touch with his age group.'

'You are the least out of touch person I know,' laughed Una. 'I don't know anyone else who keeps up with the news as keenly as you. You always have your head in the newspaper.'

'I do my best. Anyway I do agree with you about his character. He's the most arrogant young man I've come across for a long time. I can't imagine the sort of life his poor Daphne is going to lead. Poor girl, it sounds as if she's been thoroughly bullied into the engagement.'

'It makes me appreciate that I was able to marry my Fred with my parent's blessing,' remarked Una. 'I can't imagine being told who to spend the rest of my life with can you?'

'No...' Sophia paused. 'But no-one has ever offered me the chance to make that decision and anyway I was always sure I would never marry. I'm afraid I'm far too independent for any man who'd want to change me.'

She picked up the newspaper from her desk, idly flicking over the pages to cover the distraction that passed through her. I'm a woman with a past she reflected and that sounds like something out of a mystery novel. A headline caught her eye and she read out loud.

'They report that Premier Ballance has taken a turn for the worst. The poor man has been ill for months now. It says he's going to have an operation next week. I expect Seddon is rubbing his hands in glee at the chance to really lead the Government instead of just being a stand in all these weeks.'

'I always quite liked Mr Ballance,' said Una. 'But surely Sir Robert Stout would be next in line to lead the Liberals?'

'I think you'll find that Seddon will roll right over him in his determination to be top dog. There'll be a lot of lobbying going on before the election, you mark my words.'

CHAPTER EIGHTEEN

Saturday 21ˢᵗ April 1893

Sophia waited in the drawing room for her escort to arrive. A long dark blue fine wool evening cape covered her lilac satin gown, worn with new cream kid leather shoes. Tilly's diamond bracelet glittered in the gas light, on her left wrist against cream satin gloves buttoned up to her elbows with tiny pearls. Meg had proved to be expert at putting up her employers' hair into a shining sculpted chignon that was held in place by many hidden pins and two ornate tortoiseshell combs. The diamond earrings ensured a perfect finishing touch to the ensemble. Pinching her cheeks and biting her lips, to put some colour into them, Sophia pulled the curtain back as she heard the jingle of harness as the cab arrive, and admitting to some nervousness, walked out into the hallway aware of Meg watching from the kitchen passageway. She opened the front door as the bell rang and she was gratified to see Jack Butler step back as if in amazement at her transformation.

'Miss Holmes! Why you look wonderful.'

Sophia was relieved at this observation.

'Thank you. You look most presentable too. I think we'll make a fine couple don't you? We must remember to use our Christian names tonight too. It will appear odd if we are too formal.'

Her escort nodded and Sophia gave him her arm as he handed her up into the cab and sat beside her, careful not to crush her skirts. Her perfume filled the small space with the scent of spring apple blossom, and she hoped it wasn't distracting Jack from his formal purpose. When Sophia had asked him to accompany her to the Luxmore's, he'd been hesitant at first, but then, as she persuaded him it was a golden opportunity to infiltrate the environment of a liquor baron possibly to pick up some political gossip, he'd agreed. He'd told her he could use some of his police funds to hire his evening clothes, to justify this as part of his ongoing investigation into the Post murder.

Up on Tinakori Road, the cab joined a considerable queue outside the gates of 'The Oaks'.

'Thank goodness there are so many guests,' sighed Sophia peering out of the dirty window of the Hansom. 'No-one will notice us snooping around.'

'I'd rather you left that to me,' was Jack's response and then he admitted to his surprised companion. 'But I really don't expect to find out anything seriously useful. I've just come to enjoy myself.'

Finally the cab pulled into the driveway, stopping with a lurch, outside the front door of a grandiose mansion adorned with turrets, carved wooden finials and large covered verandas. Jack helped Sophia to descend from the vehicle, offering her his arm up the steps into the house. Handing her cape to a maid, Sophia gazed around at the massive entrance hall with its polished wood floor. Immense chandeliers glittered everywhere, reflected in endless ornate gilt framed mirrors hung on the dark papered walls, above chiffoniers laden with ornamental vases and statuettes. As she and Jack walked into the first drawing room, Sophia was amused to see how so much money had been spent in such bad taste.

The whole effect was not only cluttered but claustrophobic, making it difficult to walk through the room without brushing against something.

The next two reception rooms were equally as crowded with furniture and Sophia and Jack passed slowly along behind the other guests all crammed together.

'It's all horribly nouveau riche,' said Sophia softly, knowing full well how snobbish that sounded. 'A fine example of having too much money and too little taste. One gets the impression that if something is overpriced, then the Luxmores have bought it, regardless of whether it complements their decor. They must be like a pair of magpies collecting all these shiny items for their nest.'

Jack Butler nodded in agreement and Sophia could tell by his expression of distaste that he felt totally out of place in this house and even though she felt he was perfectly attired in the correct formal evening wear it seemed to do little to bolster his confidence in these surroundings.

'I mean,' continued Sophia in a scathing tone. 'Look at all these portraits. They can't possibly be ancestors can they? They're all from last century and English. I think Luxmore must have bought them to try and fabricate some sort of family history that he doesn't possess.'

'As far as I know, his father owned a pub in Feilding,' grinned Jack, who seemed glad to add some factual detail to her comments. 'And his wife's family got their money from wool farming in the South Island.'

Sophia stopped in front of an enormous portrait of a young man astride a massive chestnut hunter. It was framed in a heavy gilt surround featuring huge clusters of carved fruit and flowers at each corner.

'That looks more recent. It's surely a New Zealand landscape in the background. There are some cabbage trees... Oh,' she breathed. 'Look at his beard.'

They both moved a little closer to look at the rider in the picture who had a streaked beard exactly matching the description that Boysie Smith had given Jack.

'I see you're admiring Uncle Sinclair.'

Sophia jumped nervously as Richard Luxmore appeared beside her. Once again he smelled of whisky but was a picture of sartorial elegance with his deep blue brocade waistcoat under the latest in black evening jackets.

'Oh I didn't see you there. It is a fine painting. Your uncle you say?'

'Well he's a sort of uncle I suppose. My mother's half brother; they shared the same father. It was painted about thirty years ago I think. He lives near Christchurch but he's been staying with us for the last two months. Mama dotes on him but between you and me, I think he's a bit of a bore and so does Father.'

Sophia felt a cold chill go through her as she saw Jack paying close attention to Richard's words. To distract him she remembered her manners, placing a deliberately intimate hand on Jack's arm as she turned away from the painting.

'Richard forgive me, I haven't introduced you to my escort. This is Jack Butler, Jack this is Richard Luxmore who I literally bumped into at the races. He was most understanding, when I accidentally tipped his drink all over his jacket. I still can't imagine how I managed to do that!'

The two men nodded warily at each other.

'I thought you meant to bring a female companion Miss Holmes? Now you've arrived with a gentleman. Not quite the same thing I think? But of course you are very welcome sir.'

Richard's words fell slightly short of being jovial, his smile obviously an effort as he eyed the older man. Sophia intervened rapidly to avert any awkwardness.

'My dear friend who was going to accompany me was taken ill, so Jack was kind enough to step in at short notice or I wouldn't have been able to come,' said Sophia, quickly inventing an excuse as she patted Richard soothingly on the arm to mollify him.

'I forgive you, he said with a patronising smile. 'Just remember I've booked a dance with you. I'd better go and greet more people now I suppose. Mama hates that side of these occasions and father is closeted in the library with some of his political cronies, so it falls on my shoulders to be sociable.'

When he'd gone, Jack looked up at the painting, shaking his head over the beard.

'It must be a co-incidence. Let's wander on further and see if he's here.'

A passing waiter offered them tall flutes of champagne and Jack handed Sophia one mouthing the word "headache" with a smile. Accepting it, she sipped, and watched the groups of people coming and going through the rooms, hearing music in the distance. Stopping to talk to an elderly couple she knew, Sophia nodded at Jack to leave her with them while he mingled with the guests in an effort to find the bearded Uncle Sinclair.

Finishing her conversation, Sophia moved forward through the next room, stopping to pretend admiration for the myriad of small trinkets that crowded every possible flat space. Returning to her side, Jack pointed out a chair made of deer antlers adorned with a bright tartan cushion and she grimaced.

'It's hideous isn't it? It's really macabre. I would estimate that at least ten stags must have died or had their antlers cut off to make it.'

'It also looks supremely uncomfortable to sit on. I found Uncle Sinclair,' he said resignedly. 'But he's not our man. For a start, his beard is completely white now and he's in a wheel chair. I managed to talk to him on the pretext of my admiration for his portrait and he informed me that shortly after it was completed, the horse threw him. The fall broke his back. He took great relish in telling me that he had his workers carry him out to the stable so he could shoot the animal.'

'He sounds sadistic,' said Sophia sadly. 'Poor horse.'

'He's a really miserable old man. He kept complaining that someone has been stealing his possessions since he's been staying here. Unfortunately that got worse when I had to admit to being a policeman. He started to insist that I immediately call in a team of police to investigate.'

'Let's go and have a dance Jack. Cheer ourselves up a bit,' suggested Sophia sensing his annoyance. 'Remember you are supposed to be off duty tonight.'

The dance floor was crowded and Sophia felt Jack pull her close as he steered a course through the other couples. They moved well together but the close proximity of others made for an uneasy progress round the parquet floor. There was no chance to have any sensible conversation in this melee, so when the music ended, they moved to the side of the ballroom where Sophia noticed a stout woman making her way towards them. She wore a purple satin gown unflattering to her figure; a huge triple row of pearls sat high around her neck trying to disguise her double chin. Heavy pearl earrings gave her ears a pendulous appearance and the heavy white face powder on her cheeks couldn't disguise the fine red veins seen in the complexions of heavy drinkers. Sophia's first thought was that if this was Richard's mother, she was a very poor advertisement for drinking alcohol on a regular basis. The only thin part of her was her mouth which was prim and pursed at this instant as she came to a halt in front of them with an ungainly lurch.

'You must be the Holmes woman who picked my son up at the races.'

Sophia physically blenched at the loudness of the voice, the penetrating harsh tones and the smell of gin on the woman's breath. She gathered herself and held out her right hand politely.

'Sophia Holmes and you must be Mrs Luxmore. It's a pleasure to meet you. This is my friend Jack Butler.'

Ignoring Sophia's hand completely, Richard's mother looked at Jack with narrowed eyes.

'What do you do?'

Sophia quickly placed a warning hand on Jack's arm as she quickly answered for him.

'Mr Butler is a researcher.'

'Is he indeed? Can't he answer for himself? What do you research?'

164

They were both taken aback by her incivility but Jack managed a polite smile.

'I research criminality, Mrs Luxmore. I'm a type of forensic scientist. I'm afraid it's a bit complicated to explain and would probably be very boring for you.'

'Hmph!' muttered Mrs Luxmore, wobbling slightly on her feet. 'You academics are all smoke and mirrors. Not a real job is it?'

Turning abruptly back to Sophia she eyed her up and down.

'That's a cheap copy you're wearing. You should use my dressmaker.'

Sophia's mouth dropped open as the older woman ran her pudgy tightly ringed fingers down over the lurid sheen of her own skirts then without any further conversation proceeded abruptly away from them, making somewhat unsteadily progress towards her son who was talking to other guests on the opposite side of the room.

'She's rather difficult in a situation like this, isn't she?' Shocked, Sophia and Jack looked around at this interruption. A young woman of about eighteen stood near them obviously listening to their discourse with Mrs Luxmore. She was wearing a very suitable plain evening gown and although not pretty, held herself well, possessing a lovely smile that was directed at them both.

'I'm Daphne Parham, Richard's fiancée. I know your gown is a genuine Worth. I'm very interested in fashion, I hope you don't mind me saying this but I've been dying to have a closer look at it all evening. Don't take any notice of Hilda Luxmore, she's a bit worse for wear but not all bad.'

'I'm so pleased to meet you,' ventured Sophia.

'Richard has spoken highly of you.'

'Oh poor Richard is in for a shock. He's going to have to choose between me and Mama if he wants the marriage to go ahead. He has to break the apron strings soon or I'm breaking the engagement. He's at her beck and call all the time. It's unhealthy if you ask me.'

Once again shocked by this young woman's blunt assessment, Sophia sensed there was a great deal of truth in it. There were undercurrents in the Luxmore family that were unsettling, however it would be tactless of her to voice these thought, better to stay neutral.

'I've heard that all young women become a little nervous as their wedding approaches. You wouldn't really break the engagement would you? Richard seems a nice enough boy. Surely he will take your side if she's too domineering.'

Daphne linked her arm through Sophia's, assuming an air of instant friendship as she walked her firmly away from Jack, into a conservatory that was positively tropical in its heat and humidity, with a dense green jungle tangle of foliage. Sophia almost expected to see a brightly coloured parrot perched amidst the palms. Daphne gestured towards a wrought iron table and chairs, where she sat down opposite Sophia.

'May I talk confidentially to you? You must think it strange that I wish to bare my soul to a perfect stranger, but I sense that you most likely have the experience to help me, and besides which anyone who owns a Worth must have a great deal of wisdom and taste!'

Sophia was strangely flattered by the naivety of this sweeping statement so she smiled, deciding to encourage Daphne to confide in her uncertain where it would lead.

'Please, you flatter me, but I can be very diplomatic and discreet so I'm told. I can promise you that whatever you say will not be passed on to anyone for gossip.'

'The thing is... to tell the truth,' Daphne hesitated before rushing on with her confession. 'I don't wish to be married at all but Mr Luxmore has some sort of hold over Papa. I think it's a financial matter, perhaps some sort of loan that he made to Papa's brewery. Mama says it was agreed that he would release Papa from the arrangement if I would marry Richard. I was never consulted at all. One Sunday afternoon we were invited to tea here and the announcement was made to me, meet your fiancée! I was never so shocked in my life! To be fair, I've known Richard vaguely since we were very small, but never in a million years did I view him as my future husband.'

'That's appalling,' said Sophia with genuine sympathy. 'Are you and Richard able to be friends?'

'Sometimes he seems affectionate but at other times he ignores me. He spends far more time with his mother and his friend Quentin than he does with me.'

'So as I understand it, if you break the agreement your father could suffer financially?'

'Apparently but I feel like I've been auctioned in a cattle market. If I don't go through with the marriage, my parents will more than likely, throw me out on the streets, and perhaps my father's business will be bankrupted. I suspect in that instance, Luxmore would be able to purchase it from my father for a considerably discounted price which he would be forced to accept all because of my stupid behaviour.'

Near to tears, Daphne sniffed, searching in her

reticule for a handkerchief.

'You may be exaggerating a little but it sounds to me as if you are genuinely on the horns of a dilemma,' asserted Sophia. 'I must admit to you that Richard did tell me that he saw the marriage as a business arrangement so I couldn't recommend him to you on those grounds alone. That attitude isn't acceptable for any young woman of sense in this day and age.'

'I understand what you're saying,' said Daphne with not a hint of coyness. 'The other thing is I don't want babies for a long time and the thought of getting in to bed with him every night makes my skin crawl. It was bad enough his scraping my face with those awful whiskers every time he kissed my cheek. At least he did shave them off when I asked him.'

Once again Sophia felt a chill invade her bones. She leaned forward over the table, thinking herself ridiculous, almost unwilling to hear the reply to her next question.

'I can't imagine Richard with a beard. What colour was it?'

'Oh it wasn't a beard, just those long sideboards that they call mutton chops. What a silly name. Quite dark really, considering he has blonde hair.'

'That doesn't sound very attractive at all, but he did try to please you so that must be in his favour,' said Sophia annoyed at herself for being so suspicious of every man with a beard.

'I suppose so,' mused Daphne, not sounding as if she found this at all credible. 'With a mother as mad as Hilda, it worries me that Richard might turn out the same. When I met that awful Uncle Sinclair Montford, I wonder what I'd struck. It must be dreadful to be

168

crippled but he never stops talking about his accident and how he shot the poor horse.'

'You don't really mean she's insane do you? More likely she's too much influenced by drink,' said Sophia eager to keep Daphne on the subject.

'Oh no she's completely barmy. No doubt about that either,' stated Daphne with all the confidence of her inexperienced youth. 'She rarely leaves this house. Apparently she suffers from some strange phobia. Anyway I'm going to have to decide soon. I can't let the engagement go on much longer because the presents are starting to arrive and it will be a huge and demoralising task returning them to everyone. I feel more embarrassed about that than I do about a broken engagement.'

'If you don't marry, what would you really like to do,' asked Sophia.

'Well I know it sounds very ordinary, but I would love to work in the fashion department of a large store. I would so love helping women to choose their outfits. Then I could be independent and live on my own. I wouldn't care about being really poor if I could make my own decisions.'

Doubting that Daphne had any real idea of poverty, Sophia reached inside her bag and pulled out a small leather case. She extracted one of her business cards, offering it to Daphne.

'If you do decide to follow your heart and go out to work, you can stay with me for a while. I have plenty of spare rooms. You'd be quite safe.'

'Oh you have a telephone,' exclaimed Daphne, reading the details. 'You really are a very modern woman Miss Holmes. You've inspired me to live up to my aspirations.'

'As long as you don't tell anyone that I'm the cause of your decision,' said Sophia. 'Mum's the word. If you do come and live with me, it's better if no-one knows where you are for a while until all the furore has died down. While you should let your parents know you are safe, it would be preferable to gain employment before they know where you are living. Now you really had better go back and mingle.'

As Daphne left the conservatory, Sophia leaned back in her chair and let out a sigh. A second sense told her she might live to regret this offer to Daphne Parham, but it was impossible to go back on her word now. A loud rustling caused her to look round as Jack Butler emerged from behind a large palm frond.

'Golly, I thought it must be a snake arriving,' she gasped fluttering her hand melodramatically against her chest.

'That was a most enlightening conversation to eavesdrop on,' commented the policeman.

'Mostly the dreams of a young girl,' said Sophia. 'I did, briefly, think the beard bit might be a lead, but her description was nothing like Boysie's. I hardly think he'd mistake sideboards for a streaked beard. I can't honestly see Richard as a suspect anyway. It would mean getting his hands dirty and he appears far too fastidious for that! It's just another red herring as Meg would say.'

'Yes I think you're right. Smith is a pretty acute observer from my experience of him,' acknowledged Jack.

'Oh you're a mere academic,' grinned Sophia. 'What would you know? Forensic scientist indeed! Wherever did you dream that up from?'

'That's the future of police work, mark my words.

We won't be alive to see it but in years to come there will be all sorts of discoveries that will help us solve crimes a lot easier. The new science of fingerprinting will be old fashioned then.'

'You read too much,' said his cynical companion. 'Anyway, if it makes you feel better, I do think Mrs Luxmore was impressed even if she wasn't prepared to admit it.'

'No, she was far too drunk to work it out. What a thoroughly nasty woman.'

'I'd like to find out who Mr Luxmore is talking to in the library. Come on.'

Sophia beckoned to him, glad to leave the heat of the conservatory behind, only to find it wasn't much cooler elsewhere. Passing along a corridor lined with grand landscape paintings, they came to a door which was slightly ajar. Sophia listened and pushed it open much to Butler's astonishment.

'Ah... this is where you are all hiding,' she said in the giddiest female voice she could muster. Jack followed her more cautiously. Three men were sitting around a circular green baize covered card table, in a cloud of cigar smoke. Half empty glasses of whisky stood in front of them and an impressively large of stack of bank notes lay in the centre of the table. At Sophia's entrance they all looked up at her in surprise, George Luxmore pushing his chair back, forced by good manners to stand. The two other men stayed sitting going back to examining their cards, as if Sophia didn't exist. Before he could say anything, Sophia had moved towards her host, holding out her hand which he took hesitantly, nodding his head in acknowledgement as he noticed Tilly's diamond bracelet sparkling brightly in the lamp light.

'You must be Mr Luxmore.'

She seated herself in the empty chair next to him not waiting for any objections from the players.

'Oh goody, I do love a game of cards. Please deal me in.'

Jack 's horrified look spurred her on even though she his thoughts plainly written on his face as he wondered what on earth was she up to now? However Sophia was glad that he kept quiet as he sidled closer and sat a short distance behind her obviously ready to remove her from the room with great haste should Luxmore become unpleasant.

'I'm afraid this is rather an expensive game Miss...' the brewer searched for her name.

'Holmes, Sophia. I'm a friend of Richard's. We weren't introduced earlier so of course I don't expect you recall me with so many illustrious guests. You were so busy I didn't like to seek your attention. Perhaps you'd like to introduce me to your friends?'

'Huxley and Davenport,' was his terse response and Sophia took a closer look at the man who owned the bordello. She was quite disappointed to find him ordinary and unexceptionable but decided to take a chance that he might tell her about it if she was very charming to him.

'Ah yes Mr Huxley I can understanding you wanting to have a bit of enjoyment after the terrible murder at one of your properties.'

Conscious of Jack bracing himself in the nearby chair, Sophia fixed an ingenuous smile on her lips. Huxley lifted his drink before replying.

'And why would you be bothering your head about that? I have no control over my tenants. I'm only a land lord.'

'Yes of course but I expect it came as a shock to you just the same. After all rumours do fly around very easily in Wellington.'

'Well it was nothing to do with me, Now can we play.'

Sophia knew she couldn't take the matter any further.

'Now what did you say the ante was?'

'Fifty pounds,' was the terse reply from her host.

'Oh that's perfectly all right,' gushed Sophia as she opened her bag and took out a large roll of ten pound notes. Jack's eyes widened as she peeled off five and placed them in front of Davenport acting as banker, who with a slight smile at Luxmore, pushed a pile of chips towards her.

Taking her cards Sophia made a small opening bet but lost the first hand. She sensed the relief on the three men's faces but continued playing, losing a little, then winning it all back. After several hands, she suspected Jack was starting to relax but turning her head slightly she saw him tense again as he saw the increasing impatience in Luxmore's face.

'Well you are certainly a competent player for a lady, Miss Holmes,' said Luxmore. 'But I'm afraid this must be the last hand. I do have to make some sort of showing to my guests tonight.'

'Of course I understand. Shall we double the stakes?'

The three men stiffened as their host laughed, an unpleasantly harsh sound to Jack's ears. He'd been leaning forward in his seat which enabled him to see Sophia's hands. Poised to intervene and remove her from the room in the most diplomatic way he could think of, he could only wait to see what was going to be the outcome of her bravado. Luxmore nodded, taking a deep draw on his cigar, looking at her through the smoke with squinting eyes.

'Must say this for you Miss Holmes, you're a game girl. Double it is then.'

The other two men dropped out leaving Sophia gazing at her hand as if it was disastrous, holding it so close to her body this time that it was hidden from Jack.

'Oh dear Mr Luxmore, I don't wish to keep you from your guests any longer. I think I will have to raise you and see your cards.'

Sophia looked very pensive and doubtful over this move as she pushed all her remaining chips to the centre of the table. Jack mentally crossed his fingers when he saw Luxmore positively leering in delight as he laid down his hand with a flourish.

'Five card flush, sorry my dear,' he said and reached for the pile of notes.

'Oh well,' sighed Sophia. 'I really am dreadfully sorry too Mr Luxmore but I have these cards.'

She laid down her cards one by one, deliberately increasing the tension amongst the group of men, showing an ace, a King, a Queen, a Knave and a ten. Luxmore's face dropped and his friends clapped as she revealed her Royal Flush.

'I believe I won that hand. Now please do go and attend to all your guests,' she said as innocently as possible whilst scooping up the money from the green baize table, cramming it in her purse and rising all in one beautifully fluid movement. She handed the bag to Jack who gave her his arm and whisked her out of the room before the others could gather themselves to comment. Almost running down the hallway, Jack dragged her into the entrance way, took their outer clothes from the maid, roughly pulling her cloak about her shoulders before he ushered her out of the house into a very cold night.

'You don't need to be in such a hurry,' complained Sophia.' He won't come after us. He was cheating and he knows I spotted it. And I didn't get my dance with Richard!'

'Nevertheless, I don't think you'll be welcome back there,' said her escort as he hurriedly hailed one of the waiting cabs in the street outside 'The Oaks' and helped Sophia into it. 'Do you usually carry such a lot of money on you? Someone will accost you one day and steal the lot.'

'Don't be silly,' said Sophia. 'Look.'

Unfastening her bag she tipped all her winnings out onto her lap and found the roll of money. She stripped off the outer ten pound note to reveal a tube of plain paper pieces underneath. Jack shook his head in disbelief at her temerity and watched while she counted all the loose ten pound notes on her lap in the dim light.

'Seven hundred and fifty pounds. Not bad really. Here's your share,' she said casually as she handed him over three hundred pounds.

'I can't take that. Talk about bribery and corruption of a police officer,' he protested as he tried to give it back but she stuffed it into his coat pocket.

'Don't be silly. Tell everyone you had an inheritance. Take a holiday back to your family in Australia.'

'That's more than I earn in two years,' stated Jack stiffly, trying to bring her around.

'Oh don't be so stuffy Jack. Put it in the bank then. I don't care but I'm not taking it back.'

'Did you cheat?'

'I never cheat Jack,' stated Sophia turning sideways to give him a very prim look.

'You did the night we played at your house,' he reminded her.

'Oh! That was so I could let Meg and Bob win. You can hardly call it cheating if you don't win yourself.'

'So you didn't cheat at all tonight?' Jack persisted.

'Jack if other people are cheating then one merely adjusts the circumstances to allow for that.'

'So... let me get this correct. You cheated because you knew Luxmore was.'

'I prefer to call it neutralising,' said Sophia smoothly and Jack sensed that there was no point arguing any further. He patted the pocket that held her winnings and left them there not wishing to spoil the evening by appearing ungrateful. Sophia, on the other hand, felt her anger rapidly rising at his rejection of her generosity. All the tension of the night exploded inside of her.

'You are always so quick to criticise me. I didn't wish to be involved with all this murder and mayhem, but you and Sir James insisted, so stop complaining if you don't like my methods!'

'I'm not complaining,' retorted Jack, taken aback by her sudden temper. 'I only wish you were a little less hot headed at times. I also fail to understand how playing poker with Luxmore was in any way connected to our investigation.'

'Well you wouldn't would you?'

Her completely unreasonable reply silenced him.

'To call me hot headed is intolerable. Can I remind you that you instantly presumed I was a blackmailer? If that's not jumping to conclusions I don't know what is? I think it's best if I withdraw from this whole sorry set of circumstances and leave you to get on with the job you're paid to do. Please don't bother me with murder and arson, any more. Goodnight!'

Jack hadn't noticed that the cab had drawn up outside Sophia's house and he was taken aback by her abrupt exit from the carriage. He hurried to catch up with her, but he was too late. She disappeared inside before he reached the closed door. As he stood there alone on her door step, he wondered what had just happened between them to upset her so much. Shaking his head, he paid the driver, deciding a long cold walk home would help to calm him down and sort out his thoughts.

Sophia was tempted to run back out to apologise to Jack as she flung herself down at the kitchen table and came to her senses. Horrified at her bad behaviour, still something held her back when she thought about how self righteous he could be. She came to the conclusion that, like all men, Jack Butler expected her to fit into a certain mould, unable to accept her as she was and always would be, an independent woman who knew her own mind and didn't always act within the bounds of conformity.

CHAPTER NINETEEN

Friday 28ᵗʰ April 1893.

Evening Post Obituary.

The worst fears entertained regarding Mr Ballance have unfortunately been realised and yesterday evening he passed away, after a long and severe illness, borne with quiet heroism. His death has naturally created a profound sensation of grief throughout the colony. Undoubtedly it has been hastened by his devotion to public duty and he died in harness being engaged in official work up to the very eve of the operation under which he ultimately sank....Mrs Ballance may be assured that her husband's death is today mourned from one end to the other of the colony, for which he was Premier, and in other lands there will also be many who will hear of his death with feelings of the keenest regret.

Sophia slowly put down the paper on the kitchen table. Meg and Bayliss had listened to the news with sombre faces.

'God rest his soul,' murmured the cook.

'Amen to that,' agreed Bayliss and Sophia nodded. The three of them were silent for a few moments out of respect for the late Premier.

'Unfortunately this means that Seddon will probably take over the leadership until the Election unless Sir Robert Stout can gain enough support,' opined Sophia.

'He's not so bad though is he?'

Bayliss's question caused Sophia to think before

she replied.

'There are many women, including myself who would prefer Stout. Most of us believe Seddon has no intention of allowing the Electoral Reform Bill to be passed before the election.'

'But surely with the petition he can't ignore what so many women want?'

Sophia nodded in acknowledgement of Meg's more pragmatic reasoning.

'Oh he'll accept it and the Bill will pass in the Lower House but you wait until it gets to the Legislative Council. Somehow Seddon will organise the votes so that the Councillors won't pass it. Then he can turn round and say it wasn't his fault it failed. We can expect him to come out of it all looking as pure as driven snow.'

'But that's corruption isn't it? How can he make the Councillors decide how to vote?'

'Because he'll nominate them to the Upper House and they'll know where their loyalties should lie if they want any sort of successful political future. Remember those men don't have to be elected by a constituency,' said Sophia in such bitter tones that forbade her two listeners from commenting further. She was sure they'd both noticed her unusual moodiness since the night of the Luxmore party but Sophia offered them no hint as to the reason.

Her temper had become apparent when she'd read a particular news item in last Monday night's paper. She'd flung it down on the kitchen table and left the room. Bayliss had reached for the *Evening Post,* curious to see what had caused this sudden exit. He read aloud to Meg who didn't know what to make of her employers temperament.

'The Wellington Fire Brigade attended a small but threatening fire at the rear of 'The Oaks', property of Mr George Luxmore, last Saturday night. The fire was lit under suspicious circumstances, while a large party was being held at the house. Detective Jack Butler declined to comment or offer any insight into the crime. This reporter has learned that Detective Butler was one of those attending the party but had left before the fire was discovered. There were several suffragette leaflets scattered in the vicinity of the blaze.'

***

Another stroke of genius he'd thought as he crept away from the back of the Luxmore home. Setting the fire in the coal shed offered little risk, they'd agreed. It would entail a great deal of heat and smoke but not endanger the residence. Luckily he'd kept the remainder of the leaflets from the Susie Post 'retribution' so he'd scattered them in the same fashion as the flames started to build up. Just to tease the police, he'd left the crumpled carbon copy of the bribery letter lying on the pathway to the shed. It was a nice touch he felt. It would make certain they knew they were dealing with a man who was in control of his actions. The Police would surely believe that this arson was a strike against a liquor baron who opposed the Franchise for women.

Now, nearly a week later he was once again disappointed to find no mention of the direction that Police enquiries were taking. He felt thwarted, needing some sort of acclaim for his work, although the one who really mattered had been very pleased. Back in the cemetery, he decided to start implementing their next move against the secretary. It was imperative that he find the right two people to carry it out. It shouldn't be too hard, he reflected. Money would do the trick.

CHAPTER TWENTY

Tuesday 2nd May 1893.

'Seddon new Premier! Read all about it!'

Stopping at the newsstand on her way home, Sophia purchased an *Evening Post* from the young lad shouting out the news on the corner of Willis Street. Tucking the paper under her arm, she bent against the wind as she walked up the long hill to the Terrace. She felt quite gloomy about the prospect ahead for the Electoral Reform Bill now that Richard Seddon was confirmed as leader of the government.

Tonight she was attending a meeting of the Women's Franchise League and she wondered how the news would be greeted there. Smiling grimly as she plodded along, she wished she could discuss it with Jack Butler, but she hadn't seen anything of him since the party at the Luxmore's. It was obvious that she'd offended him at her insistence he take her winnings as well as losing her temper and telling him she didn't wish any further involvement in the Post case. Anyway, she told herself, puffing with the exertion of walking up the steep incline, more probably he was too angry with her stupid outburst and far too busy at work, to pay her a social call. She probably featured rather low on the list of his priorities. All the same she had to admit to herself that she should have apologised but it was too late now. To be honest after the event was all very well but until she made her peace with him, she would miss the slightly barbed conversations they'd had. Her curiosity to learn of any further developments regarding Susie Post's murder would have to be reined in.

Once inside her home, glad to be out of the wind, Sophia sank down at the kitchen table and smiled. Grateful for the cup of tea Meg served her, she opened the paper and read the list of new Cabinet Ministers that had been sworn in by the Governor General.

'The Hon. R.J.Seddon to be Premier, Minister of Public Works, Minister of Mines and Minister of Defence. There you are Meg. I was correct.'

'He got his way then,' said her cook, wiping biscuit crumbs from her apron. 'Well he'll get his come uppance once we get the vote.'

'Oh I hope so, I hope so,' agreed Sophia, folding the paper up in disgust. 'Realistically, though, that may be a long time coming.'

'He wants to remember that it takes three clothes pegs to hang two things on the washing line,' remarked Meg sagely.

Sophia looked at her for a moment digesting this information.

'What exactly does that mean?'

'No idea,' laughed her cook. 'But doesn't it sound wise!'

***

Joining the queue of men and women making their way into the hall, Tilly and Sophia huddled into their jackets against the cold. Tilly's nose was decidedly pink above the large fur collar around her neck. They were both grateful for the comparative warmth of the large room when they sat down, although it was only a few degrees above the outside temperature. Both women had come to a mutual decision that the abstinence from alcohol required of its members by the Women's Christian Temperance Union made them feel hypocritical as they both liked a sociable drink now and then. Having agreed on this, they decided to join the Women's Franchise League instead, which supported the vote for women but didn't expect them to be teetotal.

'I think your policeman made you feel guilty about drinking,' asserted Tilly after they'd discussed joining the League.

'Perhaps, although between you and me, he managed to make me feel guilty about almost everything I say or do,' agreed Sophia shrugging her shoulders. 'But you were never going to give up your bubbles were you? Admit it. Anyway we always drink in moderation so no harm done.'

Tilly hadn't been able to come up with any pertinent gossip that would help Jack Butler and she was disappointed that her foray into crime solving hadn't proved more successful. However she had been able to inform her friend that the fire at the Luxmore's property had also been lit with the suffragette pamphlets. This tit bit of news had come from her maid Agnes, who was friendly with the Luxmore's cook, a large lady who enjoyed a good gossip on their day off. Sophia refrained from telling her friend that this was common knowledge having been revealed in the newspaper.

'I can't believe there are no more clues. Somebody must know something about Susie Post and the fires, let alone who broke into your office.'

'The police on the night beat are ensuring they check my building regularly every night, but I can't imagine he'll return.'

As the hall filled up, Sophia noticed the black crepe draped over the stage because of the death of Mr Ballance. All flags on Government buildings in Wellington were still flying at half mast and there were many funereal displays of mourning in shop windows in respect for the late Premier. Black armbands on many jackets and coats were in evidence, all adding to the general gloom redolent of the city in the middle of winter. Cholera and typhoid were still striking down the slum dwellers on a daily basis but there seemed to be little Council action on constructing a new sewage treatment scheme for the city to solve the problem. The supremely expensive plan proposed, only producing complete inertia on the part of Councillors, when they considered the costs to the inhabitants of Wellington.

There were almost daily reports of the protracted discussions regarding the most suitable type of memorial to be erected in memory of Ballance in his home town of Wanganui. Like the rest of the population of New Zealand, Sophia supposed that eventually a decision would be reached with a statue placed in a public park for future generations to gaze at trying to remember who he was.

With a sharp rap of her gavel, the chairwoman called the meeting to order and asked for everyone to stand and observe a two minute silence in memory of the late Premier. This dispensed with, she smiled and welcomed everyone.

'As some of you may have read, today the new Cabinet was announced. As expected Mr Seddon will lead the Government. It is to be hoped that he will persuade the new Ministers of the urgent necessity of passing the Electoral Reform Bill before the next election. It is essential that our organisation keeps pressure on these men to ensure they fulfil the expectations of the women of New Zealand in being granted the right to vote. Each and every one of us must demand that these men exercise their integrity and honesty in listening to our demands. They must be certain that this matter will not be allowed to lapse, as happened last year, and that we will be even more insistent this year and raise our voices louder than ever before!'

Pausing as she received loud cheers and shouts of, 'Hear hear,' the chairwoman took a sip of water and consulted her notes.

'It is pleasing to see ladies and gentlemen here tonight, from all walks of life, for this is precisely the reason Mrs Kate Sheppard helped to found this League. She wrote, "*To accomplish our aim we gladly enlist rich and poor, high and low, Priest, Levite and Samaritan.*" Kate was well aware that not everybody wished to join the Christian Temperance Union but that those of every faith and belief should be included in our league.

Of course we commend and support the temperance movement and it is with a combined force that we will be successful.

I have the greatest of pleasure in announcing with great excitement, that Mrs Sheppard is to make a visit to Wellington in about three weeks time and has agreed to address you all at our next meeting. It is to be hoped that her presence in the town will draw added attention to the cause and I urge you all to attend and listen to her inspirational words.'

There was a loud hum of excitement from the audience at this announcement and she held up her hand to quieten them.

'We must pack this hall to welcome and listen to her. There can be no turning back now. We must achieve the vote for women before the coming election. Please hand in your signed petition lists to the Secretary before you leave and remember that we will be marching to Parliament on this Friday in a peaceful demonstration of our cause. We will rally at the central Post Office at eleven o'clock sharp. All of you willing to carry a banner should wait behind tonight to collect them. Thank you everyone for attending tonight.'

Tilly and Sophia walked outside to where Tilly's carriage was waiting. Climbing inside they settled back.

'We finished early tonight. Come back home with me and we'll have a cup of chocolate,' said Tilly.

Her friend nodded as the brougham conveyed them back and they chatted about the meeting.

'I shall go on the march,' declared Tilly. 'I hope the weather is fine or it will be most unpleasant.'

'Yes,' agreed Sophia. 'Unfortunately I have to work. We're very busy and it's really not fair to leave it all to Una.'

'I must remember to write the date in my diary when we get home. My mind is like a sieve these days and I don't want to forget to turn up.'

Later, as they drank their chocolate by the fire in Tilly's extremely fashionable but cosy parlour, she took her diary from a side table and made an entry for the march the coming Friday. Watching her friend, Sophia suddenly sat bolt upright nearly slopping her drink over her blouse.

'That's what's missing!'

'What?' said a startled Tilly.

'Surely a woman like Susie Post would have kept a diary? But I don't recall Detective Butler talking about it. It obviously wasn't in her bag when he looked for the receipt or he would have certainly mentioned it?'

'You're quite correct,' observed Tilly. 'She'd have to write down her appointments wouldn't she? Couldn't have two men turning up at the same time I suppose. That could be very awkward,' she said with a very knowing look.

'So...' Sophia said slowly, thinking her way through the problem. 'Perhaps she would have made a note of the man who wanted the receipt. He sounded really important to her when she told us about his donation. We need to ask Jack Butler what has happened to the contents of her room. I'll make a telephone call to the Police Station tomorrow to see if he's there. I'll just have to swallow my pride and apologise to him at the same time.'

'Ah we are so modern here in Wellington aren't we? Who would have thought a few years ago that we would be so blasé about electric lights in the streets and shops and owning our own personal telephones,' mused Tilly, and Sophia was grateful her friend was wise enough not to seize on the mention of apology to Butler.

'And yet we still have overflowing sewage in the streets, rampant disease and a very irregular water supply,' Sophia said in disgusted tones. 'I for one would rather have better sanitation than instant communication.'

'I second that,' agreed Tilly as she finished her drink. 'Now it strikes me that if we could get into Susie's

188

room, I'm quite certain you and I would see clues that a man would miss. Why don't you ask Butler if we can have a look at her personal possessions?

'I expect Mrs Protheroe has re-let the room by now but it's worth a try.'

The two friends nodded at each other then turned their thoughts to more trivial matters.

'I was horrified to read in the Saturday supplement that crinolines might be coming back,' said Tilly with a grimace. 'I, for one, will never wear such a contraption again, not after mine blew over my head a few years ago. I was strolling along Oriental Parade with Arthur and next thing a huge gust of wind positively raged in from the harbour, lifted up my skirt and blinded me.'

Sophia burst into laughter at the sight this must have presented, but Tilly was quite upset by the memory.

'Really it wasn't at all amusing at the time. I felt as if I was captured inside a huge dark tent. I was certain I was going to be blown up into the sky like a hot air balloon! Poor Arthur was tugging at the frame to try and bring it under control. I swear I was nearly blown into the sea at one point.'

'But knowing you, you were wearing your prettiest frilly bloomers so not all was revealed,' giggled Sophia.

'Well yes of course,' recalled Tilly complacently. 'But it was traumatic. I'll never forget it. Everyone stared at me and some of the young men made lewd comments. I blushed red as a beetroot and Arthur had to summon the carriage straight away to take me home. I must have used a whole bottle of smelling salts to calm myself down!'

'I don't think I've ever seen you blush Tilly. Are you sure it was a bad as you say?'

'Absolutely,' said Tilly with the hint of a smile. 'Actually I think Arthur needed the smelling salts more than me! He's so modest, always so protective of his dignity.'

'And he always is...,' reassured Sophia. 'The utter picture of dignity.'

'Yes...' sighed Tilly. 'I must admit to wishing, just occasionally, mind you, that he was a bit more fun; a little less rigid would be welcome.'

'He's a good husband. You know that's true.'

Tilly nodded, rising as Sophia stood to collect her coat to return home.

'I'll let you know when I've talked to Detective Butler,' called out Sophia, as she climbed into the carriage, waving good night to Tilly.

CHAPTER TWENTY ONE

Saturday 6th May 1893.

Waiting rather nervously in the carriage outside the Protheroe residence, neither Tilly nor Sophia were willing to get out into the street until the arrival of Jack Butler. Although it was one of the more salubrious houses, set well back in its own grounds, they could see the environs of Grainger Street were less than wholesome. The abundance of brothels in this one road made it a most undesirable place for two respectable women to be seen in. The gutter overflowed out into the roadway with foul detritus, forcing the coachman to park the vehicle well away from its edge. Even the horses looked offended by the overpowering odours emanating from the area, tossing their heads in what could have been interpreted as disgust at their surroundings.

'I hope he's not going to keep us waiting much longer,' said Tilly holding her handkerchief to her nose. 'I don't think I can stand this smell anymore.'

'It's a wonder how people can exist in places like this. What an eyesore right in the city,' agreed Sophia.

When she'd finally managed to pluck up her courage to telephone Jack Butler yesterday, he'd sounded friendly to her relief, but she was still surprised when he'd agreed to meet them to have another search of Susie's room.

'It's certainly worth having a further look in there because I'm no further forward with my enquiries, but I must warn you it's not a very pleasant place.'

There was a tap on the carriage window heralding the arrival of the detective and, keeping their skirts well clear of the ground, they followed him up a short driveway to a double storied house built of peeling weatherboards badly in need of a coat of paint. Despite this, the property appeared tidy with a neat shrubbery to one side and clean windows draped with lace curtains. Pointing out the place that Boysie Smith had hidden, Butler rang the door bell. After a few minutes it was opened by a neatly dressed but somewhat elderly maid who recognised the policeman and ushered them into the hallway.

'Mrs P. says to go right up. She doesn't want to see you and anyway you've got the only key,' she observed in an unfriendly fashion.

Butler led the way up a steep staircase to the upper landing, where he went down a long corridor to the back of the house, stopping in front of the last door, which he unlocked.

Before opening it, he looked at them both questioningly.

'I decided not to let Mrs Protheroe in here until we finish the investigation so no-one else has touched anything since we found Susie. Are you quite sure you are still happy to go in?'

Both women nodded, although Sophia noticed Tilly swallowing hard as the stale stench of the room reached them when the door was pushed open. Butler quickly walked ahead to a large window that looked out towards the rear of the property, pulling it up to allow some fresh air to circulate then stood quietly to watch the two women. He'd been pleased to receive the phone call from Sophia, reasoning that it must have been hard for her to swallow her pride and therefore there was no point in prolonging their estrangement. He had to admit her logic and intuition had become too valuable to him to lose at this point in the investigation.

Gazing around, Sophia noticed a faded green velvet upholstered chair near the window with a small side table beside it on which stood a decanter and some glasses. The bedclothes had been pulled off the sagging stained mattress, and then dumped in a heap on the floor. Stooping down, she pulled a large suitcase out from underneath the bed and opened it gingerly. It contained nothing more interesting than several pairs of well worn boots and shoes. Returning it to its dusty home, Sophia tried the lid of a portable writing desk that stood on top of a chest of drawers, only to find it locked.

'Tilly, where would she keep the key do you think?'

Pondering this, both women moved towards the wardrobe at the same time as Jack laughed at their mutual thoughts. Opening the doors, Sophia revealed the colourful and novel collection of Susie Post's clothes all smelling strongly of camphor moth balls and cheap scent. The top shelf was full of hats, and feather boas. Standing on tip toe to reach behind these, Sophia ran her hand along the shelf until she felt a hard surface. Pushing aside an enormous hat decorated with a whole army of chicken feathers, she put both hands up and withdrew a very beautiful jewellery box. Excitement built in her as, carrying it over to place it beside the writing desk, she briefly admired the rosewood and mother of pearl inlay pattern before trying to open it. They all leaned forward in anticipation of the contents but to no avail.

'Oh! This is locked too,' she exclaimed. 'Jack did you find any keys in her bag?'

'No, nothing at all,' said Butler. 'The key must be somewhere though.'

He walked over to the mantelpiece above the small cast iron fire hearth. There were possibly a dozen cheap china trinkets packed onto this shelf and Jack proceeded to lift each one, shaking it and checking underneath. He found nothing and watched as Sophia searched among the cosmetics and jewellery that lay scattered on the dressing table.

'It must be here,' said an exasperated Tilly, walking back to the pile of blankets on the floor. Pulling them apart in a very fastidious fashion she suddenly grasped something that was hidden to Jack and Sophia.

'There,' she said triumphantly holding up a rather battered doll. Its china face was worn and the original silk dress was tattered but around its neck was a fine silver chain with a small key dangling from it.

'Oh well done Tilly,' admired Sophia. 'Let's see if it fits either of these.'

The key fitted the jewellery box and as Sophia lifted the lid, all three of them gasped. Lying in the red velvet interior tray was a collection of precious items that were far beyond the earnings of Susie Post. Tilly lifted up a pair of emerald drop earrings in admiration turning them in her hands with almost professional examination.

'These are worth a small fortune. They can't belong to Susie surely?'

Sophia carefully lifted out and placed the jewellery piece by piece on top of the chest of drawers and took an inventory.

'Two diamond bracelets, two diamond and ruby brooches, a pearl choker necklace and five rings with sapphires, diamonds and rubies set in white gold as well as the earrings,' she listed in amazement. 'I've never seen such wonderful things outside of a jeweller's window.'

Jack Butler looked as astonished as the two women.

'Well they are either stolen or taken as payment for her services,' he guessed. 'But I'm more inclined to believe the former. I'll have to take them back to the Station and check the stolen items list but I really can't recall anything of this description being reported missing. I'm sure I would have remembered.'

'She'd have to be a top class whore to be paid with these types of jewels,' was Tilly's down to earth comment. 'Quite honestly, and not wanting to speak ill of the dead, I don't think she was in this league. This is almost the sort of jewellery one would wear to meet the Queen!'

Staring at the emeralds, Sophia nodded but looked puzzled.

'You know I have a strange feeling that I've seen these before, or some very similar, but I can't recall where.'

'You wouldn't forget someone wearing these in Wellington,' suggested Tilly. 'They're unique and spectacular.'

'No you're absolutely correct about that. Perhaps it will come to me, anyway, let's get back to business, we still haven't found the key to the desk.'

'There may be a secret cavity in here. I used to have one similar.'

Pressing around the base of the box, Tilly heard a faint click and a small panel slid back. Reaching inside with a finger, she hooked out another small key and handed it to Butler.

'Don't you think it's odd that she must have felt that the contents of her desk were more valuable than those of the jewellery box? Most women would have hidden the key to the desk on the doll and locked the other one in the desk,' asked Sophia.

'Well we shall see,' said the policeman as he unlocked the writing desk and opened it out. The flat leather surface for writing on was worn and faded. Lifting up the bottom half of it revealed only some sheets of new notepaper and two envelopes. The top half that sloped upwards was harder to lift and producing a pen knife, Jack slid the blade carefully into the crack and gently levered it up. Sophia put her fingers into the crack and tugged and the lid fell back to fold on top of the lower one. The interior of the desk was packed with small paper parcels, a very puzzling sight to the women but not so extraordinary to Jack. He lifted one out and unfolded it to reveal the powdered contents.

'Opium. She must have been supplying it to her clients. There's a great deal here. It may explain the jewellery being in payment.'

'Oh how dreadful,' said Tilly. 'Do you think these men were stealing their own wives jewels to pay Susie for this?'

'No wonder she thought this was more valuable than the diamonds,' said Sophia. 'But it doesn't get us any closer to her killer. He evidently didn't realise this was here or he would surely have taken it. No-one would have ever known it was missing. It's pure luck we found it.'

'You're right about that,' agreed Jack. 'Do you think this desk has a secret drawer? We still haven't found a diary.'

Tilly felt all around the box but to no avail.

'You'll have to dismantle it at the Police Station,' she suggested. 'There's bound to be another compartment somewhere but I can't find it.'

Walking around the room restlessly, Sophia put her head on one side and then going back to the door, she swept her gaze slowly around.

'I'm trying to put myself in his place,' she explained. 'He would have come in here to wait for Susie not knowing how long she was going to be, so how did he fill in the time?'

'How did he get in? That maid said you had the only key Detective Butler,' asked Tilly.

'I can only presume that Susie gave him the key. She must have trusted him not to be inquisitive while she was away. The key was still in the door outside when we arrived. He didn't even bother to lock it when he left. Smacks of arrogance doesn't it?'

'What do men do when they have to wait for a woman?'

'Have a drink usually,' laughed Jack Butler, then something dawned on both him and Sophia as she turned to look at the decanter on the small table. Sophia reached it first. Peering into the glasses without touching them, she pointed at one.

'This one has been used. There are still a few drops of liquid in the bottom. Do you think you can find finger prints on it?'

Taking out his handkerchief, Butler wrapped it loosely around the base of the tumbler, held it up against the light from the open window then placed it in a large inside pocket of his overcoat.

'I'll do my best. I don't really have the equipment yet but the more evidence we can collect the better. I'll take the two boxes back with me. Can't leave them here, with these valuable contents.'

'We'll take you back in the carriage,' offered Tilly. 'It's far too difficult for you to carry those back on your own. Much too risky too.'

'Thank you. That's a good point,' said Jack.

They left the room with Sophia carrying the jewellery box. Jack tucked the writing desk under his arm. Locking Susie's door after them, Tilly put the key into Jack's hand as they made their way outside.

The coachman jumped down and opened the door for them to climb in and as they sat in rather close proximity, Jack smiled at his two helpers.

'That was a good morning's work ladies. You are both very astute when it comes to investigation I must say.'

'Praise indeed for us amateur sleuths,' said Sophia dryly.

CHAPTER TWENTY TWO

Monday 22nd May 1893.

Over two weeks had passed since their foray into Susie Post's room and Sophia had not heard anything from Detective Butler. Her curiosity gained in strength as the days went by, forcing her to wonder whether she should contact him. This very morning, unable to contain her frustration about the lack of communication, she had rolled a piece of note paper into her typewriter and written him a short note enquiring about any further news. Writing his name on the envelope, she left Una to manage the office and braving the weather, set off to the Police Station, where she handed the letter to the desk Sergeant.

'Please ensure Detective Butler receives this as soon as possible,' she requested.

'Does it pertain to a police investigation,' said the man rather pompously, eyeing her with suspicion. 'I do not pass on billet doux.'

'I should think not,' replied Sophia, becoming embarrassed at this unforeseen question. 'It's a legitimate request regarding the Susie Post murder. I am helping Detective Butler with an enquiry.'

'Oh yes?'

His cynical response infuriated her and she put the envelope on the counter, patted it firmly with her hand and walked briskly out of the waiting room not wishing to waste any more time on this conversation.

To calm herself down and distract her thoughts from the incivility of the sergeant, she took a longer way back to her office, walking up Lambton Quay to window shop. Halting outside Kirkaldie's, she inspected the range of serge materials displayed in the window. At four and sixpence a yard they seemed quite reasonably priced and she resolved to bring Meg down to the store to purchase a few yards to make herself a new skirt and jacket. Poor Meg, she thought, she's worn cast off clothes since she came to live with me so it's about time she had something new. For herself, Sophia gazed at the silk robes but decided that it would be the height of frivolity and most impractical to spend sixty shillings on such a flimsy garment in the middle of winter. However that didn't prevent her from imagining how it would feel to own one and enjoy the way silk whispered against one's skin! Wistfully, she thought it a garment that needed a man to appreciate the wearer! Stick to flannel, she thought!

Arriving back to find Una hard at work, Sophia felt guilty that she'd wasted time daydreaming about silk garments. With her blouse cuffs folded back, she sat at her desk and started typing a very long and boring report of a Board meeting held by a local factory owner. Whilst she was screwing up her eyes to decipher the looped and scrawled writing of the clerk who had taken down the minutes, she was interrupted by the door bell. Stretching her back as she walked through to the counter, she was astonished to be confronted by Hilda Luxmore who, once more, was attired completely in various shades of purple. The only relief to this was the brown fox fur that served the dual purpose of keeping her warm and disguising her ample chins.

'Mrs Luxmore? What can I do for you?'

Hilda Luxmore seemed at a loss for words and when she did finally speak, she let forth in such a bellow of rage that Sophia took two steps backwards.

'Where is she? You wretched woman, what have you done with her?'

'Who?'

Sophia was caught off guard at this attack and racked her brains to make sense of the questions fired at her in such a vituperative tone.

'You know very well who I mean! Daphne Parham of course. You've lured her away from my son haven't you? I saw you two chin wagging at my house that night. What did you say to her? She's disappeared and Richard has received the engagement ring back from a servant! So humiliating for him! My poor boy is beside himself with worry about her.'

Most unlikely, thought Sophia uncharitably, but she took a deep breath before she replied.

'First of all, Mrs Luxmore, you must believe me when I say that I haven't seen Miss Parham since that night so I have no idea of her whereabouts. Secondly, our conversation was private, but I certainly made no suggestions that she should run away, if that's what she's done. Good heavens, do you really think I would encourage an eighteen year old girl to break off an engagement and run away from home? What sort of person do you think I am?'

The challenge to reply to this appeared to be too difficult for Hilda Luxmore. She stared at Sophia, who noticed how dark her small eyes were under their sagging eyelids. After a long moment, the older woman suddenly shook her head. Looking around vaguely, she blinked several times, lifting a purple gloved hand to her face in a gesture of puzzlement. When she spoke, her voice had lost its stridency and came out as a hoarse whisper.

'Where is this place?'

'It's my secretarial agency,' replied a surprised Sophia. 'Mrs Luxmore? Are you feeling unwell?'

'No! No!' came the sharp response. 'I'll be quite well when I get home. I need my medicine, that's all.'

Making a slow turn towards the door, Hilda leaned against it, but before Sophia could move to help her, she had made her way to her carriage which was parked outside. Watching this extraordinary exit, Sophia couldn't work out what had happened to Richard's mother to change her demeanour so suddenly. Returning to her desk she realised that Una had overheard.

'What did you think about that?'

'I thought it was very strange,' said Una. 'There's something odd about her.'

'She just seemed to run out of steam,' said Sophia. 'It was almost as if someone had switched her anger off and she couldn't recall anything. Perhaps Daphne Parham was correct in thinking there's some type of mental weakness in Hilda Luxmore.'

'I wonder what the medicine is that she mentioned? Perhaps she's an alcoholic. After all you did tell me you thought she was drunk on the night of the party.'

Una's comment was food for thought but Sophia doubted that a lack of alcohol had caused Mrs Luxmore's temper to disappear so fast.

'Goodness only knows. Fancy coming in here and talking to me like that. I only hope that Daphne is really safe at home with her parents, trying to avoid her ex mother-in-law to be.'

***

Later that afternoon, the Holmes Secretarial Agency received another visitor, but this time it was a welcome one as Jack Butler came through the door. He appeared thinner in the face and quite pale.

'I'm sorry I haven't been to see you,' he smiled apologetically. 'I went down with a bad dose of influenza a few days after we visited Mrs Protheroe's and I've only just returned to work. You can't imagine the amount of paperwork that was piled up on my desk!'

'Are you well now? I can see you've lost weight,' said a concerned Sophia glad that he was in such a good mood.

'Well enough not to lie in bed anymore,' he groaned. 'So unfortunately I'm not much further ahead with any of the things we found, except that none of the jewellery is listed as stolen.'

'Ah well, I must admit to being far too impatient. It's a weakness of mine to wish for quick results. Come and have a cup of tea, while Una and I tell you of an extraordinary visit we had this morning.'

Jack Butler listened with astonishment as the two women regaled him with their account of Hilda Luxmore's outburst and her sudden deflated behaviour.

'Here is a woman who had the nerve to criticise my Worth gown and you should have seen her clothes today. Everything purple, from hat to boots.'

'Even her earrings,' said Una laughing. 'Great big chandeliers they were too. They must have been made of glass though, to get the colour matched to her outfit.'

'Yes,' agreed Sophia. 'She has these long stretched ear lobes. She must have always worn very heavy earrings....Oh my goodness...that's where I saw them!'

'Saw what,' said Una puzzled at this sudden exclamation.

'The emerald earrings we found in Susie Post's jewellery box,' she said turning to Jack. 'Do you recall we were looking at the portrait of Uncle Sinclair? Well perhaps you didn't notice, but next to it was a much smaller picture of a young girl and she was wearing the same earrings. It must have been Hilda when she was first married. I'm almost certain they were identical. I noticed them because they were painted in such fine detail.'

'Probably the most beautiful thing in the composition,' said Butler sarcastically. 'I think I vaguely remember it, but we'll never get back into that house to check the picture now. Can you imagine what the response to a request like that would be?'

'I could pay a call to enquire after Mrs Luxmore's health, I suppose,' was Sophia's doubtful reply.

'No I don't think that's a good idea at all,' said Butler shaking his head, 'What we've got to work out is how the Luxmore earrings found their way into Susie Post's jewellery box.'

'And also, does the rest of the jewellery belong to her too,' posed Sophia. 'She said she was in need of her medicine and... I know this sounds farfetched, but there was something strange about her eyes. Very dark and staring somehow.'

'Horrible little piggy eyes she had,' said Una unkindly.

'Are you suggesting she's addicted to something? Wide open irises are often a sign of drug addiction, said Jack. 'She could be addicted to laudanum. Perhaps her Doctor prescribes it for her.'

Sophia digested this idea but shook her head in rejection.

'What if the jewellery was payment for drugs? The opium that Susie was selling?'

'But that amount of jewellery would buy year's worth of opium,' pondered Butler.

'Yes but if she didn't want her husband to find out, she could have used it to pay. If he asked about the jewels, she only had to say they were safely in the bank and I doubt he'd question that,' said Sophia. 'Women like her never carry cash in their purses. There'd be no need for that. She'd have charge accounts at all the stores. I doubt she'd even have a personal bank account.'

'I suppose it's possible but she would have never dealt with Susie personally. Can you imagine her going cap in hand to the brothel? She must have had someone buy for her, who wouldn't appear to be out of place there.'

'Richard, do you think? He might be addicted too. He does seem to have mood swings that aren't quite natural. But there's nothing to link him to Susie Post unless you can find his finger prints on the whisky tumbler.'

'The only trouble with that supposition is that Mrs Luxmore appears to still be using whatever it is. Since Susie's death, her supply from that source has stopped so whoever she trusts to buy the drug must have access to another supply and another way of paying for it even if it is Richard.'

'Perhaps your Chinese friends in Haining Street might know.'

Jack Butler shrugged.

'If they do, they wouldn't tell me unless they don't trust him or dislike him intensely. But it's one place I could try and there's another in Cuba Street. There are always suppliers on the wharves. Often a boat docking from Hong Kong will bring sailors who are looking for opium buyers. They may have an idea who it is. I'll get one of my Constables to do a bit of undercover work down there.'

'We're still no further forward with the murder though. This business of the jewellery seems to be another line of enquiry all together doesn't it? Something we've stumbled on by accident but with no real connection to the case.'

Jack nodded and took a sip of his tea. Then he reached into his coat pocket, producing a small black leather covered book.

'All this talk of the Luxmore's and I completely forgot this,' he exclaimed. 'I had to break the desk open to find it. I haven't had a chance to read it yet, but let's take a look now.'

Sophia and Una leaned closer as he turned the pages over, until he found the week before Susie's death. They could see words written on the page and waited for him to read them out.

'It says here simply "L" then a plus sign, then the number five.'

He flicked the pages over and came to an entry for the night of the Temperance Union meeting.

'Here she's written "WCTU 500" and then "receipt".'

'That's obvious, but nothing about who the receipt was for?'

'No,' said a disappointed Butler. 'There are other initials further back in the diary but we'll never guess who they are.'

'What can "L+" mean?'

'Well a plus sign means something added on I suppose,' offered Una. 'Something extra.'

'Something more? L+ for Luxmore? It's a very simple way of coding a name. Rather similar to shorthand,' said Sophia.

'So perhaps we can presume that the entry refers to Richard Luxmore purchasing five packets of opium on that day?'

The two women nodded at Butler's suggestion. He went back to the beginning of the year in the little black diary.

'There are regular "L+" entries so she had contact with Luxmore for at least the three months prior to her murder. I might ask Boysie Smith if he knows, or can find out who was supplying Susie Post with the drugs. There's always a possibility she told them who was such a regular customer with her.'

Placing the diary back in his pocket, Jack stood to take his leave.

'I'll keep you informed if I find out anything,' he smiled.

'Oh I hope you start feeling well as soon as possible,' said Sophia. 'Do take care of yourself. Before you go, is there any news on the fire at the Luxmore's?

'Nothing at all I'm afraid, except it was the same modus operandi as Dixon Street. The leaflets scattered around and also, and this is interesting, the screwed up carbon copy of the bribery letter. I suppose we can cross off the Luxmores from our list of suspects. They'd hardly condone the risk of their own house possibly being burned to the ground in order to place suspicion with the suffragettes. Even with my cynicism, I find that too hard to swallow.'

Shutting the door behind him, Sophia sighed and returned to her desk and the mundane task of typing the minutes. My life seems to bounce between very dull and over exciting, she thought. Tonight I am determined to put my feet up in front of the range, read the newspaper and start settling into a comfortable middle age!

***

Finally reaching home that evening a little later than usual, Sophia walked round to the back door and let herself in, calling out as she went down the passageway to the kitchen.

'Here I am at last Meg.'

Meg appeared behind her, coming out from the wash house.

'I won't be long Miss Holmes. Just putting in some laundry to soak. Bayliss is out getting the coal. Oh... there's a lady waiting to see you. She's in the kitchen, a Miss Parham. I made her a cup of tea.'

'Oh no, fancy her coming here,' Sophia muttered and braced herself for the inevitable awkwardness of the meeting..

Entering the kitchen, Sophia expected to find Daphne seated at the table but the first thing she noticed was a smashed cup lying on the floor by the table and the poker sticking out of the grate, as if someone had been interrupted in stoking the fire. Hearing a strangled sound she turned to find Daphne standing behind the door, captive in the grip of Richard Luxmore who was holding a knife to her neck.

'What on earth are you doing?'

Sophia was utterly taken aback by this sight. She backed up to the table, trying to assess the situation.

'Richard let her go at once. I'm sure we can talk about this calmly.'

'You bitch!' he snarled at her and she saw the young girls eyes widen at his language. 'Daphne is coming with me. You're all the same you bloody Franchise League women. Hell bent on destroying normal family life, wanting girls to ignore what's best for them. That Kate Sheppard ruined my mother's life, but I'm not going to allow it to happen to me!'

Sophia hesitated before she reached out a placatory hand to him but withdrew it quickly as she saw the knife move closer to Daphne's neck causing the terrified girl to whimper. The young man confronting her now had no resemblance to the boy she'd dallied with at the races. In his place, a cruel faced youth who was suddenly showing his true character. The situation confronting Sophia made her almost physically ill as she was forced to face one of her worst nightmares but her overwhelming fear for Daphne prompted Sophia to try and placate him again in the calmest tones she could muster.

'Whatever you're thinking Richard, this is no way to treat one of my visitors. Put the knife away and let her go. I'm sure we can sort this out,' she pleaded.

Richard Luxmore ignored her entreaty as, to her horror, she saw him press the blade into the tender white skin at the base of Daphne's neck and draw blood. Daphne moaned as the wound started to sting and small red droplets oozed over her white blouse collar. Sophia made a decision walking over to the coal range where she pulled the poker, now red hot, from the fire and trying to keep her hands steady, she advanced on Richard, holding it out towards the hand that held his knife.

'Drop the knife immediately.'

'Or you'll attack me with the poker? Don't be ridiculous, you'd never dare do that Miss High and Mighty Holmes.'

His next sound was a scream as Sophia touched the red hot metal to his hand. The knife went flying across the floor, ending up under the table and Daphne tore away from his grip. Keeping a firm hold on the poker, Sophia edged nearer to Luxmore who was nursing his burnt hand almost in tears as the smell of his burning flesh permeated the kitchen.

'I'll give you a head start, Richard before I call the police. Get out of here now and never bother Daphne again.'

At this moment both Meg and Bayliss came rushing through the open door, alerted by the sound of Richard's yelling. Sophia was incredibly pleased to see them.

'Ah... Bayliss. Please show Mr Luxmore out of the house and ensure he leaves,' she said, keeping her voice as steady as possible as the full import of the situation dawned on her.

Without a word, Bayliss took Richard by the arm and started to pull him out of the kitchen. However, his captive turned and looked venomously at the three women.

'You haven't heard the last of this. My lawyer will be in touch. I shall charge you with wounding me unlawfully.'

'You'd be wasting your time Richard,' Sophia's voice was full of scorn. 'I think you'll find that I have no case to answer in view of you wounding Miss Parham and attempting to abduct her in front of witnesses. Just get out.'

On Richard's departure, Daphne sunk down in a chair and started to cry. While Meg fetched a clean cloth and a bowl of hot water and dabbed at the blood on her neck, Sophia returned the poker to the coal scuttle. Coming back into the kitchen, Bayliss looked shocked.

'What a mouth on him! I haven't heard swearing like that since I was in the navy. He must have sneaked in the back door when Meg was busy. I was out in the garden and I never heard a thing.'

Sophia swallowed hard and taking a clean tea towel out of the dresser drawer, she bent under the table and carefully used it to pick up the knife by the blade. Laying it on the table, she realised what a dangerous knife it was and she experienced a cold chill as she inspected the razor sharp blade with a horror it was hard for her to hide from the others.

'That's a Bowie knife,' said Bayliss. 'I recognise it because one of my sailor mates had one. They're made like that on purpose to give a better stabbing motion. You can disembowel someone with one of these!'

Bayliss indicated the top edge of the slim eight inch blade which was thinner.

'Well I think I'll give it to Detective Butler,' agreed

Sophia with a shudder at his description, wrapping it carefully in the towel. 'He's very keen on this new finger print science and it may add to his information although this bone handle probably won't yield anything useful.'

Placing it on the dresser top, she turned to Daphne who had recovered from her sobs, addressing her in what she hoped sounded like bracing no-nonsense tones.

'I think you owe us an explanation Miss Parham. This morning I suffered a visit from Mrs Luxmore who said you'd run away from home, disengaged yourself from Richard and she accused me of suggesting it to you. I didn't really believe her story and of course I denied having anything to do with it, but now it appears you did take matters into your own hands. Thank goodness I arrived when I did. Richard was completely maddened.'

'I thought and thought about what you said to me,' sniffed Daphne, dabbing at her nose with a small lace handkerchief. 'I felt that I should be braver, that it would be hypocritical to enter into marriage with Richard when it was the last thing I wanted.'

'But what about your father's position?'

'That made it even more difficult, but in the end I decided that I wasn't responsible for his debts and I came to the conclusion that I was worth more than a loveless marriage. My father will have to face up to his own problems and not use me as a pawn to capture the castle.'

Daphne's tones became increasingly defiant as she spoke but Sophia wasn't impressed. She had had enough of recalcitrant sons and daughters for one day.

'Very eloquent I'm sure,' she stated. 'But there will be consequences that you have to face now. First of all you must explain all of this to your mother and father. It seems hard I know but I imagine they won't be too angry when they hear of this episode. I'm happy to come with you as a witness. Secondly you have to persuade them that you wish to find a job and be independent. That may be much harder for them to cope with.'

'My mother is obsessed with having grandchildren,' muttered Daphne. 'It was all she talked about when I got engaged. Not once did she ask if I was happy with Richard. Not once.'

Understanding that Daphne was sinking fast into a negative mood of blame and self pity, Sophia decided to give her a brisk smile and change the subject.

'I think you'd better spend the night here with us. You'll feel much more the thing after a good night's sleep and some of Meg's wonderful cooking. Tomorrow I'll take you home and we'll see how things turn out with your parents. They must be made to understand your point of view even if they find it hard to agree with. When did you leave home?'

'Early yesterday morning before the maid was up. I did leave my mother a note to say I was going to stay with a friend. I booked into a ladies hostel last night but it wasn't very nice. I've been wandering about today, trying to get a job in a drapery store but there aren't any positions available at the moment.'

'Do you wish to charge Richard with assault? I shall have to tell the police about this when I take this knife into them. It may be vital evidence in another case.'

Daphne started sniffing again, keeping them waiting until she'd regained her composure.

'I think I'd better talk to my parents first don't you?'

Her appeal was wasted on Sophia who was almost at the end of her patience.

'You really have little choice Daphne. He's a very dangerous man and might attack someone else. You can't have that on your conscience can you?'

'No...I suppose not,' whispered the girl. 'It will cause such a terrible scandal though won't it? The Luxmores' will try and make out it was my fault.'

'It depends on their genuine knowledge of their son. They may be as shocked as we are.'

Shaking her head in confusion Daphne lapsed into silence, overawed by the enormity of what could be unleashed if she went to the police. Sophia came to the conclusion that there was nothing else she could say to make the young woman come to a decision. Meg looked at her employer and started to lay another place at the table for the evening meal with resignation written all over her face.

CHAPTER TWENTY THREE

Tuesday 23ʳᵈ May 1893.

For once the next day dawned fine and still. Sophia sent Bayliss to her office with the keys so that Una could take charge of the business. Daphne came downstairs to the kitchen, where she ate a large breakfast and appeared to have recovered well. The scratch on her neck had started healing and Meg had managed to sponge off the droplets of blood that had spattered on to her cotton blouse.

Around nine o'clock, Sophia accompanied her charge to her family home on Tinakori Road, a few houses away from the Luxmore's, where they were greeted by a distraught Mrs Parham who threw her arms around her daughter and then broke into a tirade of scolding. Daphne bore it all stoically, finally managing to quieten her mother.

'I'm quite safe Mama thanks to Miss Holmes who looked after me and saved me.'

'Saved you from sin?'

Mrs Parham's immediate assessment of what her daughter had been up to, found little sympathy with Sophia, who cleared her throat in a warning sound to Daphne who, she could see, was about to protest to her Mama.

'Mrs Parham, your daughter has suffered a dreadful experience at the hands of Richard Luxmore. I found him holding her at knife point in my kitchen last night. He was completely enraged by her breaking off their engagement but that was no excuse for his outrageous behaviour. It was fortuitous that I came home when I did, or the results may have been tragic.'

Sophia felt rather pleased with this explanation even if it did sound a little melodramatic. She noted that Mrs Parham took a deep breath, before she turned to Daphne.

'Is this true? Did he attack you?'

'Yes Mama. I went to visit Miss Holmes to ask her advice. He seemed to know that I would be there. It was terrifying. Look what he did to my neck.'

At the sight of the wound, all Mrs Parham's anger against her daughter evaporated. She put her arm around the girl and stroked her cheek.

'I think we'd better have a long talk about all this my dear. Perhaps I was a bit hasty in judging your actions.'

'Daphne is undecided if she wishes to go to the police about this. I expect you and Mr Parham will need to think very carefully about that. I do feel obliged to hand in the knife to the Police as I'm sure you'll understand,' proposed Sophia, with a knowing look at Mrs Parham. She was relieved to see complete understanding in the woman's eyes.

Satisfied that all was well between mother and daughter, Sophia took her leave, flagging down a passing cab to take her to the Police Station where once again she was faced with the pompous desk sergeant who'd delivered her letter to Detective Butler.

'Oh it's you again Miss,' he said impatiently folding his arms. 'What is it this time? Apprehended a murderer or two have we? Or maybe you want to join the force?'

'Oh it won't be long before you will be working alongside women police,' smiled Sophia sweetly. 'Then you'll have to mind your manners and smarten your attitude. I'd like to see Detective Butler if he's available please.'

'Oh and I suppose it is deadly urgent,' was the sarcastic reply.

'Deadly indeed, as I'm sure you'll find out in due time,' said Sophia.

'Take a seat and wait like everyone else,' was his gruff response.

A few minutes later, Jack Butler appeared and ushered Sophia through into the passageway. As she walked past the Sergeant who was eyeing her with contempt she whispered to him, causing him to turn bright red.

'What was that all about?' Butler asked as he opened the interview room door.

'He was abominably rude to me so I told him his trousers were unbuttoned,' said a cheeky Sophia.

'And were they?'

Jack was trying to keep a straight face.

'No,' said Sophia. 'But it made him most uncomfortable to be told that by a woman. It serves him right.'

'Well what brings you here?'

Sophia recounted the events of the previous night and then reaching into her bag she brought out the tea towel containing the knife. As it lay on the table between them she wrinkled her nose in distaste, as she described the smell of Richard's burning flesh.

'I didn't think I could ever do anything like that but I was so angry I never gave it a thought.'

'It appears that you made the most of the only weapon at hand. Not many men would stand up to a red hot poker being waved at them by an irate woman. I'm proud of you.'

'I'm so glad you see it that way, because he threatened to have me charged with assault. It doesn't seem likely that he would do that but I could need all the support I can muster.'

'Protecting Miss Parham from the knife was the main thing in your favour and this particular knife is a very nasty object.'

'Indeed it is. Bayliss tells me that it's an American style Bowie knife but made in Sheffield. I thought perhaps there might be finger prints on the handle, which is why I wrapped it so carefully.'

'You really are up to the mark,' admired Jack Butler. 'Most people would have handled it and ruined any prints but not you.'

'It's all due to your tutelage I'm sure.'

'Which brings us to the vexed question of whether Richard Luxmore is our murderer? If I can obtain finger prints from this knife that match those on the whisky glass we may be a lot closer to discovery.'

'He was quite vicious towards Miss Parham. There was no sign of the pleasant young man we've met before. He said something strange about Kate Sheppard ruining his mother's life. What on earth could that mean?'

'I have no idea but it does seem to be an odd remark to make when holding a girl at knife point.'

'Do you suppose there is something in Hilda Luxmore's past that's affecting her son's behaviour?

'Families can sometimes be a policeman's worst nightmare. Past events can influence behaviour for years to come in my experience,' Jack sighed. 'If he's carrying out some sort of vendetta on behalf of his mother it's convoluted to an extreme and beyond my comprehension.'

'She's speaking tonight,' said Sophia abstractedly.

'Who is?'

'Mrs Sheppard. She's visiting Wellington for a week to talk to us and ensure we are all enthusiastic. She's rallying the troops, in a manner of speaking. Tilly and I are so looking forward to hearing her. Why don't you come with us?'

'I'll try but it depends how busy we get in here. It might be better if I ask Sir James if he'll arrange a meeting for me with Mrs Sheppard before she returns to Christchurch. She may be able to throw some light on Mrs Luxmore's past. In the meantime I shall issue a warrant for Luxmore's arrest. I can't let him roam around anymore until we have an explanation for his bizarre behaviour. He may or may not be a killer but he needs to be questioned regarding the episode last night.'

Sophia nodded, took her leave and went back to work where, because of her late arrival, she had to go into long explanations to Una regarding the events of the last evening.

'What a dreadful thing to happen. Mr Luxmore is even worse than his mother from the way you describe it,' was Una's only comment as she returned to her typing.

***

If an onlooker had deemed the usual Franchise league meetings well attended, they would have been astonished at the number of people at tonight's gathering. Arriving almost half an hour early, Tilly and Sophia were only just in time to find two spare seats at the very back of the hall. As they waited, more and more people crammed in, standing in every available space. The buzz of conversation heightened the impression of excitement as the patient crowd contemplated the evening ahead. At last the pianist appeared, sitting down at the upright piano on the side of the stage. Arranging her music, her skirts and flexing her fingers, she kept everyone in suspense until finally she put up the lid of the instrument and struck a grand series of chords. All those sitting rose to their feet, singing the national Anthem with an unusual fervour. 'God Save the Queen' rang out so loudly pedestrians, passing outside in the street, stopped to listen.

Tilly and Sophia craned their necks to watch as a small procession of ladies made their way on to the stage from a side door. Mrs Sheppard stood next to the Chairwoman as thunderous applause greeted her. She smiled modestly before she sat down and the audience quietened. The Chairman stood, greeting everyone in the overcrowded auditorium.

'Tonight we are honoured by the presence of Mrs Kate Sheppard who has travelled up from Christchurch to address us. As many of you are aware, Mrs Sheppard is the Franchise Superintendent of the Women's Christian Temperance Union and a founder of the Woman's Franchise League. I hardly need tell you of her attributes and her loyalty to the cause of suffrage. I'm sure you are all in awe of her extraordinary hard work, her focussed efforts, her writing skills and her absolute devotion to ensuring women achieve the vote in time for the next election. Please show your appreciation.'

Once again the applause was deafening as Kate Sheppard rose to her feet and walked to the lectern. She stood waiting for quiet, a dignified woman of nearly forty five, dressed soberly in a well cut jacket of dark blue wool, with a matching skirt. Her silvering hair was swept back from a kind face that smiled eagerly out over her audience. Lifting a hand in acknowledgement, she consulted her notes, and began to speak in a well modulated voice that still held the slightest hint of her youth in Liverpool.

'Ladies and gentlemen, thank you for this wonderful welcome. It's heart warming to travel all this way and find like minds and hearts so full of energy and enthusiasm. I don't need to tell you all of the urgency that we face in putting our petition together to influence our politicians to vote for the Electoral Reform Bill before the next election. Before I came to Wellington I read back on some of the entries in my diary from two years ago when the Bill was defeated in the Upper House by seventeen votes to fifteen. I will read you what I wrote then in the hope that you will be even more determined in your striving for this achievement for the women of New Zealand. I reflected as follows,

"To sit down and mourn, however, would be worse than foolish, and it may be that our temporary defeat will have the effect of spurring on all who consistently desire to see this reform carried to greater zeal and energy so that the majority favourable in the House of Representatives next election may be so great that the Legislative Council will not throw the Bill out again."

Those were my sentiments in 1891 and those are still my sentiments, ladies and gentlemen. We cannot retreat in this matter and accept defeat. However much our Parliamentary representatives may procrastinate and attempt to change the wording of the present Bill, they must not be allowed to forget that nearly half the population of this colony has been denied the right to decide its future until now. All we ask is for democracy to be achieved, equality to be achieved and as soon as possible!'

As she finished speaking the audience rose en masse in a standing ovation. Not one single heckler raised his voice. Kate Sheppard clapped her hands in a gesture of appreciation towards everyone and sat down.

'Thank you Mrs Sheppard,' said the Chairwoman, when the noise had abated, 'your words are truly inspirational to all of us. I am sure we will leave tonight fired anew with enthusiasm and vigour.'

'Wasn't she wonderful,' commented Sophia to her friend, her hands quite sore from clapping.

'And so well dressed,' added Tilly, ever the fashion commentator.

CHAPTER TWENTY FOUR

Thursday 25th May 1893.

Another invitation had arrived by the first post for Sophia. Sir James wished her to come to his office to discuss progress on the investigations over an afternoon cup of tea.

Later that afternoon, as she entered his office, she was most surprised to find that Mrs Sheppard was also sitting at the tea table with her Godfather.

'Come in my dear. How are you? Let me introduce you to Mrs Sheppard,' said Sir James seizing her hand and planting a kiss on her cheek. A wave of shyness swept over Sophia as she extended her hand to the woman she most admired. Kate stood and smiled at Sophia as she shook hands.

'My dear Miss Holmes what a pleasure to meet you. James is full of your praises.'

'Oh... Mrs Sheppard, how do you do? I attended your talk last night. It was so inspiring to us all. We've been looking forward to your visit for several weeks.'

Feeling her cheeks grow pink in the company of this woman, Sophia sat down next to her at the table and tucked her muddy boots out of sight under the long tablecloth.

'We're waiting for Detective Butler to arrive. He did warn me he could be running late. It was his suggestion that we convene this little meeting,' said Sir James fussing with the cups and pouring the tea.

Kate Sheppard looked at Sophia who sensed approval in her eyes.

'I can see there is an air of responsibility about you that is entirely in keeping with your fond Godfather's description,' she smiled. 'I am so eager to hear what progress has been made with regard to the anti-suffrage acts that have occurred so recently, because it's apparent that my worries over the troublesome events associated with suffrage here in Wellington were entirely warranted. Murder, arson and bribery are surely the worst crimes and to try and make it look as if they were part of the plans we laid to get the vote is despicable. I never thought that anyone would be in such dreadful danger.'

'Whoever is responsible has a very twisted sense of vendetta,' replied Sophia respectful of Kate's quick grasp of the situation. 'We do have a suspect but lack of evidence is a problem.'

Jack Butler's arrival heralded more introductions and another cup of tea being poured. Sophia noticed how at ease Mrs Sheppard was with the policeman, not at all intimidated as many women would be.

'Perhaps, Sir James, I could briefly summarise the events for Mrs Sheppard then bring you all up to date on the investigation.'

Proceeding from the first meeting with Sophia and Sir James, Jack Butler related all the details of the Post murder, the Dixon Street fire, the attempted bribery of the MP and the break in to Sophia's office, right up to the fire at the Luxmore home. Every so often Mrs Sheppard or Sir James would stop him to ask a question, but Sophia was impressed with the clear and lucid way he set out all the facts. Nothing was missed out, from the fingerprints to the discoveries in Susie's room. Last of all he described the attack by Richard Luxmore on Daphne Parham at Sophia's house on the previous Tuesday night.

'Good heavens! This has developed into a litany of crime,' gasped Kate Sheppard.

'What I would like to ask you, Mrs Sheppard, if I may, is do you have any connection with the Luxmore family or Hilda Luxmore? Richard's comments about you didn't make any sense to us.'

Kate Sheppard shook her head sorrowfully and biting her lips together, took a deep breath.

'It was all so long ago. I can't believe it wasn't long forgotten...Hilda was a spiteful girl but if this is all of her doing it's malicious to the extent of being evil.'

'So you did know her in the past?' Butler urged her to respond.

'No, in fact I've never met her. Oh... it's a long story. I arrived in New Zealand with my family in 1869. I was twenty and we lived with my married sister in Christchurch. The next year I met Walter Sheppard. He was a successful business man, also he'd been a Councillor on the City Council. We became engaged and married in 1871. When our engagement was announced, Walter received a most vitriolic letter from Hilda Montford, as she was then. She accused him of abandoning her, after making promises of marriage. It was all a pack of lies, according to Walter who said that the only connection between them was that they attended the same family gatherings. He told me that they shared the same Great Grandmother so it was hardly a close connection. We put her feelings down to something like a school girl attraction and tried to forget about it. More imagined than real you might say.'

225

She paused and took a sip of her tea.

'Unfortunately for us all, she refused to accept my husband's version of events. She came after him at his place of work and threatened to sue him for breach of promise in front of all his staff. It was all quite ghastly for us. Poor Walter wrote to her father and sent him her letter. He was completely honest, both to me, and to Mr Montford, about the circumstances of their meetings and that there was never any question of marriage being discussed between them. Mr Montford replied promptly and apologised. He said that Hilda had been unwell, that she was now in a convalescent home and that was the last we would hear of the matter. Obviously he didn't wish to have a scandal on his hands. After listening to your account Detective Butler, it occurs to me that perhaps this was an early sign of her addiction. I recall reading an engagement notice in the *Christchuch Press,* about a year later saying she was marrying George Luxmore . That's really all I can tell you.'

'Distant relatives,' commented Sophia dryly, looking intently at her Godfather, 'What a trouble they can be.'

'I'm trying to understand why she would let something like that fester away over the years,' puzzled the policeman. 'One can only presume her husband knew nothing about it.'

'It occurs to me that perhaps she never recovered and brought Richard up on the story and encouraged him to think how ill used his Mama was by Kate and Walter. Daphne told me how she thought he was tied to his mother's apron strings,' was Sophia's suggestion.

'Some sort of mental complex perhaps,' suggested Mrs Sheppard. 'She must have drummed it into poor

Richard from birth to make him commit murder and arson if he is indeed the guilty person. His mind must be as addled as hers.'

'Well until we catch him in the act of some other dreadful deed, or get a confession we still can't pin anything on him,' said Butler. 'I've put out a warrant for his arrest on the charge of assaulting his fiancée but he's disappeared of the face of the earth. His father insists he's innocent and says he has no idea where Richard is. He says it's quite normal for him to go off for days with his friends. I wasn't permitted to speak to Mrs Luxmore. She was deemed far too unwell to discuss her son with me.'

'Probably in a dreadful state if she's not able to get her doses of opium,' said Sophia.

'I hope you're not feeling any sympathy for her?'

Sophia pulled a face at Jack which was noted with amusement by the others.

'Certainly not.'

'So...' said Sir James trying to sum up in true legal fashion. 'Are we saying that there is a possibility all these events have been planned by Richard Luxmore to avenge his mother's twisted belief that Kate took Walter away from her. It's almost ludicrous to imagine such a scheme. Our belief that it was the brewers carrying this out must be wrong in that case.'

'Yes, I think we can all agree on that, but on the other hand, what better way to hit back at Mrs Sheppard than to create a scenario that put the Franchise movement and the liquor barons in the role of perpetrators and all with the purpose of harming the thing dearest to her heart. Oh! Apart from your husband Mrs Sheppard of course,' said Sophia with an apologetic smile.

'Well he might even argue with that,' responded Kate Sheppard, somewhat bemused by the alacrity of Sophia's surmising. Surveying the others around the table she suddenly felt a great fondness for them. That these complete strangers had taken such an interest in her comments to Sir James touched her and momentarily she wished that they didn't live such a long way from her so that she could improve her fleeting acquaintance with the two of them.

'So given that you cannot find Richard Luxmore, is there anything else that can be done to prove he is the villain,' she asked Jack Butler.

'As I mentioned before, we can try taking fingerprints from the glass and the knife. If they match we can at least prove he was in Susie's room at some stage and perhaps that he was purchasing drugs from her using Hilda's jewellery as payment. If I can find him then my superior has given me permission to ink his fingers and take prints that we might be able to match. I have managed to buy some very fine talcum powder from the pharmacy in Willis Street and I'm going to use it to dust the other items for prints. I've been reading a book written by Sir Francis Galton which has been most instructive on the means of identification. We have a photographer who is keen to record anything I can discover.'

'Most commendable Butler,' approved Sir James. 'It's good to know that our New Zealand Police Force is able to use all the most modern science available to fight crime.'

'I can't let myself become too hopeful though Sir James. We could go to all this trouble and find that the Judge won't accept it.'

'Ah well if it comes to that perhaps I can arrange a sympathetic Judge,' winked Sir James. 'Although alas it cannot be me, owing to my relationship with Sophia.'

'Even so, any evidence we present has to be watertight, because the Luxmore's can no doubt afford to hire the best advocate in the land to defend themselves.'

'You said, "themselves",' asked Sophia. 'Does that mean that Mrs Luxmore could be incriminated in all this?'

'Certainly if we can link her to Richard's actions. But I imagine any lawyer worth his fee, would make sure she was certified unfit to stand trial.'

'Yes...that's true,' said Sophia. 'Anybody representing her wouldn't know what sort of mood she was going to display in court.'

'That's a long way ahead of us, but for now all we can do is wait and see if Richard appears so that we can catch and question him. I've taken the step of advising the authorities in Sydney by telegraph, in case he's jumped on board a boat to escape there.'

'I wish you luck,' said Mrs Sheppard, 'The sooner you find him the better, in case he does anything else awful.'

They all agreed on that sentiment and soon after the meeting broke up as Kate was due to board her boat for Christchurch that evening.

***

Sophia walked back to her office, intending to return to work for an hour or so before going home. Una smiled as she entered.

'There you are. I was going to leave you a note. A

woman came in earlier to ask if you would go and see a client. Apparently he's an old man who can't get in to see us here. She said he wants some documents copied as soon as possible. Here's the address.'

Sophia took the piece of paper Una had made her notes on.

'This is quite a way to walk. I'll get a cab. Can you lock up for me tonight please?'

Ignoring the rather surprised look on the cab drivers face when she gave him the address, Sophia eventually reached the narrow street on the western side of the city where she'd been directed. Paying the cabby she saw that the address she'd been given appeared to be an empty two storied shop. She hesitated and then rang the bell on the side door and stood there in the gathering gloom of early evening.

The door opened slowly revealing a young Chinese woman in traditional dress who remained silent, although she smiled at her visitor and ushered her into the hall way where lanterns hung with red fringes offered only the dimmest of light. As the door closed, Sophia turned quickly as she heard the girl turn a key to lock it, which she removed and placed in a hidden pocket under her black silk tunic top.

'I've come to meet Mr Chang. I'm from the secretarial agency. Will you tell him Miss Holmes is here please?'

There was no response from the girl and Sophia wondered if she spoke English.

'Why have you locked the door?'

'You come with me please,' was the soft polite answer as the girl glided past her on black satin slippered feet and led her up a steep flight of stairs and then down to the far reaches of a dark hallway.

Bewildered, Sophia had no choice but to comply. She kept her eyes on the long plait that hung down the Chinese girl's back as it swayed sinuously like a shining snake against her tunic. Reaching a door at the rear of the upper floor, the girl slipped inside, gesturing to her guest to follow. The sights and smells that greeted Sophia were ones she would never forget. The large room was almost dark with only a few candle lamps providing any light. A haze of smoke hung in the air adding to the lack of visibility and Sophia strained her eyes to find any sign of her possible client. On closer inspection she made out figures lying on low beds, everyone of them supine and quiet. Breathing deeply in her efforts not to panic, she refused violently when the girl offered her an opium pipe. Her realisation of what this place contained hitting her with a considerable shock.

'No! No!' she cried out, pushing the girl away and made an effort to see her way back to the door.

'You all right,' the girl said still holding out the smoking pipe. 'You smoke. You feel better then. Sit here.'

She pointed to a comfortable padded chair that had a strange air of normality in the surroundings of this room and with surprising strength pushed Sophia down into it, keeping a firm hand on her shoulder while she place the opium pipe on her lap. Without thinking, Sophia picked it up in another effort to return it but she was too late, the girl had vanished into the haze. Aware that the smoke was starting to affect her judgement, Sophia tried to stand up but when her legs weakly refused to hold her, she collapsed back into the chair gasping with horror. How was she to escape? No-one knew she was here. Lying back in the soft comfort of the armchair, she felt inertia creep over her even though her breathing was as shallow as she could manage.

Struggling to keep her eyes open, she saw her father approach her through the mist.

'My dear girl,' he said, bending over her. She started to raise a feeble hand to touch him when his face dissolved into a demonic goat's head and blood poured down his chest. Attempting to scream, nothing would come from her throat. Once again a figure came up to her, dressed in the most fashionable clothes.

'Tilly,' she tried to say. 'Save me Tilly.'

The creature she supposed was her best friend let out a cackle, revealing rotting blackened teeth behind garishly painted scarlet lips. The stylish outfit dissembling into filthy rags that barely covered the creatures' body which was that of an ancient crone, wrinkled with drooping flesh and overgrown finger nails. Shutting her eyes tightly was the only response Sophia could make to these nightmarish apparitions. Slowly the opium fumes worked on her and she slid into a deep sleep, slumped in the chair like a large rag doll.

'Get her out of here!'

Sophia gagged as she was pulled to her feet roughly and lifted over the shoulder of a burly man. Hanging over his back she managed to lift her head to see that she was being carried along the hallway, down the stairs and out of the building into the cold night air. She was almost dropped onto the ground in the street, curling up into a ball before a hand shook her hard.

'Come on Miss! Time to wake up now and face the world.'

Sophia was horribly sick, just missing the front of

her coat but this appeared to make no difference to the rough treatment meted out to her. Hauled to her feet by an unseen person, she was half dragged, half carried to a large enclosed carriage which she was thrown up into as her legs refused to climb the steps. Feeling around in the dark she found a bench seat and managed to achieve a sitting position on it, although a persistent pain in her head was urging her to vomit again. Her mouth dry and foul tasting, she felt a lurch as the coach started off and put her head in her hands

After a few minutes she felt a little better, not so faint and began to realise where she was. Plain board seats along the sides of the vehicle spoke of only one answer. She was in a police wagon. Had she been arrested? Her muddled brain couldn't find an answer to that but she was very much afraid it was the truth. There was little fresh air in the wagon to revive her and no windows. She found her bag which had rather astonishingly been placed in with her, taking out a handkerchief to wipe her mouth and give her nose a good blow, which she hoped might dispel some of the effects of the opium she's inhaled against her wishes. Opening a bottle of eau de cologne, she put some on the cloth and wiped her face clean, the refreshing scent reviving her at last. It was the only time that she wished she was like Tilly who always carried smelling salts with her. A sniff of their sharp acrid ammonia smell would have been welcome at this time to clear her head and bring her to her proper senses.

As the wagon came to a halt, voices shouted but Sophia couldn't discern the words. The door to the vehicle was opened and she was taken by the arm and helped out.

'This way', was the instruction from a young constable who held her arm tightly as she staggered when trying to follow him. A doorway led off the alley where the police wagon had parked, opening into a back entrance to the Station. Sophia, hustled along at a smart rate, had no time to take in her surroundings until she was pushed into a tiny room, containing a bench seat and little else.

'You'll be dealt with in the morning,' was the only comment offered by her gaoler as the door slammed shut behind her.

Gradually her eyes became accustomed to the darkness as a faint glimmer of light edged through the tiny barred gap in the door. No windows meant that the cell was cold and airless, it's atmosphere redolent of former inmates. Stale sweat, dirty clothes and urine odours assailed her as she tried to catch her breath sitting on the narrow seat. Waiting for the opium fumes to slowly clear from her brain and her bloodstream, Sophia admitted to a fear of the results of this night. It also occurred to her that she'd been enticed into the drug den and deliberately placed in a situation that she couldn't explain easily. Quite certain that Una hadn't realised that the woman who left the message was deceiving her, she started to wonder if this been put in place by Richard Luxmore? If so, where was he and was he the one who'd informed the police of her whereabouts? Was this his promised revenge on her?

Struggling with all these suppositions became too much for her. Placing her bag on the end of the bench, she unpinned her hat, placing it on the floor. Using the bag as a pillow, she pulled her legs up, lying down on the narrow shelf and closed her eyes, allowing the remains of the drug to lull her into sleep.

CHAPTER TWENTY FIVE

Friday 26th May 1893.

'Wake up Miss!'

Sophia lifted her head, blinking as the cell door opened to reveal a policeman carrying a small lantern. He placed a tray with a mug of water and a plate of bread and butter, on the floor beside her then left. Groaning from the pain in her cramped limbs, Sophia sat up, reaching for the mug, taking deep gulps of the frigid liquid. The bread was fresh, its yeasty aroma going a long way to cover the obnoxious odours of the room. Sophia devoured it with haste, her empty stomach receiving the plain food gratefully, as if it were a feast. She stood, testing her legs, stretching her back before she realised how much her head ached. Reaching for her bag she found a comb and attempted to put her hair in to some sort of order. Many of her hairpins had disappeared over night and in the end she pulled out all those remaining, plaited her hair like the Chinese girls', before pinning her hat firmly back on top of her head to cover the worst of the style. I should have had it cut short, she thought, how much easier it would have been to keep tidy.

There was little else she could achieve to neaten her appearance, so she sat down again, her mind still aghast at what had happened to her. It was obvious she had been arrested, but as yet she hadn't been charged. Was it illegal to be in that den? Sophia started to realise how innocent she was of such matters but then recalled hazily something that Jack had told her about the elderly Chinese men in Haining Street. She thought he'd told her the police left them alone unless they recruited any new people into the opium den. Was that the reason she'd been detained? Never mind that she'd sat in Courts and listened to her father defend innocent and criminal alike, she lived in another country now and perhaps the laws were different in these matters? Mentally trying to put together a defence of her actions, she hoped she could find a good lawyer to defend her if it should come to that. She felt disgraced by her actions. How naive of her to be led into such a place. Meg and Bayliss would surely be out looking for her by now although she had no idea of the time, only guessing that it must be early morning.

She lapsed into a mood of utter dejection until she heard footsteps and voices outside the door. Lifting her head she watched as it opened to disclose Jack Butler on the threshold. The sight of him was both a huge relief and a huge embarrassment to Sophia and she looked away as he came into the cell.

'Good morning Miss Holmes,' he said formally. 'It appears you have broken the law.'

'Oh...' sighed Sophia. 'It wasn't on purpose. You must believe that... and now...' she broke off as tears welled up, spilling down her cheeks, causing her lips to tremble violently. 'B...Bother,' she sobbed as her normal calm demeanour completely deserted her.

A large clean handkerchief was placed in her hand and as she opened it out and wiped at the betraying tears, she was overcome by a dreadful thought that brought on a fresh paroxysm of weeping.

'I'm going to be an addict now...' she finally

managed to gasp. 'I can't bear it.'

She felt a gentle hand patting her shoulder reassuringly, as Jack Butler sat beside her on the bench.

'Of course not. You can't get addicted from one short session. The police found you before too much could happen.'

'But I was unconscious,' moaned Sophia. 'I don't know what happened to me.'

'Can you recall how you got to the place?'

'Oh yes,' she said, gradually calming down, 'A woman came into the office and told Una a new client wanted to meet me there. I've never done anything so stupid in my life. I fell straight into the trap. I presume it was a trap?'

She turned her tear stained face towards the detective who took his hand away from her arm and pulled out the morning newspaper from his pocket.

'I'm afraid so. It appears our friend is up to his tricks again. A small boy told the beat policeman where you were, but not immediately it would appear.'

Opening out the front page he showed her the headlines.

'*Well known business woman found in opium den,*' read Sophia out loud. 'My God, he must have told them before it happened. Look what rubbish it says here, "*Businesswoman and leading light for universal suffrage, Miss Sophia Holmes was last night discovered in a Cuba Street drug den when Police acting on a tip off, raided the upstairs apartment.. Our reporter has been reliably informed that Miss Holmes was in a drug induced state, being incapable of walking. She has been taken into custody pending charges.*" I was trapped. You do believe me don't you?'

'Yes of course I do,' said Butler patiently. 'But it's

238

going to be difficult to sort out unless we can persuade the Chinese in the house to tell us who asked them to do this.'

'Perhaps you could bribe them into telling the truth. I'll pay them if necessary or offer a reward,' said Sophia in shameless desperation. 'Perhaps I could go to the reporter and tell him my side of the story? Insist that he write a retraction.'

'Just leave all that to me please. The first thing to do is get you out of here and back home. I'll release you and Sir James will, I'm sure, vouch for your good behaviour.'

'Oh no...,' groaned his prisoner. 'I suppose he'll have seen the paper by now. I'll never live this down. It will ruin my business.'

'Let's deal with one thing at a time. Come on, I'll call a cab to the back entrance and spirit you away.'

Sophia nodded, picking up her bag, brushing down her crumpled skirts and followed him out of the cell, her mind full of how she was going to explain this awful event to everyone.

**

At last night had fallen and he was protected by the darkness. What a marvellous day it had been. The next stage in their plans had worked perfectly, nothing had gone awry. The symmetry of the execution enthralled him almost as much as the beauty of his blade. Sitting on the edge of his bed, he read over and over the report of Sophia's arrest, his eyes glittering in the dim gaslight. Watching from an alley across the street, he'd nearly drooled with pleasure as the policeman carried her out of the house. For a brief instant he had wished it was him who held that slender body over his shoulder, imagining her perfume and her fresh sweet hair against his face. He pushed the thought firmly away; women like Sophia Holmes were not for him. He required submission, adoration and no questions asked when he came home in the early hours of the morning. No chance of that with the Holmes woman, who would no doubt wish to be in full control of all aspects of a man's life.

Taking out his knife, he carefully cut the news report out. Folding it into a tiny shape he placed it in his wallet next to the receipt for the donation to the Temperance League. When all this was over and the result they required was achieved, he thought he might start a scrapbook to hold all his little mementos. How sentimental you're becoming, he chided himself silently laughing. Lying back on the bed in his rented room, he pondered his next move with relish, as he envisioned the process of attaining the next step in the scheme. The instructions, all those weeks ago, had been clear, but the actual delivery of the idea had been trusted to him to work out. It would take more precise planning to judge the right moment but he was fast becoming an expert at that. He was beginning to pride himself on his ability to seize opportunity when it arrived. There was just the small matter of removing Miss Homes for good before he could proceed any further against Kate Sheppard. The secretary was getting far too close to him and without her around to help the police, he felt sure their investigations would grind to a halt.

A knock on his door, roused him and he stood up, stretching and went to open it.

'Here's your supper sir,' said his landlady,

handing him over a covered tray with an ingratiating smile at her tenant.

Thanking her, he closed the door and sat at the small table near the window to eat. Stupid woman, he mused, good cook though. His landlady had completely accepted his story of being an undercover policeman. She raptly listened as he'd explained that his work took him out at all hours of the night. It had been so easy to fool her but he'd come to feel indulgent towards her, wished her no harm. He had to remain focussed on the plan and would not allow himself any diversions.

Tonight he would wander down to the docks again. In time he would move the plan forward again and he found the sea air and the rough taverns a good stimulus to his mental and physical wellbeing. Well disguised, he could pass off as any sailor or dock worker which would be a blessing when he came to make his trip to Christchurch to eliminate the Sheppard woman.

CHAPTER TWENTY SIX

Saturday 17th June 1893.

Drawing her bedroom curtains that morning, Sophia lamented the pouring rain that lashed down over the front garden. Once again the city was all but obscured by low cloud, with strong southerly winds pushing up the white caps on Wellington Harbour. Thankful that she didn't open her office on Saturdays, she dressed warmly before descending to the kitchen. As she waited for Meg to cook her breakfast, she started to read through the pile of newspapers that had lain on the table for two days as she'd been too tired to look at them. Over the past three weeks she'd felt exhausted by her ordeal in the opium den, the ensuing explanations and the sheer shame of what had happened to her.

On her arrival home from the Police Station, she'd been greeted in great consternation by Meg and Bayliss and no amount of talking would alleviate their anxiety.

'When you didn't come home that night, I sent Bayliss to your office but there was nothing to see. Mrs Johnson had already gone so I couldn't ask her,' related her cook.

'I asked around in the street, if anyone had seen you but no-one had so I came home hoping you'd be here,' added the gardener. 'We didn't know what to do so Mrs Williams bravely telephoned Mrs Sergeson...,'

'But she was out,' interrupted Meg. 'I didn't know what to do then so we just had to wait until this morning and then Bayliss was going to go down to the Police Station and report you missing.'

'Thank you both. I do appreciate your concern but here I am and in one piece although my head is still aching.'

'Best you go up to bed and I'll bring you a nice cup of tea,' was Meg's wonderful idea which Sophia obeyed to the letter and spent most of the day catching up on her sleep. She'd been reassured of Butler's attention to detail when a newspaper report appeared a few days later saying the police were treating her visit to the drug house as entrapment and were actively seeking the perpetrator who they said was a person they wished to interview regarding other crimes in the city. Much to her relief, her clients had, for the most part, been sympathetic, indeed quite curious as to the circumstances. Several of them were most insistent that she describe the room where she'd been taken in all the lurid detail she could remember! Reminding herself that perhaps this was the nearest they had come to this type of experience, she indulged them with all the details, sometimes even embroidering them just a tiny bit!

Now, restored to health, she only wished to get back to normality and continued her perusal of the newspaper.

'You may like to hear this Meg. Somebody has written a piece called "Woman Defined". First of all they say,

"Woman is man's conscience and it is a good thing for him to have his conscience always with him."

This must be written by a married woman by the sound of that. Oh... I like this observation,

"Woman is the mother of mankind since Adam. It is the maternal muscle that has spanked the race into decent manners and good behaviour."

'We'd better tell Hilda Luxmore about that one. She seems to have got it quite wrong with her son!'

'Is there any news about him yet?' Meg asked as she expertly turned fried eggs over in the sizzling pan. 'It's been over three weeks now since we found him in here with Miss Parham.'

'Nothing,' sighed Sophia. 'It's all a bit deflating when we felt we'd got so close to solving everything. Detective Butler called in very briefly yesterday to tell me that there hasn't been a single sighting of him. Even Boysie Smith can't track his whereabouts. I'm wondering if people aren't too frightened of him to turn him in to the police. After what happened to me it's obvious he hasn't left Wellington, so someone must be sheltering him.'

The arrival of Bayliss interrupted her train of thought, but even during breakfast her mind was working on where Richard Luxmore might be. Pushing back her empty plate, she tried to forget him as she continued to read the paper and gradually, became totally absorbed in the progress of the Electoral Bill and the length of time it was taking to debate each clause.

'I cannot understand why these politicians are so bound up in whether shearers and commercial travellers should be allowed to vote. If this is to be a universal franchise, then everyone must vote, no matter where they are on Election Day. Surely if they are registered then their votes can be checked against that list before they are counted? And as for this expression "abandoned women", what does that imply? Can you picture heaps of women lying in the street like rubbish Meg? It's laughable. If women are abandoned it's because of men. Some don't have any choice but to take up prostitution.'

'I've been known to be a bit abandoned myself after a couple of gins. In my youth that is,' grinned Meg. 'Didn't mean I was going to go out whoring.'

'Exactly,' said Sophia tartly. 'Oh the English language is a marvellous thing but you have to be so careful in understanding the correct meaning of a phrase and that particular one is open to many different translations and connotations. I'm amazed that the person who wrote this Bill should leave the interpretation of it so wide open to such an extended debate. If you or I or any woman for that matter, wrote a document so important, we would be sure to have no ambiguity what so ever. All these trivial arguments are being seized upon as delaying tactics. Haven't they heard of writing in plain English? Instead of which we have the use of two words where one will do, all through the Bill so it naturally becomes misleading.'

'You understand so much about it. Perhaps you should stand for Parliament when women are allowed to?'

Meg's suggestion hung in the air between them tempting Sophia to imagine it for a moment before she shook her head.

'I think that may be a few years away, but it's a thought,' she giggled. 'You know how much I like arranging people's lives! Maybe I could do it on a national basis? But in reality I'm sure that Mrs Sheppard would make a far better candidate than me. She'd be outstanding. People would crowd the public galleries to hear her speak at debates. She'd put all those old men to shame in no time.'

'I'd like to be housekeeper to a Member of Parliament,' said Meg wistfully. 'That would be very grand, give me a very high status with the grocer!'

'It would be better for us, if he gave you a very high discount,' laughed Sophia.

CHAPTER TWENTY SEVEN

Thursday 6th July 1893.

Winter dragged on in the capital. The inhabitants became accustomed to the rain and wind that accompanied them everywhere in their daily lives. Grit filled eyes and wet feet were the normal way of things and letters to the papers, complained on an almost daily basis, about the muddy roads and the dirty street lamps. Like many other women, Sophia sat up late at night, hemming up her work skirts a few inches shorter in an effort to keep them clean. Even Una decided to lift her hems to avoid the chore of drying and brushing her clothes every night. Discussion of the Electoral Reform Bill was apparently an endless part of Parliamentary sessions, the delaying tactics becoming increasingly ridiculous in the eyes of the public, whilst the collection of signatures on the Franchise Petition grew almost daily.

Jack Butler had obtained finger prints from the blade of the Bowie knife used on Daphne, and the glass from Susie Post's room but without matching prints taken from Richard Luxmore personally, he was resigned to the case not being closed.

'If we can't trace Luxmore, we have no choice but to admit we can't solve it. I suppose we could try him in absentia but it would be almost impossible to bring the case without the suspect being in court. It's frustrating but I have to accept we may never bring him to justice.'

'Yes,' agreed Sophia. 'It might be possible to get

somewhere if you could persuade Mrs Luxmore to talk to you, but as long as she refuses, nothing can be learned.'

'I've tried to get George Luxmore to answer questions but he appears to be in such a state of shock about his son that he's in denial of anything being wrong with him. He's still insisting that Richard is away with friends. I even briefly entertained the idea of showing him the jewellery but I couldn't see that it would achieve much. He would just say it had been stolen by a maid or some such story.'

Now as the afternoon sky darkened with the ever present grey clouds, Sophia decided to close her office early. Una had been confined to bed for the past two days with a hacking cough. The weather had kept customers away from the city centre and the pile of work that usually sat in the filing tray had dwindled. Reaching to turn off the last gas lamp, Sophia heard the front door bell ring and leaving the light burning she went out to see who had arrived. She was confronted by a tall dishevelled man in a long oilskin raincoat and a large brimmed hat. As he removed this, his greasy blonde hair falling down over his forehead, she stepped back in amazement. Richard Luxmore stood before her, his whiskers grown long, his eyes narrowed, a wolfish grin on his face.

'Ah...Miss Holmes, you didn't expect to see me again did you? But I'm a man of my word. I told you, you hadn't seen the last of me and here I am.'

Fear crept through Sophia. She looked over his shoulder through the window at the street outside. Willis Street was empty for a rare moment, no-one likely to appear to whom she could wave out and appeal to.

Swallowing, she took a deep breath, summoning her courage to find a brave voice.

'It is a surprise, you're absolutely correct. What can I do for you?'

Luxmore lifted up the folding part of the counter and pushed her into the dimly lit back office before she realised what he was doing.

'It's not what you can do for me, more what I'm going to do to you,' he sneered as Sophia backed away from him towards her desk. She watched horrified as he reached inside a pocket, a knife appearing in his hand that she recognised as a twin to the Bowie in Jacks' possession. It seemed to Sophia as if time came to a halt. The clock on the office wall appeared frozen as Sophia noticed how, in this low light, his long newly grown side whiskers and the goatee beard he now wore on his chin gave the same impression that Boysie had recounted. The bare skin either side of his mouth gave the appearance of light streaks in a beard. This discovery only increased her fear and she carefully kept her hands behind her skirts, leaning back away from him as her fingers touched the edge of her desk, slowly reaching under it for the catch that would release a hidden drawer. To distract him she turned her head to look pointedly at the telephone some yards away. She saw him follow her gaze.

'That's not going to help. It's such a shame to do this to you,' smiled Luxmore unconvincingly sympathetic. 'I really liked you Sophia, but you poked your nose into things that had nothing to do with you. That was fatal I'm afraid.'

Holding the knife out towards her in his right hand, he came closer, his breathing fast and rasping. Sophia cowered back against the desk as he advanced, waiting for a chance of escape but he appeared able to read her thoughts.

'There's no way you can escape. I'll try and make it a quick death. One slice across your throat and in a few seconds all will be over for you. I'm quite good at it, practised on a few sheep. Don't be afraid,' he whispered in almost soothing tones that increased his repellence to Sophia who could barely recognise the languorous youth she'd first met at the races. In his place a hardened killer had appeared, showing no mercy, eager to murder again.

'You're in enough trouble Richard. Please don't make it worse,' Sophia said then gave a loud cough to cover the noticeable click of the drawer catch as she pressed it and reached inside with her right hand to find what she required. At the same time she pulled out the folds of her skirt with her left hand as if arranging them, disguising her intentions. Licking her dry lips, she swallowed hard never removing her eyes from the knife blade with its razor sharp edge glinting so close to her.

'Well that's just it isn't it? It really can't get worse for me can it? May as well be hung for five murders as four, and anyway no-one is going to catch me my dear. They can only execute me once and I do so love the thrill of killing so it's worth the risk. You know,' he said reflectively, pausing for a moment in his advance towards her. 'It's far more exhilarating seeing the blood spurt from an artery than taking any drugs. You should know what that's like Sophia? Did you enjoy your little sojourn in Cuba Street?'

'No I certainly didn't but I guessed you were behind it,' she stated in the strongest voice she could muster with a knife pointed at her.

'Shame, shame but I've always found that a little

session with a drug like opium can enrich one's thoughts no end. Of course one has to be careful as Mama found out so sadly. I suspect she might have been a different person without the laudanum all those kind Doctors prescribed to her. In the end she couldn't do without it and I had to step in, didn't I? Papa couldn't have cared less even if he had noticed. I couldn't bear to see her in such a state and it was so easy to buy the opium that made her happy again.'

'Drop the knife Richard,' Sophia commanded as she saw her chance with her captor musing about his mother's addiction, his concentration on her, slightly out of focus. Richard found himself confronted by a small pearl handled gun that she held out in front of her with both hands, in a very determined and well practiced fashion despite her palms becoming sticky with perspiration.

'Oh look what you've got! ,' he nevertheless said sarcastically. 'A little pea shooter. You don't really believe that's going to stop me do you, stupid bitch?'

'Drop the knife,' demanded Sophia again, as she took the safety catch off. 'I'm not joking, I will shoot you.'

Holding his hands out to the sides of his body in a mock gesture of surrender, he let the Bowie knife lie casually in the palm of his right hand, laughing loudly as he took a deliberate taunting step forward, giving Sophia the perfect target. His laughter turning to a scream as a bullet tore through his right wrist, sending the knife jumping out of his hand. It flew across the room and its tip penetrated the wooden panelling of the far wall causing it to hang there, embedded and vibrating from the impact.

'What the hell did you do that for?'

Richard whimpered as he clutched the wound, blood seeping through his fingers.

'Go and sit in that chair over by the wall,' ordered Sophia her courage surging. 'And don't think of trying to disobey me or you'll get a bullet in your knee cap. You should know that I'm a very good markswoman regardless of your scorn for this weapon. That wasn't a lucky shot. It was completely deliberate and I won't hesitate to shoot you again.'

Luxmore continued to whine and complain as he backed away from her, collapsing into the wooden office chair, where with a great deal of noisy suffering he wrapped his wrist in the clean tea towel that Sophia tossed him from a safe distance.

'Now I'm going to telephone the police. Do not move,' she told him, her aim unwavering. She picked up the mouthpiece from the telephone that stood on her desk and rattled the receiver until an operator answered.

'Would you put me thought to the Police Station please? ...Is this the desk Sergeant? This is Miss Holmes speaking. No don't interrupt me! I'm in my office at the Wellington Secretarial Agency, Willis Street and I'm holding a man at gunpoint...Yes that's right, at gunpoint. It's Richard Luxmore. There's a warrant for his arrest. Yes that's correct. It is Detective Butler's case. Please send some men as soon as possible and you will need a Doctor. Yes Sergeant, a Doctor. I shot him, only in the hand but there's a lot of blood. Thank you.'

Replacing the mouth piece, Sophia pulled out her chair and sat facing her prisoner at a safe distance, the gun still steady in her left hand. As an afterthought, she reached for her shorthand pad and a pencil. As she started to question him she managed to write some of his answers down in the long strokes, dots and curlicues that Doctor Pitman had so well invented despite her shaking hand.

'Would you like to tell me why you behaved in such a deplorable manner?'

It occurred to her that she sounded like a nanny admonishing a naughty child.

'You wouldn't understand,' was his defiant response, his eyes darting from left to right in an effort to see if he could escape.

'Try me,' she said bitterly. 'Shall I get you started? Is this all because you believe your mother's story about Walter Sheppard jilting her? She made the whole thing up at the time and even when she was proved wrong she has apparently persisted in her belief that his engagement to Kate ruined her life. Kate has never even met your mother. Did she own up to that?'

'No,' he said sullenly. 'But I always believed Sheppard had done something cruel and malicious to her and nothing has changed that. She wouldn't have harboured this grudge for all these years if it wasn't true.'

'Your mother was a very sick girl at the time. She had to be put into a special hospital for a while.'

'And then her parents forced her to marry my father. He couldn't have cared less about her. Oh he went through the motions of appearing a loving husband, giving her all that fake jewellery and things like that.'

Sophia gazed at him thoughtfully, mulling over this information.

'Is that why you used the gems to pay Susie Post for the opium? You were quite sure she'd think they were real and not worthless?'

'Yes. She just adored any cheap bauble. I remember she was overjoyed when she got her hands on Mother's stuff. I laughed all the way back home, thinking of the greedy expression on her face as she put those green earrings on.'

'I expect she was happy,' commented Sophia quietly. 'Susie was no fool. She knew the jewels were real, Richard. Your mother lied to you. I suppose she realised you would have pawned them for yourself if you'd known. We found them in a jewellery box in Susie's room. Detective Butler has had them valued by an expert. Your father did love her very much to give her such beautiful gifts.'

'It doesn't matter. Mother got her opium and she was all that I cared about. We're very close, Mama and I. I'd do anything for her, anything she asks for I go running. She rewards me. She knows what I like,' he almost whispered smiling to himself at some memory that Sophia intuitively knew she wouldn't wish to have explained. However, this assertion played on Sophia's mind as she pressed on with her interrogation.

'How did you pay for her drugs after you killed Susie Post?

'Just pawned the trinkets that are lying around all over the house. No-one ever noticed, except Uncle Sinclair, the old bastard.'

'You said that I was going to be the fifth murder you'd carried out? Who was the other person?'

'Oh some lout down at the wharf the same night I did Susie. He kept pestering me for money so I stabbed him. He fell into the harbour. I watched but he never surfaced. Too bad eh?'

'And was it your mother who came up with the plan to implicate the suffrage movement in this way?'

'Partly, but mainly it was my idea. When she said she wished to strike at something dear to Mrs Sheppard, I realised immediately how it must be organised. I did it rather well don't you think? The way I manipulated Susie to get the receipt, spied on your business and then accidentally on purpose bumped into you at the races. That was my stroke of genius. It gave me the opportunity to keep an eye on you to find out what you knew. Setting the fire off at home on the night of the party must have really thrown you all off the scent,' he boasted with obvious pride. 'And then your little jaunt to Cuba Street was a piece de resistance. Peng Shua, the owner, was most obliging I must say. I positively ached with laughter when they carried you out!'

'I, on the other hand, just ached...' came Sophia's terse response. 'For days.'

'Oh come on it was fun wasn't it? I bet you've always wanted to know what goes on in one of those places?'

He leaned forward as if sharing a confidence with her, but Sophia simply lifted her gun an inch closer and he subsided back into the chair and watched as she wrote.

'Where have you been hiding all this time?'

'In lodgings, in Thorndon. I have a most obliging landlady. She thinks I'm a policeman! What a laugh!'

Sophia was aghast to think that he'd already been aware of her existence before the day of the race meeting, and of the nonchalant way he was talking to her about his activities, but before she could question him further, she heard the bell jangle and suddenly the room was full of policemen. A hand removed the gun from her stiffening fingers.

'Don't think you'll need that anymore,' said Jack Butler, putting on the safety catch, emptying out the bullets and placing the small weapon in his pocket. 'Have to confiscate this for evidence.'

Turning to the prisoner he said curtly,' Richard Luxmore in the name of her Majesty I am arresting you for the attempted abduction and assault of Miss Daphne Parham, the suspected murder of Miss Susie Post, and the arson of the Dixon Street boarding house leading to the manslaughter of two inmates. There will also be charges relating to breaking and entering these premises and bribery of a Member of Parliament, setting a deliberate fire at your own home 'The Oaks' and the deliberate enticement of Miss Holmes into an opium den. There may also be a further charge of assault against Miss Holmes after I have questioned her. You may remain silent but anything you do say may be used against you as evidence in Court. Do you understand?'

Richard Luxmore nodded and grunted with pain as he was hauled to his feet and hustled out to the police wagon waiting outside, by two burly Constables. Looking back, his venomous look was wasted on Butler.

'You didn't tell me he was a bloody policeman,' he spat at Sophia.

'You never asked,' was her tart reply, and at last Jack turned to her with an anxious look.

'Are you all right Sophia?'

'Yes I think so. It all happened so fast. One minute I was turning off the lamps and the next he was in here advancing on me with a knife. It's over there stuck in the wall,' she pointed as she sat down, her knees starting to tremble.

Butler pulled the knife carefully from the panelling, by the blade using another tea towel to preserve any finger prints.

'I'll buy you some new towels when this is over,' he smiled then he noticed how she was shaking.

'For God's sake Sophia, you're in shock. Here...'

Taking off his long overcoat he wrapped it around her shoulders. She pulled it close over her chest, smelling the damp odour of the tweed and feeling the comfort of his body heat captured inside the garment.

'I'll make you a strong sweet cup of tea and then put you in a cab home.'

Sophia hated sugar in her tea, would have preferred a hug and a shoulder to lean on or even a large shot of whisky, but Detective Butler was businesslike and she supposed this was the correct method the police followed when dealing with victims of crime. Trying not to pull a face, she sipped at the tea and gradually calmed down as Butler waited for her to recover.

'His mother told him the jewellery was fake,' was her only comment.

'Did he admit to anything?'

'Yes, to Bob William's murder definitely but I'm sure he'll try and deny everything else. He did say the idea of implicating the suffrage movement was his idea not his mother's but she seems to have invented a lurid story regarding Walter Sheppard that he absolutely believes in. She seems to have a very strange relationship with her son; most abnormal from the sound of it although he didn't put it into precise words. Oh...I remember now, he did say I was going to be his fifth murder so that is an admission that he did the others I suppose. Anyway I wrote some of it down. Perhaps Una can transcribe my notes for you in the morning. It's probably not permissible as a statement in Court but it does answer some questions we couldn't.'

She motioned towards her pad on the desk. Jack agreed to leave it for Una to interpret when he saw the symbols that meant nothing to him.

'It's probably time you went home now. I'll call a cab for you. I can't come with you I'm afraid. I do have to get back to the Station and file all these charges and notify George Luxmore that we've arrested Richard.'

'You can expect an army of lawyers to descend on you then I'm sure,' stated Sophia as she handed him back his coat.

'Nothing's simple in major cases like these,' he said as he helped her on with her jacket and watched with interest as she pinned her hat on firmly. 'Now promise me you'll get an early night and be well rested because I want you to come down to the Station to make a statement, as soon as possible in the morning.'

'Yes Sir, said Sophia meekly as she climbed into the cab and waved goodbye. For once she felt obliged to accept his advice as she sunk back in the darkness of the carriage.

CHAPTER TWENTY EIGHT

Monday 28th August 1893.

The audience hushed as the Chairwoman rose to address them. There were many in the crowd who were uneducated but this was no barrier to their interest in the proceeding of the Electoral Reform Bill; they waited eager to hear the latest news regarding progress. Their Chairwoman was well aware of this and she waved a handful of press cuttings at them as she stood and cleared her throat preparatory to speaking.

'Ladies and Gentlemen the time is drawing near to achieving our goal. I believe that in a matter of days our politicians will have reached a decision that will have historical implications for this nation.'

There was a loud burst of applause and several cheers.

'Over the past month the momentum has been building and for the benefit of those who do not have access to the newspapers I have continued my practice of cutting out some of the more salient items from the *Evening Post* to read out to you. Often when we read things retrospectively, they make more sense and we can concentrate on the relevant facts more easily. I have compiled quite a large scrapbook about events as they unfold this year.'

She selected the first cutting from her pile and smoothed it out on the lectern.

'The editorial of the 9th August remarks on how

trusting we woman are of our politicians,' she smiled and paused as groans issued from various parts of the hall. 'It talks of the power given to Ministers to appoint the members of the Upper House and I quote,

"It was to give the Government a fair chance of carrying its policy measures in the Council that the power to add twelve members to that body was granted by the Imperial authorities. It might have been expected that in using this power and making the appointments Ministers would take care that they were increasing the support which their more important policy measures would receive in the Council, not calling thither men whom would oppose their policy. Yet what do we find? Out of the twelve appointments made, five of the appointees are opposed to the principle feature in the main policy measure ostensibly promoted by the Ministry. The proportion of votes on either side of the Womanhood Suffrage question has been altered by two, an alteration not sufficient to ensure the acceptance of the proposal by the Council! Can it be doubted that this matter was very carefully arranged by Ministers? – that in making their selection of new Councillors they were as careful not to alter the relation of Parties in the Council as to make absolutely certain that the enfranchisement of women should take place? Had Ministers been sincere in their desire to admit women to the possession of political rights, they would have considered any doubts as to a man's views and vote on this all-important question an absolute bar to his advancement to a seat on the Council."'

Pausing to take a sip of water, the Chairwoman looked out over the audience ad heard the rumblings of discontent at the revelations in the editorial.

'We are up against strong forces my friends,' she resumed. 'We must all be thankful to the Press for their support in writing such articles as this one. Sir John Hall has presented the last of the petitions for the Woman's Franchise, bringing the total signatures up to 29,548 and together with others previously put forward by Mr Palmer and Mr Mills, the total is now 31,872.

Ladies and gentlemen, you will all be aware of the pessimism expressed in these reports and I ask you to hold your heads up high and not be down hearted. There are many, many influential supporters out there who are doing what they can to help us.

The following are extracts from three letters written to the *Evening Post* over the past weeks. On the 15th August, "Excelsior" wrote in favour of women Members of Parliament,

"As a general rule women on the platform do not strive after the oratorical effect aimed at by men, and as a consequence the quiet, restful feminine tones in Parliament would carry with them a feeling of peace and tranquillity, which would produce the same soothing effect on the mind as does a calm sunny morning after a wild tempestuous night."

The letter proceeds to say that the whole business of Government would benefit by allowing women to stand for Parliament. I'm sure we are all agreed on that.'

There were noises of approval and 'Here, here's', from the audience. In the back row, Tilly whispered to Sophia, 'It sounds marvellous but what a large wardrobe one would have to have! Imagine having to look one's absolute best every day? It's easy for the men just having to wear the same old baggy suit week in and week out. Everyone would comment on her clothes before they gave credit to her ideas. I'd probably be the guiltiest!'

'I think I'd be exhausted after the first week,' said Sophia. 'It will take a very special woman like Kate Sheppard, to enter Parliament and I think she'll have to have a very loud voice to be heard!'

'Not to mention a very thick skin, nerves of steel, endless patience and a strong sense of humour,' added Tilly.

Raising her hand for silence the Chairwoman continued almost as if she'd heard Sophia's comments.

'The writer raises an interesting point. I seem to recall that Shakespeare said about one of his characters that *"her voice was ever soft, gentle and low."* However, like many of you, it seems to me that a woman in Parliament will have to be possessed of an extremely strident voice to be heard above all the childish banter that the men indulge in! This next letter from "J.W." which was penned on the 21st August starts,

"The reasons put forth by the opponents of Womanhood Suffrage in the Council may well make the women and men too of New Zealand draw their breath in astonishment and ask themselves what manner of men are these our "lords"?...Nature teaches us everywhere that things which are longest coming to maturity are the most stable, and looking back on the history of women from the earliest ages, the woman of today is fast becoming as triumph of evolution, and possesses a solid force and power which is growing steadily, and which cannot fail to be productive of good to the country whose law-makers are wise enough to profit by it."

Ladies I would suggest to you that we were always well evolved but held back in expressing our talents by the male sex!'

Another loud roar of approbation met her comment and smiling she proceeded to read the last letter.

'On the 22nd August Mr H.J.L. Augarde of Majoribanks Street, writes,

"Re the Female Franchise, I am surprised at the narrow-minded statements – I cannot call them arguments- brought forward by several of the members of the House against the granting to women this just and equitable demand and right – a right that will have to be given sooner or later, The women ask for it and the country will demand it...Many Women are bound to be in our Houses of Parliament sooner or later. What an improvement! What a tone it would give educated women, compared to what we see many times in the reports of speeches. Some members seem to be frightened at the Bill passing. Be more manly, gentlemen. Pass the Bill, and don't be afraid of a woman."

And lastly here is the editorial in today's newspaper.

"The fate of Womanhood Suffrage rests in the hands of the Government. We desire that there should be no mistake upon this point, and that all Liberals and all women should clearly understand it. The decision of the legislative Council will be in the direction the Government really desires. If Ministers are honest and sincere in their professed desire to enfranchise women, they have sufficient influence in the Council at the present moment to ensure the granting of the franchise. If, as we believe to be the case, they are utterly insincere, it will be through their influence that the enfranchisement of women will be refused by the Council. It will be because many members know that by voting against the Womanhood Suffrage clauses of the Bill they will be really

acting in accordance with the genuine wishes of the Government and carrying out its true policy that they will vote against those clauses.

Last year the Government had it in its power to carry the enfranchisement of women. Had Mr Ballance been able to keep his place in Parliament, it would have been carried. Mr Seddon and his colleagues intrigued so as to ensure its defeat without appearing to cause it."

'I don't feel I need to continue as I'm sure you are all now well aware of the blatant tricks our Ministers are capable of performing. Will we now have to watch while the performing dogs of the Legislative Council jump through their hoops at the commands of Ringmaster Seddon? Or will they hear the lionesses' roar in contempt of their efforts? The fight is not over yet ladies and gentlemen. I suggest that every one of you who are able, write to a Minister of the Crown asking how he intends to vote and demanding an honest answer. Let us ensure the Government is doubly aware of our insistence that the Electoral Reform Bill be passed!'

Gathering up her papers, the Chairwoman sat down and acknowledged the applause. Sophia and Tilly cheered and stamped their feet in unison with the audience, both feeling uplifted and elated by the spirited advice.

'I shall write as soon as I get home,' declared Tilly. 'Whilst I'm still feeling inspired by this meeting.'

'Yes, but I think I'll sleep on it and type mine tomorrow,' said Sophia. 'I tend to make silly mistakes if I dash something off in the heat of the moment. Some of the things I tried to write when I was trying to hold my gun steady on Richard Luxmore made no sense at all.

Remember we are supposed to be the cool calm voice of reason?'

'Have you any news about Richard Luxmore?'

'Only that he's awaiting trial but the legal professions seem to move extremely slowly. I should think there is a mountain of evidence for Detective Butler to sort through and he'll want to ensure it's all absolutely correct. I heard that George Luxmore has hired a top criminal defence lawyer from Sydney, so it has taken time for him to arrive and start on the case. Somehow, I imagine, a series of Doctors will be brought in to certify Richard and Hilda as insane.'

'So he'll escape the gallows? Just because his father is wealthy and can afford to hire the best.'

Tilly was indignant in her disapproval, shaking her head in such annoyance that all the feathers on her hat bobbed and weaved in a syncopated motion.

'That would be correct. I'm sure Jack Butler will be devastated at the result of the trial if that occurs. I do know he's worked extremely diligently on the collection of fingerprints left behind by Richard. We can only hope the Judge will allow this type of new evidence to go before the Jury. It will be terribly disappointing for Jack if that doesn't happen, but he won't be able to do anything about it. I can foresee that Richard will spend the rest of his life living in a comfortable secluded house carefully attended by loyal medical staff in the pay of his father. His mother will quite likely join him. They'll never have to face the consequences of their crimes, whereas, we the victims, will always have to live with the memories. '

'It certainly doesn't feel as if justice will be done,' mused Tilly. 'But at least we know you'll be safe from their murderous intent. Kate Sheppard must be relieved it is all over.'

'Yes she is. I had a letter from her thanking me and hoping I had recovered from the attack. Oh I forgot to tell you, I met Daphne last week. She's found employment in James Smith's. She's working in their haberdashery department with the promise of promotion to Ladies fashions upstairs in a few months. Apparently her parents have forgiven her and she is still able to live at home.'

'That's a happy ending then. Let's hope the next few weeks are better,' smiled Tilly. 'We must be positive.'

CHAPTER TWENTY NINE

Saturday 9th September 1893.

The report in the *Evening Post* was eagerly perused by those unable to attend Parliament that day. Later that night sitting at her kitchen table after tea, Sophia read it to Meg and Bayliss who were as attentive as two school children in class.

"It was an exciting time in the Legislative Council yesterday when the first Order of the Day was called on. It was 'Electoral Bill; Third reading'. All sorts of rumours were flying around and the galleries were full. Sir John Hall and Sir Robert Stout were anxiously watching the proceedings, amidst a large group of members of the House. No-one seemed to know how the division would go."

'It s full of suspense isn't it? Like a mystery story', interrupted Meg.
'Yes,' said Sophia. 'The next bit is just a list of all the Councillors who wanted to vote against the Bill. It goes on to say,
"Sir Robert Stout and Sir John Hall looked down gloomily, and the opponents of the Bill above and below beamed radiantly. Then with a Sphinx-like air, the Hon. E.C.J.Stevens rose. On his lips hung the fate of women."

'That sounds so dramatic doesn't it?' said Meg. 'Like one of those penny comics?'

'It appears from this report that while he was opposed to women voting, he had analysed all the previous voting on the matter in Parliament and by the Council over the past two years and come to the conclusion that,

"He would not wreck the Bill and prevent women voting at all simply because they were not to vote the way he wished." Mr Reynolds then rose and stated that he did not like some of the details of the Bill, he resented the manner in which it had been forced through the Council, but he had always held that women should have votes, and now he would not prevent their securing that privilege. The Bill was safe."

Imagine that, we received the franchise by only two votes, twenty to eighteen. It says here that when they heard the news,
    "the Premier and the Minister of Labour looked very much annoyed at the unsuccessful result of their labours in the lobby!"

Oh I would have loved to have seen their faces,' chuckled Sophia. 'Tilly telephoned me last night to say that her husband heard that Mr Stevens and Mr. Reynolds only voted for the Bill because they were so annoyed at Mr Seddon's manipulations and wished to spite him. So we won the vote because of King Dick's unpopularity with his fellow politicians, not because they really believed we should have it. There's a lesson to be learned from that if you're a politician, I would guess.'

'Makes no difference how you got it,' said Bayliss wisely. 'You just make sure you girls use it wisely.'

'My dear Bayliss, how very perspicacious of you,' said his employer.

CHAPTER THIRTY

Monday 18ᵗʰ September 1893.

The trial of Richard Luxmore had finally commenced after long discussions between defence, prosecution and the presiding Judge. It had been decided that only cross-examination by these gentlemen would prove his mental state, since no Doctor could be found who would commit a definite opinion on his sanity. His mood swings were extraordinary but for the main part, he appeared quite normal if that adjective could be applied to one who had committed such crimes. Jack Butler and the Crown prosecutor by mutual consent had expressed grave concerns about Richard being certified and not having a fair trial. They were both convinced he was perfectly capable of answering the accusations; determined to let his future be decided by a jury and not by the medical profession.

      The first day of the proceedings went smoothly, with the jury members chosen and leading statements made. Some fifty witnesses were to be called, many of whom had been put forward by the defence to provide good character references to the accused. On the second day, Butler listened carefully to school teachers, Luxmore employees and friends as they took their places in the witness box to extol the perfectly delightful person they had encountered in Richard Luxmore. Much to Sophia and Tilly's chagrin, they were not allowed to attend and listen to any of the proceedings until they had given their evidence. They had to rely on updates from Jack to whet their appetite. Tilly, of course, had spent a great deal of time choosing her outfit for her appearance in front of the Judge but Sophia had made copious notes to remind herself of every detail she could recall of her association with Richard.

On both evenings Sophia read the account of the day in court, but the details reported were fairly uninteresting as they were mainly concerned with the choosing of the jury, and discussions in chambers between the Judge and the lawyers. All Sophia could glean from this that there was a strong debate regarding Richard Luxmore's sanity or lack of it. Early on, before the trial started, Jack Butler had been asked to present his finger print evidence to the Judge in chambers, but as they had suspected, it was ruled this new science as yet being unproven in New Zealand laws courts, was not admissible. Justice Vantham did, however, commend Detective Butler for his detailed description of how finger prints could prove a persons' guilt but in this instance he felt that owing to there being a lack of the correct equipment in the Wellington Police Station, any attempts that had been made to link the prints were only of an amateur status.

If Jack was disappointed about this, he hid it well when he spoke to Sophia and Tilly at more length about the Judges' decision, later that night at the kitchen table where they had all been convening for several evenings before the trial opened.

'I had to try,' explained Jack. 'At least now it's raised interest higher in the ranks and perhaps I will be given the chance to take it further with the right equipment.'

CHAPTER THIRTY ONE

Wednesday 20th September 1893.

On the third day, the two women were finally summoned to attend the trial, sitting nervously in the witness room before they were called. Tilly was the first to be sent for and she squeezed Sophia's hand briefly as she left.

'Good luck Tilly. You look wonderful,' said her friend knowing this would bolster Tilly's confidence more than anything else she could say. Daphne Parham had gone before them and although pale, she had assured them that she was quite staunch in her evidence, especially her recall of the night in Sophia's kitchen. Left on her own, Sophia crossed her fingers, hoping that all was progressing well in the examining of evidence even if she did have great faith in her ability to answer any tricky questions that would come her way. Sir James had rehearsed her well in how the defence would concentrate on her attacks on Richard and she felt prepared to give clear explanations as to her behaviour.

Half an hour after Tilly had left the room, the door opened and a young constable beckoned to Sophia to follow him. In silence he accompanied her to the door of the courtroom where she was met by another official and escorted to the witness box, where he asked to her to place her right hand on the Bible.

'I solemnly promise to tell the truth and nothing but the truth. So help me God,' Sophia read out from the card held up in front of her. In the few moments that ensued before the Crown prosecutor rose to his feet, she swept a look around the room. The Public Gallery was filled to capacity and she could just see Tilly in the very back row. Across from her sat Jack Butler in his best black suit and he gave her a faintly encouraging smile. The accused sat behind and above the policeman in the high sided confines of the prisoners' bench. Only visible from the chest upwards, Sophia had no doubts that he was handcuffed as befitted such a serious and dangerous criminal. Luxmore hardly raised his head, looking down at the floor for most of the proceedings. Clean shaven and dressed in a sombre black suit, he had obviously taken advice from his lawyer not to appear too flamboyant in his attire.

The Crown prosecutor Mr Le Quesne stood, pulling his gown around him and approached the witness with a warm smile.

'You are Miss Holmes of The Terrace, Wellington?

'Yes sir.'

'And you are the proprietor of the Wellington Secretarial Agency in Willis Street?

'Yes sir.'

'Miss Holmes please would you tell us how you first came to meet the accused?'

Sophia quietly and proficiently recounted her encounter with Richard at the races, but omitted to say that she had deliberately spilled her drink on him to enable that meeting. In her discussions with Le Quesne, he had decided that as Richard had told her that it was he who had engineered the meeting, she shouldn't give the defence the slightest chance to question it.

'Very well Miss Holmes. Then you were invited to the Luxmore residence to attend a social gathering?

'That's correct. I was surprised as I had only met Richard once, but he was insistent I attended.'

'Precisely... do you think he wanted you to be a witness to the fire he lit that night?'

'Objection your honour,' shouted the defence lawyer jumping to his feet.

'On what grounds Mr Levine, said Judge Vantham peering over the top of his gold rimmed spectacles.

'On the grounds that it has not been proved that my client was responsible for the arson at 'The Oaks'.

'Sustained,' said the Judge making a note. 'Please rephrase your question Mr Le Quesne.'

'When you later read about the fire, Miss Holmes, did it occur to you that this might be another attempt to set back the suffrage movement and remove suspicion from the opposition?'

'Yes I did, especially as it appeared that the same method had been used as in the Dixon Street arson. I mean, leaving the pamphlets scattered around.'

The day passed as Mr Le Quesne led Sophia slowly and patiently through all the details of her experiences over the past months that had a bearing on the case. Through all of it, Richard sat immobile, sometimes gazing around the room, but mostly, with his head hung, staring at the floor. The only time he showed animation was when Sophia described using the poker on him in her kitchen and also how she shot him in her office. At those moments he gave her a smug smile as if to say that her actions were to blame for everything. This was wasted on Sophia who looked away hastily as she was giving her testimony, but sharp eyed Tilly noticed and told her that night as she and Jack sat at the kitchen table eating supper with Meg and Bayliss, who were all ears about the day's events.

'That defence lawyer is very sharp my dear. It wouldn't surprise me if he was brutal in his questioning of you tomorrow. He's come from Sydney where he must have represented some very dubious characters and he won't mince his words!'

'I can only agree with that,' said Jack pushing back his clean plate. 'Levine is highly sought after by the criminal fraternity in Sydney. It's rumoured he's a very wealthy man from other people's crimes, but you didn't hear that from me!'

'Ooh...' said Meg. 'From what you say, he's almost a felon himself then.'

'Not quite, but he certainly benefits greatly from the proceeds of villainy. His fees are astronomical according to Sir James.'

During all the discussion, Sophia had remained unusually quiet and as soon as her two guests had left, she went to bed, her mind churning with the strain of the day and the vulnerability she was open to if the defence had delved into her past.

CHAPTER THIRTY TWO

Thursday 21st September 1893.

Day four of the trial was fine causing even more would be spectators to queue outside the Court House in the hope of gaining access to the limited seating in the Public Gallery. Tilly had persuaded an usher to save her a seat and she was ensconced on the very front row of the balcony when Sophia entered the witness box for the second time to face up to the defence questioning. Glancing up at her friend, with a faint smile, Sophia gave her attention to the men of the jury. They had been carefully chosen by both lawyers but Butler had told her that Levine had thrown out many of the working class men on quite weak excuses, so that he could ensure the jurists were of a higher class and more in tune with the Luxmore's way of life. Recalling that, she saw how well dressed, the majority of them appeared. Sitting somewhat uncomfortably between these upright citizens, were no more than five ordinary clerks and labourers, all scrubbed and neat but their shiny suits and tweed jackets with leather patched elbows were strongly in contrast to the other men, dressed in bespoke tailoring. If we had the vote, there would be women on this jury, was her overwhelming thought.

Hearing her stomach give a nervous gurgle, Sophia settled in the hard, straight backed chair. Judge Vantham smiled at her as she caught his eye and she felt slightly reassured in the face of, what she anticipated, could be a very difficult session for her.

Levine, tucked is hands behind his back beneath his black gown and wandered over to stand near her, in an overly casual manner and she braced herself.

'Good morning ladies and gentlemen. Good morning Miss Holmes,' he said cheerily but his smile at Sophia belied this with its essence of guile. Ah, she thought, I can see what you're up to Mr Levine, your face gives you away. I wonder if that was how Jack Whicher knew people were guilty, from their facial expressions and the way they held their bodies, but her ideas were curtailed as Levine started his questioning with a deliberate rapidity, barking his responses in a manner designed to throw her off her stride.

'Would you say that you are an aggressive woman Miss Holmes?

'No sir. I would say I was assertive. They are two quite different characteristics.'

'So... not aggressive but... admittedly assertive. Yet, Miss Holmes on two occasions you have seriously injured my client. What do you say to that in your defence?

'Exactly what I told Mr le Quesne sir. I hit your client with a hot poker to stop him cutting Miss Parham's throat and I shot him to prevent him doing the same thing to me. I have already described those moments in graphic detail. Dealing with this man was not a game of tiddly winks! Both times I gave him fair warning to cease his violence, both times he ignored me, taunted me in fact.'

There was a stir in the room, a few people laughing softly in the gallery. Levine frowned and walked back to his table where he consulted his notes. Jack Butler stretched his legs out, enjoying this encounter in a vicarious way. Levine was going to have a hard time putting Sophia in the wrong, of that he was certain. She wasn't the daughter of a top class barrister for nothing and he knew she'd attended many hearings such as this as assistant to her father. Oh yes, he thought to himself, Sophia knows all the tricks defence lawyers can pull out of the hat.

Pouring a glass of water from the carafe provided, Sophia sipped and contemplated the options available to Mr Levine. He would no doubt discard this line of questioning and move on another tack. Would it be the hysterical female ploy or some slur on her suffrage affiliation? Maybe he would bring up the idea that her incursion into the opium den had damaged her thinking or what...? She had prepared for all those slurs on her character, rehearsing her responses but she still felt nerve wracked when she thought about the questioning that lay ahead of her. She watched as Levine returned to stand close to her. He was of mid height with black hair oiled back, flat and smooth, either side of a centre parting. His eyes were sharp and he sucked in his lips, releasing them with a smacking sound, before he delivered the next query.

'Miss Holmes I gather you have been attending Franchise League meetings this year, is that correct?'

'Yes.'

'Would you say that your "*assertive*" attitude has been increased by these rebel rousing gatherings of like minded women, the so-called screaming sisterhood?'

'No sir. I have always had a mind of my own. I am used to being decisive.'

'And sometimes your decisions have had terrible consequences I might say.'

Sophia remained silent as a strong premonition of what he was implying starting to erode her confidence.

'Oh you don't wish to answer that question then?'

'I'm so sorry Mr Levine,' Sophia said with a mock sweetness in her voice.' I didn't realise it was a question. I thought you were merely making a statement of your personal belief about my character. I must say I think that is entirely inappropriate since we are complete strangers!'

Keeping a straight face with difficulty, Judge Vantham intervened, as she looked up at him with an innocent face.

'Please keep to the facts Mr Levine. You may give vent to your imaginings in your closing address but not at this stage of the trial. The jury will ignore Mr Levine's opinion.'

A slight reddish tinge grew on Levine's cheeks but he was not to be deterred.

'Wouldn't you say that a severe burn and a bullet through the hand were terrible consequences to your actions?

Relief at this question flooded Sophia's being. It was entirely the opposite of her expectations.

'Indeed they were Mr Levine and to Mr Luxmore's actions also. He incurred them by his behaviour and, to correct you, if I may, it was his wrist I shot through, not his hand. I was taught that if you are to disable someone who is holding a knife, aiming at the wrist is more effective.'

Levine appeared to splutter but covered it by whipping out a large white handkerchief to cover his mouth. Wiping his lips, he looked malevolently at the witness.

'You have accused my client of breaking into your office and type writing a threatening letter to a Member of Parliament, is that true?

'I believe it is the police who have accused him, but if you want my opinion, then yes I do think it was your client. The receipt found in his wallet when he was arrested surely proved that he had the signature to copy and forge on the letter. It's too coincidental to think otherwise.'

'Do you think you are a reliable witness Miss Holmes'?

He changed his direction again.

'Yes.'

'You have recently been arrested after being dragged from an opium den. Is that the behaviour of a reasonable and respectable woman?

'Not if she did it on purpose but I would remind you that I was lured there against my will. I was tricked by Richard Luxmore to discredit me. I would never attend such a place willingly.'

'But you did go there willingly Miss Holmes. No-one forced you did they?'

'Only by trickery, which Richard admitted to me after I shot him.'

Sophia immediately wished she could take back her answer.

'I would think any man would confess to things he didn't do if confronted by and shot by a mad woman. Do you agree with that Miss Holmes?

'No. Neither do I agree that I'm mad.'

Levine digested this and allowed a moment to pass before he started his questioning again.

'Let us talk about the night of the Luxmore party. You met up with Miss Daphne Parham and she told you she was thinking of ending her engagement to Richard Luxmore. Is that correct?'

'Yes.'

'I put it to you that this disclosure secretly delighted you? You saw a way to further your acquaintance with my client did you not?'

Shaking her head at this, Sophia gathered her thoughts.

'No to your first question and also no to your second. My reasons for attending the evening were entirely differently motivated.'

'Ah... and do you wish to enlighten us on those motives?'

'No because they have nothing to do with this case.'

'I think that the jury must be able to decide that Miss Holmes so I will ask you again, why did you go to the Luxmore house that night?'

Sophia looked at the Judge and gave a shrug of her shoulders as if to say this was a ridiculously trivial question.

'First of all, sir, for the simple reason that I was invited. Us ladies like a night out,' she said coyly hesitant to divert him. 'Not too many chances come my way to enjoy an occasion like that. Secondly, I was hoping to have a game of cards.'

'A game of cards... Miss Holmes?'

Levine's voice assumed incredulity as he looked at her with mock astonishment.

'There you have it, Mr Levine, you've prised my secret vice out of me,' said Sophia in a chatty, confiding voice as if they were only the only two people in the room. 'I do so enjoy a game of poker. It is one of my weaknesses so I'm told. I'd heard that Mr Luxmore senior would more than likely be dealing a hand or two during the evening. I'm rather ashamed to admit that I invited myself into the game.'

'And did you win anything Miss Holmes?'

Levine looked as if it pained him to ask this.

'Of course, I won the lot with a Royal Flush. I'm known to be very lucky at cards, if not in love. So you see I had absolutely no designs on the son, only on his father's money!'

'Miss Holmes I hear that you are a very good shot so let me ask you, in these fits of 'assertiveness' have you ever killed anyone?'

There was a gasp of tension in the room and Sophia' mouth dropped open as sudden terrible images were aroused in her mind.

'I...' she stammered and looked up at the Judge, her mind racing.

'Answer the question Miss Holmes. Have you ever killed someone? Yes or no?

'Yes,' whispered Sophia, her mouth dry as she started to shake. She looked across at Jack and saw his expression darken as her reply registered with him. There was a sudden upsurge of noise in the room as people started to talk about this revelation by the star witness until the Judge banged his gavel and called for order. Levine stood back and peered at her with a triumphant gaze. She saw his fingers tighten on the papers he gesticulated with.

'Yes indeed you have Miss Holmes. In fact for one so young you seem to have been in the habit of getting yourself into violent situations more than frequently. Perhaps you would like to tell the Court what happened in London two years ago.'

'That has nothing to do with this case,' said Sophia, trying to gather herself into some sort of composure. 'It was proved to be self defence.'

'Nevertheless it might help the Jury to know the circumstances especially as you seem to have a particular aversion to knives,' said Levine.

Sophia looked pleadingly at the Judge but his stern glance told her there was no point in appealing to him. She played for time asking for a glass of water and then raising her eyes she started to speak about something she had hoped to never confront again in her new life in New Zealand.

'My father was a defence lawyer in London. He was extremely successful and dealt with some cases where it seemed almost impossible to sway the Jury, but he was persistent. Naturally he mixed with people who were not always the cream of society or as honest as they might be. He was asked to defend a man who was known to be a petty thief against a charge of murdering a fourteen year old girl from a good family. She'd been found dead in the Thames near the bottom of her parent's garden. Apparently she was prone to sleepwalking and one of the servants had mistakenly left open the back door to the house against the wishes of her father who had issued strict instructions about keeping the house secure to prevent her wandering outside. On this night the accused man had been walking along the tow path trying to scout likely houses to burgle and he admitted to this. He came across the girl in her nightdress and not realising she was asleep he tried to talk to her to see where she came from. He had children of his own and was genuinely concerned about her. His intent was to escort her back to her home but she woke and took fright. Before he could stop her she turned and ran out onto a landing stage. When she reached the end she tripped and fell into the water. He raced after her but she'd completely disappeared and he couldn't swim. He ran back along the path to the nearest pub to raise the alarm but she wasn't found until two days later further down the river. It was proved she had hit her head and was unconscious when she fell in and even though he was arrested, the man was proved innocent but her mother never accepted the verdict and blamed my father.

A few weeks later I heard my father answer the door quite late at night. I was on my way down stairs to see if he and his visitor required any refreshments when I heard the most dreadful screaming and my father shouting out. I went to the hallstand and took my father's revolver out because we always dreaded situations like this and I entered the library. I was confronted by the sight of my Father lying in a pool of blood with a woman standing over him holding a large knife. She saw me and started to scream again and then ran towards me holding the knife out and I shot her. I am a good shot and I did intend to hit her in the shoulder but I missed and found her heart. She dropped instantly and all I could think of was saving my father but it was too late, he was bleeding so profusely I couldn't stop it. Our maidservant had been behind me and witnessed the whole scene. I was absolved and certainly yes, I do have an aversion to knives but surely that is understandable?'

'No more questions for this witness at this time your Honour,' said Levine quickly.

'In that case we will adjourn for lunch,' said Judge Vantham looking at the clock over the door.

***

The court convened again at two o'clock and after the two lawyers had approached the bench and had a muttered conversation with the Judge, Le Quesne armed with a thick wad of notes waited behind his table while it was announced that the accused would now be questioned. Levine looked distinctly uneasy about this turn of events but it was obvious to all present that Judge Vantham felt that the prosecution had put up a water tight reason why this should happen.

Allowed to sit upstairs and watch the proceedings unfold, Sophia tried to recover from the morning's events and Mr Le Quesne's somewhat frosty attitude to her now. Over a hasty meal she had found Tilly and Jack to be most sympathetic but she couldn't imagine that the information she had been forced to reveal hadn't tarnished her reputation. She struggled to give her attention to the court room with its long windows bare of drapes. Behind the Judges bench a Union Jack flag was displayed under the royal crest. To the left was a large oil painting of Her Majesty Queen Victoria in full ceremonial robes.

Le Quesne approached the prisoner and smiled kindly at the young man who gave him a sullen acknowledgement.

'Mr Luxmore, do you understand why you are here today?'

Richard nodded in reply which served to satisfy the lawyer.

'Mr Luxmore, would you say you have a very close relationship with your mother Hilda?'

'Yes,' answered Richard quite clearly. 'Mama and I are very close. We always have been.'

'So when she suggested to you that she wanted a misguided revenge on Mrs Kate Sheppard you agreed to help her?'

'Poor Mama. Of course I did. It was a wonderful plan we put together.'

'Mr Luxmore you told Miss Holmes that your mother rewarded you when you did her bidding. Is that true?'

'Oh yes. Mama knows what I like and I know what she likes. Opium or laudanum, she's not fussy anymore.' He turned in his seat and addressed the listeners in the room. 'I hope someone is looking after her?'

'So you and your mother schemed together when she was drugged? Is that a fair description?'

'Suppose so,' was Richard's disinterested comment.

'How did she reward you Richard? Please tell the jury what Mama did to you?

The men of the jury all leaned forward at this direct question. Some of them started to shuffle in their seats as if anticipating the response and finding it unacceptable.

Richard remained silent for a few minutes but Le Quesne was patient.

'In your own time... Mr Luxmore.'

Richard started to sway in his seat, humming under his breath and then said in a sing song voice, 'Who's a naughty boy then? Who's a naughty boy? Mummy will have to smack your bottom won't she? Lie down here over Mummy's knees.'

He put his thumb in his mouth but, undeterred by this admitted aberration, the lawyer pushed on with his questioning.

'She beat you? What else?'

'Oh it wasn't a beating,' said Richard in a perfectly normal voice, after removing his thumb and inspecting it minutely. 'It was all in fun...well...most of the time unless the drugs were wearing off. Then she got a bit rough with me. And then other times, she'd cuddle me and stroke me,' he said nodding at the jurors. 'They'll all understand how enjoyable that is for a man. Oh the pleasure Mama could give me. Sometimes it was nearly as good as the killing!'

A communal gasp came from the attendees of the trial as Le Quesne gathered himself.

'What killing would that be?'

'Well, all of them I suppose,' admitted Richard and shrugged.

'Richard Luxmore are you telling this court that you are guilty as charged?'

'No, said Richard in his childish voice again. 'I'm mad as a hatter. Mama says that's what mad people do so it was quite safe. They lie and cheat and murder and steal and get away with it...'

He was interrupted by the Judge banging his gavel loudly to silence everyone.

'Order! Order! I am adjourning this session. Court will open again at ten o'clock tomorrow morning when prosecution and defence will present their closing arguments.'

Everyone stood as Vantham left the room for his chambers. Richard was hurried down into the holding cells and the occupants of the room slowly filed out. Out in the street, Jack Butler met up with Sophia and Tilly.

'Is he really insane?'

Jack shook his head in puzzlement.

'Well if he isn't then he has a death wish which could hardly be described as normal either!'

'I'm so glad I'm not on the Jury,' said Tilly. 'What a difficult decision they'll have to make.'

'I'm sure when they take another look at all the evidence, they'll realise what they have to do, said Sophia. 'I can't make up my mind about his sanity. At times he's perfectly lucid but that performance in court, if it was genuine, makes me doubt he's normal in any way at all. The jurists were most uncomfortable at his perverted relationship with his mother but...'

'That doesn't necessarily make him insane' suggested Jack. 'I agree he may be shamming but there's no doubt in my mind that he has a very warped mind and attitude. It will depend if they feel any sympathy for him over having to deal with Hilda as a mother. Which one of us could say we would cope with the situation, faced with a drug addict for a mother and the natural leaning of a child to please their parents?'

'We wouldn't turn murderers I'm certain of that,' said Sophia emphatically. 'I noticed that George Luxmore hasn't been in court. How could he have been so unaware of what was going on in his own house?'

'Quite easily apparently. Daphne said she hardly ever saw him on her visits there. He spends all his days at work or travelling round the country to his breweries. I suspect as his wife became more and more obnoxious he just put it down to bad temper and alcohol, blamed it on her time of life and kept away from her. She must have been able to hide her addiction from him in the early stages of their marriage. Addicts can be very cunning. It's not uncommon I'm afraid.'

'Well we could waste hours in conjecture,' said a practical Tilly. 'Let's go and find a cafe and have a cup of tea. Coming Jack?'

CHAPTER THIRTY THREE

Thursday 25th September 1893.

Sophia seated herself in the public reading room at the new library. She read steadily through all the reports on the passing of the Electoral Reform Bill, in the various provincial newspapers.

The *New Zealand Herald* of the 11th of September noted that,

> *"So complicated is the position, and so obscured have been the real merits of the question in the manner of its determination that it is hardly too much to say that the enfranchisement of women has been accomplished by her enemies."*

An anonymous verse in the *Christchurch Press* brought a smile to her lips.

> *Henceforth small boys shall wear their clothes without a spot or stain,*
> *And those who pull their buttons off shall sew them on again.*
> *Then, at the age of 25, each solvent single male,*
> *Shall make a solemn choice between the altar and the jail.*

The same newspaper, which had been aggressively against suffrage, was forced to admit on the 19th September,

"We have now got the Female Franchise as surely as we had the measles. It has come to stay, and we must make the best of it."

There were many reports of the jubilation of women around the country as the Bill was signed by the Governor General. Susan B. Anthony, President of the National American Women's Suffrage Association wrote,

"New Zealand women are no longer political pariahs – I am rejoiced with you."

To Sophia's mind the best letter came from Catherine Wallace who had written from Melbourne,

"Your long, patient, faithful, untiring, earnest, zealous effort is finally rewarded, which means so much, not for you and the women of New Zealand only, but for women everywhere on the face of the globe. It will give new hope and life to all women struggling for emancipation, and give promise of better times, of an approaching millennium for all the down-trodden and enslaved millions of women, not only in so-called Christian countries, but in India and the harems of the East. Right glad I am and proud of New Zealand.

CHAPTER THIRTY FOUR

Sunday 3oth September 1893.

At last the weather had improved with a touch of Spring in the air. Up in the Botanical Gardens, large swathes of daffodils stood tall and proud against the grass and late camellias gave colour to what had been a drab and wintry park a few weeks before. On the previous Tuesday at 11.45.am, the Governor General had assented to the Electoral Reform Bill when it was presented to him by the Clerk of Parliament.

Thousands of women were now being urged to register their intent to vote in the General Election. The *Evening Post* had included a copy of the registration form in each of its issues with clear instructions as to how to fill it in. Every man or woman of twenty one years of age, being a natural born citizen or naturalised British subject, who had been resident in the colony for twelve months was entitled to vote, as long as they had also resided for three months in the electoral district where they were registered.

Every white camellia in Wellington had been picked and presented to all those Members of Parliament who had supported the Bill as a symbol of the suffrage movement.

Congratulations poured in from the other British colonies to all those who had worked so hard and long towards this achievement. Mrs Kate Sheppard received many plaudits. The Sydney Daily Telegraph stated that,

"New Zealand is entering on a political object-lesson which, no matter what the issue may be, must make the world wiser in statecraft than before. New Zealand, to begin with, is in civilisation in the foremost rank, and peopled by a race who, socially, intellectually, and politically, have perhaps as little to learn from outside as any in the world."

On this fine day, Jack Butler had invited Sophia to walk with him around Oriental Bay. Disembarking from the horse tram at the start of the promenade pathway along the beach, he tucked Sophia's arm firmly in his as they commenced their stroll. It was a gentlemanly gesture as the path was a little rough in places but she felt there was a hint of possession inherent in his action.

The sandy beach was busy with children bravely paddling, squealing as the cold water lapped over their toes. Dogs raced freely along the waterline revelling in the fine weather and young nursery maids struggled to push heavy perambulators through the sand.

Halfway around the Bay, they reached an empty bench and by mutual tacit consent seated themselves to watch and enjoy the view before them. Wellington harbour stretched like a mirror to the misty shores of Lowry Bay to the east. A few ripples caused by the occasional boat, lapped intermittently at the shoreline but there was little to disturb the tranquillity of the water which appeared clean and clear for once.

'Looking at all this domesticity and enjoyment, it's hard to believe there are people like Richard Luxmore in the city,' remarked Jack. 'But not for much longer. His hanging date is due soon. I'm so relieved to get that result out of the jury and have the trial over. I thought it might have lasted a great deal longer.'

'I am sincerely glad it was so quick after his unpleasant revelations. I certainly won't forget them in a hurry,' said Sophia with a dramatic mock shudder.

'No, of course not,' Jack said hastily. 'I believe it was his perversion that hardened the decision from the jury. There's no sympathy for that sort of thing even in wealthy families. He paused and then said, 'I can honestly say that I will never forget the sight of you pointing that ridiculous gun at Luxmore.'

'It may look ridiculous but even those tiny bullets hurt a great deal, you can be sure of that. You know now that I have shot someone before, but even so I didn't hesitate to shoot Richard. Before, in London, all I could think of was saving myself so that I could reach my father in time. I've never felt so angry and unrestrained which was also very frightening but this time I was quite shocked at my lack of emotion.'

'I did warn you that when the Press heard of it, they would probably dub you as some sort of Calamity Jane.'

'They can't decide between her or Annie Oakley as you suggested. Oh... I read about Jane recently. Isn't she appearing in Buffalo Bill's Wild West Show?'

'That's right but please don't become too like her. She's supposed to be a terrible alcoholic.'

'Perhaps her aim is better when she's drunk,' laughed Sophia. 'However I expect it's not nearly as dangerous as it sounds. Not as dangerous as being a detective I imagine?'

"I can think of far more risky occupations than being a policeman,' he countered.

'Oh? Yes I suppose one must think of mining, whaling or soldiering as being extremely perilous,' offered Sophia after some thought.

'Well...' Jack hesitated. 'I'm quite sure that being a secretary is the probably the most dangerous job I can think of, at this moment.'

Sophia laughed at him.

'You know I think you may be correct. There's always high drama in the office when either of us breaks a finger nail!'

'I was thinking more of being involved in murder, bribery, corruption, and arson, not to mention being dragged from a drug den and thrown into prison. If that's what shorthand and typing involves it must come high on the list of hazardous work.'

Jack sighed deeply and shook his head at this pronouncement and watched as Sophia smiled then started to delve into her bag. Finding what she was searching for, she held it out to her companion.

'A pipe? Please don't tell me you're intending to take up smoking? It could lead to all sorts of accidents if the last few months are anything to go by! I can see the headlines now!'

Sophia ignored this barb as he threw his hands up in mock horror.

'No. Don't you recall I found this at the meeting where I met Susie Post. After I showed it to you I put it away and forgot all about it until today. That strange man sitting along the row from me who dropped it as he left, do you know, I think it was possibly Richard Luxmore on his way to meet Susie? He left early so she wouldn't see him there.'

Turning the carved pipe over in his hands, Jack looked at the initials and frowned.

'Yes now I do remember, S M? That must stand for Sinclair Montford, Richard's uncle? This might be one of the items he claimed was stolen from him. Richard was intending to pawn it presumably. I'll keep it and see if I can trace the ownership.'

Placing the pipe in his coat pocket, Jack reached inside his jacket.

'I feel rather guilty that I haven't had more time to speak with you and thank you for helping me in this case. Despite our frequent disagreements, I must acknowledge your skill in uncovering many helpful details that I, as a mere male, would have probably missed. Can I call on your talents in the future if I need to?'

'I'd like that but please don't worry about our arguments,' said Sophia gazing rather fixedly out to sea but Jack heard the tone in her voice that bespoke the opposite. 'I'm quite sure you've been far too busy to find time for me. It must have taken hours and hours of work to put your case together.'

'Perhaps I can make it up to you,' he said and handed her an envelope that was addressed to her and sealed with a blob of red sealing wax impressed with a coat of arms. 'It struck me that in dealing with this case it was all about relatives and I realised that your only kin was Sir Arthur Conan Doyle and that maybe, although you appear to believe to the contrary, he would be interested to know how you were faring, so I wrote to him about you after the attack, including my police report on the Luxmore case. He replied almost instantly and this is for you. It only arrived yesterday on the mail boat.'

'How kind of you but I doubt he would remember me, as I told you, when we first met,' said Sophia diffidently turning the envelope over and over in her hands. Finally, to Jack's relief and curiosity, she opened it and pulled out the sheets of notepaper it contained. Unfolding them she read out loud.

'My dear Sophia, It was with great interest that I received the letter from Detective Butler regarding your heroic efforts in the Luxmore case. To say that I was impressed is an understatement. Thus I have put pen to paper immediately to write to you so that this will catch the next mail steamer to New Zealand. I hardly think Sherlock himself would have acted any more astutely than you did in the circumstances. I think if I were to write about this as a novel, I would have to entitle it, "The Case of the Distant Relative" and the readers would have a hard time guessing which one it was! Please write back to me and relate all in your own words. I do wish to keep in touch with you as I do have such fond memories of your father and his sound legal advice.
Your affectionate distant relative,
Arthur Conan Doyle.'

There was a long silence between them then eventually Sophia carefully folded the letter back into the envelope and placed it in her bag, before turning to look at Jack.

'There's something else I thought might interest you,' he said and produced another scrap of paper on which he had scribbled a few words.' Do you recall we were discussing Jack Whicher? I told you that Charles Dickens loosely based his character Inspector Bucket on him? Well I took a look at Bleak House again when it was quiet on my watch a few nights ago. I found this quotation which seems entirely appropriate. Listen to this,

"Very strange things comes to our knowledge in families," says Bucket. *"Aye and even in gen-teel families, in high families. In great families... you have no idea... what games goes on."*

'Indeed it is very apt,' agreed Sophia smiling at him. 'Have you ever been married Jack? You've never really talked about your family.'

Her question came out of the blue catching Jack by surprise but he reckoned she deserved an honest answer.

'Yes I was, a long time ago. We were both very young. Adele was an orphan employed by my father as a book keeper in the office of his hardware shop. I was barely twenty, just starting off as a constable and she latched on to me because I suspect, she wanted to belong to a family. Oh, we were happy enough and my parents adored her, but she became very discontented about the hours I worked. It was hard and lonely for her. I had to work fourteen night shifts in a row, then. After a year she hadn't become pregnant and that was blamed on me. To cut a long story short she had an affair with my best mate and became pregnant by him. There wasn't any point in being angry about it, so I divorced her. They're happily married with four children now. My mother then recalled a bit late in the day that I'd had a mild case of mumps when I was fourteen so the problem of infertility probably lay with me.'

'And you've never met anyone else?'

'No.'

Sophia noticed a slight hesitation before he

replied.

'To tell the truth, after I realised that it was my fault Adele didn't fall pregnant, it didn't seem fair to get involved with another girl. After all, most women want children.'

'Do they? I certainly don't,' said Sophia quite fiercely. 'I don't have a maternal bone in my body. It used to worry me but then I realised that I wasn't the type of woman to coo over babies and there was nothing wrong with that. Not everyone is suited to be a parent. Children should have parents that have time for them, lots of patience and no other interests or ambitions in life.'

Jack digested this statement for a few moments as he watched the seagulls wheeling overhead.

'Well now that you're one of the new emancipated women, how does it feel?'

'I'm not sure to tell the truth. I do so like being a single woman with supposedly equal rights but there are limitations.'

'Such as?'

'It's not something a man would understand. I haven't even discussed it with Tilly.'

'Try me and I promise not to laugh.'

Sophia gazed out to sea, her profile set and a small frown between her eyes.

'It is wonderful to be able to vote and make our own choices but there are still many places where females are subject to rigid societal rules. For example I can vote about the control of liquor licensing but I can't enter a public bar. There are still so many areas of life where we have to seek the approbation of men. What really worries me is the fact that we women are brought up to guard our virginity as being the most precious thing we have to offer a husband. It's regarded as a saleable commodity in their daughters by many parents. The trouble is that if, like me, a woman doesn't wish to be married, but would still like to enjoy a close companionship with a man, why should she deny herself that opportunity in order to preserve her maidenhead? To what purpose? There is no future husband who's going to value it, is there? It's easy for men to have affairs and keep mistresses, but single women can't take a lover to ease the problem, without some sort of scandal.'

Jack drew a deep breath as he considered his response then chose his words very carefully, summarising what she had just told him.

'So what you're saying is that you or should I say an unmarried lady who wishes for male companionship of a very intimate nature, outside of wedlock, would find it difficult?'

'Exactly... Having an affair with a married man means possibly wrecking a marriage and one couldn't countenance that. Supposing one found a suitable single man who didn't wish to be married, where could one go to do... it? Renting a hotel room seems so tawdry and well, let's be honest I could hardly take a man home and announce blatantly to Meg that we were just going upstairs to bed! Can you imagine her response?'

Indeed Jack could and the effort of keeping a straight face forced him clench his teeth. He looked out over the harbour, his jaw rigid before, finally, managing to answer.

'I do see your problem. I suggest you would have to find a gentleman who was of a like mind, who owned his own home where the two of you could enjoy your relationship in any way you liked, in complete privacy.'

'Yes that would be ideal,' she said, a little too promptly as she saw the grin spreading over his face that he could no longer contain.

'It would appear that I would qualify for the position if you wish to interview me.'

'Oh Jack,' said Sophia and had the grace to blush a deep shade of pink. She reached over and placed her hand rather immodestly on his outstretched leg well above his knee. 'How do you understand me so well?'

'Well...' said Detective Butler moving closer to her. 'It's elementary my dear Miss Holmes. It's elementary.'

BIBLIOGRAPHY.

Pierce, Jill — *The Suffrage Trail*. National Council of Women 1995 Wellington.

Grimshaw, Patrica — *Women's Suffrage in New Zealand*.1987 Auckland University Press.

Harrison. Michael — *The World of Sherlock Holmes.* 1973 Frederick Muller Ltd.

Summerscale, Kate — *The Suspicions of Mr Whicher.* 2008 Walter & Co. New York.

Yska. Redmer — *Wellington, Biography of a City*.2006 Reed Publishing (NZ) Ltd. Auckland

Price,Hugh & Susan — *.Old Wellington in Colour.* 2008 Steele Roberts, Wellington.

Johnson, David — *Wellington by the Sea.* 1990 David Bateman, Auckland.

Johnson, David — *Wellington, A Pictorial History*.1995 Grantham House Auckland.

Ward. L.W. — *Early Wellington.* 1975 Capper Press, Christchurch.

Boon, Kevin — *Kate Sheppard.* 1993 Kotuku Publishing, Wellington.

Randall.B, Price.H — *Wellington at Work in the 1890's.* 2009, Steele Roberts. Wellington.

www.paperspast.co.nz

www.angelfire.com

If you enjoyed *The Case of the Distant Relative* you may like to read other books by Jill Darragh.

Writing as Carole St Aubyns

> *Sweet Bitter Waters*
>
> *Sweet Bitter Revenge*
>
> *Creating Infinity*

Writing as Jemma Daintree

> *Vote for Love*   (18+) *The Aphrodite Club Book 1*
>
> **Spy for Love*   (18+) *The Aphrodite Club Book 2*
>
> **(Due August 2018)*